USED

THE PLAYGROUND CLUB
BOOK 1

SHANNON ELLIOT

Used

The Playground Club Series

By Shannon Elliot

Copyright © 2024 by Shannon Elliot

To request permission or for more information, contact the publisher at pa@authorshannonelliot.com.

Paperback ISBN 978-1-964117-18-8

Ebook ASIN B0DCZY33KG

Second edition December 2025

Edited by Bookcase Media

Proofed by Bookcase Media

Cover Art by Eve Graphic Designs

Formatting by Creative Shannonigans

www.authorshannonelliot.com

CONTENT AWARENESS

Please take the following under advisement before reading.

Your mental health matters.
<u>Hate, Discrimination & Oppression</u>
Fatphobia & body-shaming, Misogyny, Slut-shaming
<u>Abuse and Relationships</u>
Abandonment (Parental), Abuse (Parental), Neglect (Parental)
<u>Pregnancy and Childbirth</u>
Abortion Rights Discussion (No Impact on Characters), Birth
Complications / Trauma (Off-Page, Historic), Infertility (Failed
IUI), Pregnancy
<u>Death and Loss</u>
Death of a parent & guardian (Off-page, Cancer), Grief & loss
depiction
<u>Violence and Crime</u>
Home invasion, Guns
<u>Kink Related</u>
Breeding, Free Use Agreement, Use of Adult Toys
<u>Other</u>
Politics

This book contains "spice", or graphic sexual content, and is intended for persons of legal age. The content of this work should not be used as a manual or a realistic depiction of kink, fetish, or BDSM activities, and all characters are of legal age. This novel is intended for entertainment purposes only.

RESOURCES

Your mental health and safety matters to me.

Please make note of the resources below if any content in this book is triggering for you:

Dial 988 for the Suicide & Crisis Helpline or visit their website for more resources. (https://988lifeline.org)

For support after losing a loved one to suicide, call 1-800-646-7322 or visit the Friends for Survival website. (https://findahelpline.com/organizations/friends-for-survival-suicide-loss-helpline)

Call 1-800-662-HELP (4357) for SAMHSA'S national helpline (Substance Abuse and Mental Health Services Administration) or visit the website for more resources. (http://www.samhsa.gov/find-help/national-helpline)

*To anyone who's ever been made to question their body or their rights
to it.
You are perfect, just as you are. Don't let anyone tell you otherwise.*

WELCOME TO THE...

Playground Club

1

ELSIE

March 6

God may be a woman, but she fucked up when she decided to make periods a bitch.

Cunt.

After coming off of birth control over two years ago and now four rounds of Intrauterine Insemination (IUI), I know what my symptoms look like.

I've always had periods on the heavier side, but even the minor spotting and cramping I experienced last week was a tell-tale sign that my period came and went.

No wonder I wanted to cry.

My past two periods are a reminder that my last round of IUI didn't work.

I'm sitting in the waiting room of my OBGYN's office, walls covered in photos of happy mothers with their children.

Every time I go to the office, all the photos on the walls make me think of the little mini-me I want to have. I imagine their bright blue eyes and auburn hair mirroring my own. Hopefully, they have my smile or my nose. Though, they are welcome to be taller than my 4' 11" curvy frame.

For now, I'm waiting to be taken back for yet another appointment that will disappoint me. I already know I'm going to pee in a cup and have them confirm what I already know in my broken heart.

I'm not pregnant.

Which feels devastating to admit after wanting a child of my own for so long.

Thus far, I've planned my life meticulously, but I never thought to plan for a relationship, much less a baby.

Then, two years ago, I reached the same age as when my mother had me, and it became the only thing I could think about.

Previously, my life centered around work. Long days and sleepless nights are what helped me conquer my little corner of the Tech market in Texas.

Being a woman in tech is hard enough, but adding a passion for ocean conservation will suddenly put you in the oil and gas world.

I left my job as a researcher at twenty-four. For the past ten years, I've worked my ass off to build up Coral Crude, the leading consulting and technology resource for oil companies looking to offset their environmental impact by building up coral reefs around their offshore oil platforms.

In college, I studied at the Flower Garden Banks National Marine Sanctuary, which lies 80-125 miles off the Texas and Louisiana coastlines.

The Flower Garden is proof of the Gulf's capacity to house thriving coral reefs. Reefs protect coastlines, host hundreds of marine species, and aid in the development of treatments for cancer, arthritis, and viruses.

After only a few years working as a researcher, I knew there was a need and a market for resources that energy companies looking to offset their environmental impact on the Gulf.

Thus, Coral Crude was born.

It's been my baby ever since.

But something changed around my 32nd birthday that kicked my biological clock into overdrive.

Suddenly, my focus shifted from conservation to conception.

The desire to start a family consumed me, and I started consulting with my doctor about options for entering "My Motherhood Era."

Family has always been a tricky subject for me.

My father and I went no-contact nearly four years ago after years of trying to have a relationship with him as an adult. But the truth is, he was never the parent I needed him to be, even as a child. He was gone for work more than he was home. Between the neglect and cruelty toward me, our relationship was always superficial.

In many ways, it was purely business. I served a purpose for him. I gave him the public persona he wanted everyone to see him for. In return, I was given food, shelter, and an education. But I was never his daughter.

He never showed me *love*.

After beginning to unravel all of the trauma he caused with my therapist, I realized it was healthier for me to go through my life on my own than with him in it.

Parenthood is no different.

Doing this whole motherhood thing alone was the only way I ever saw myself having a family.

So, I poured over hundreds of records for sperm donors, and once I found a suitable donor, I started rounds of IUI and fertility treatments.

Two years in, my hope is waning.

I am waiting for the news from my doctor today, and the disappointment to follow will surely crush me.

The patient room the nurse led me into is painted a plain, soft eggshell color, creating a calm and neutral environment. However, it's still just like any other doctor's office, with its familiar medical equipment and sterile atmosphere. The most notable difference is the personal touch added by the blown-up photos of patients with their babies and children, which are proudly displayed alongside the medical posters that hang around the office. These posters depict various aspects of women's health, such as prenatal care, childbirth, contraception, and reproductive health, offering educational information while reinforcing the clinic's focus on caring for both mother and child.

Since being guided into the room, I've been scrolling through my endless emails, all of which have already been culled by my assistant, Oliver.

I'm trying to distract myself with work from the dread forming in my chest when my doctor knocks on the door.

"Ms. Snow. How are you doing today?" Dr. Taylor says as she enters the room.

"Fine," I answer shortly.

"Alrighty. Well, let's just dive in, shall we?" She glances down at my patient chart with a blank face. "I know we've been working towards building up your family."

I nod curtly, bracing myself for the news I know is coming.

"Well, I believe congratulations are in order then." The doctor says with a smile on her lips. "You're pregnant."

She pats me on the knee before returning to my chart and discussing the information I should be paying attention to.

I wish I could absorb anything that she's saying right now. Instead, all I can think about is those words.

You're pregnant.

I'm having a baby.

A *baby*.

My baby.

I'm going to be a mom.

But... *fuck*.

I *know* my period came and went. Twice.

"Excuse me," I say, interrupting the doctor mid-sentence. "My last period was last week, and my cycle also came the month before. How can I be pregnant?"

"You've been tracking your ovulation cycles, correct?" She asks.

"Of course." I snap a little too curtly. "And we did my last round of IUI during that window two months ago." I sigh. "I've had two periods since then. They came and went, though my most recent one was a little late."

"Well, what has your sex life looked like recently? If I recall correctly, you haven't been partnered during the time we worked together. Has that changed?" She asks, head tilting in curiosity before continuing. "With the fertility treatments, your body would be more receptive to any additional introductions of semen around your ovulation periods."

"I haven't..." I stop.

Shit.

The weekend of Selene's engagement party.

Shit. Shit. Shit.

I only remember that night through a haze of hormones, but I definitely had sex at The Playground Club that weekend.

The Playground is a membership club that caters to swingers and kinksters.

It's a sex club.

Horny doesn't begin to explain how needy I was that weekend.

How was I supposed to say no when he offered his dick up on a silver platter?

I was sober, with no alcohol or drugs in my system, but by the end of the night, I was drunk and high on orgasms. He fucked me for hours, and I came enough times to where I nearly blacked out, but he didn't stop fucking me.

I wanted it.

Desperately.

Almost as desperately as I've been wanting a baby.

But that night, I'd been feeling low after having just had my period recently. I knew my body had failed at its job once again. So, I went for it and just tried to enjoy the night along with my friends.

But this wasn't the plan.

The possibility that my dreams have come true because of a one-night stand?

That doesn't sound like a dream. It sounds like a nightmare.

Because now there's a second parent involved. One who *hasn't* signed away rights to the child growing in my womb.

Which is a problem I'm not ready to deal with.

I'm wringing my hands, trying to cling to the last shred of sanity that remains, when the doctor's voice shakes me from my panic. "How about we schedule you to come back next week to discuss things more? In the meantime, here are some resources for you to look over."

Before she leaves, she hands me a stack of papers and pamphlets, but I only give them a quick glance before tossing them to the side.

Then I reach for my phone. I scroll back through my photos before the doctor even closes the door to the room.

"Where are they?" I ask, my heart racing a million miles a minute. "Fuck!"

"Fuck!" I repeat under my breath when I still can't find them after a few minutes, and the nurse knocks on the door to check on me, signaling I should leave soon.

I drop back onto the examination table and stare at the ceiling until my vision crosses. My hand comes to rest on my stomach, and underneath the mounting panic, a small flutter of excitement forms in my chest.

I'm having a baby.

My baby.

No matter the other half of the DNA, this child is *mine*.

2

ELSIE

March 6 — 9 Weeks 4 Days, Kumquat

Driving home from the Medical District happens on autopilot, my heart pounding for the full 30 minutes it takes to get back to River Oaks and park in the garage before taking the elevator up to my penthouse apartment.

When I reach the top floor, my shoulders sag, and I let out a breath I did not realize I was holding.

My apartment is the one place in the world where I have complete control. It's my safe haven from the world.

When you enter through the front door from the elevator bay, you walk into the large open floor plan. To the left is the kitchen with white cabinets and marble countertops. The layout flows seamlessly into the living room, with an entire wall of bookshelves around the television.

It is decorated in a minimalist, modern style, and I keep the space immaculately clean and organized. The entire place is in various shades of white, cream, and gray, with accents throughout of my favorite color, rich emerald green.

Turning to the right from the front door takes you down a

hallway that leads to the primary bedroom, my office, and a guest bedroom that I planned to convert into a nursery when the time comes. In the opposite direction is the den and two more bedrooms, one of which I've converted into a yoga studio that overlooks the city.

Placing my purse on the kitchen island, I immediately head to my bedroom for a shower and a mental breakdown under scalding water.

The water beats down on my back and face as I go through my shower routine, but the panic hits again just as I'm lathering my hair with shampoo.

Sinking down on the shower bench, I struggle to breathe in with all the steam surrounding me. Everything goes fuzzy, and my thoughts swirl.

Something twists in my chest as I fixate on the doctor's words.

You're pregnant.

Am I happy about this? Absolutely.

It's what I've been trying for these past two years.

But like this?

Having a baby after sleeping with a man only once?

He has to be the dad, right?

I haven't slept with anyone else.

How could this have happened, though?

We used condoms!

Realization dawns, and my eyes grow wide.

My hidden album.—I finally remember.

Without shutting off the water or rinsing the shampoo out of my hair, I scramble out of the shower. I throw a towel around my body and race to the kitchen.

Dripping wet, I search through my Mary Poppins bag for my phone, which I find under all the crap I keep in there.

When I try to unlock my phone, facial recognition doesn't work, and my wet hands struggle to type in the passcode.

I wipe my hands and the phone screen on my towel to dry off everything and try again.

Just having my phone open makes a breath rush out of my lungs in relief.

A puddle of water and sudsy bubbles form on the floor around my feet. I know they're here, the photos and videos from that night. I specifically asked him to take them on my phone so I could control what and with whom these were shared.

I navigate to my photos and wait for facial recognition to open the album of hidden pictures and videos. I stop when the folder opens.

The photos and videos are right there, but I can't bring myself to click on them.

To watch my choices unfold before me.

But I want this. I have wanted this more than anything. This has been my goal, and what I have been trying to achieve.

I turn and slump to the floor, my back resting on the cabinets under the kitchen island counter. Once settled, I force myself to click on the last video saved in the album.

Thirteen minutes and twenty-three seconds.

In thirteen minutes and twenty-three seconds, I'll know for sure.

Clicking on the small icon, the video begins to play. It starts with a frame of my face, which is surrounded by my mess of curls. It then moves down to show my breast, which fall to my sides and every roll of my stomach. When the recording reaches my waiting pussy there's a glorious cock sheathed in a condom there as well.

I let out a relieved breath at the confirmation that we used a condom.

On the screen, I watch myself visibly shiver under his touch. The sight of us, our bodies, together is mesmerizing.

I unmute it just as he runs his dusty pink head up and down my slit, paying extra attention to my clit.

Then, after positioning himself at my entrance, he stops.

"You want more of my cock, little princess?" He says in his deep growl.

The camera scans back up my body just in time to catch me rising up on my elbows to glare at him, but the expression quickly turns to pleasure.

Even with it offscreen, I remember him slowly entering me and the way my body rippled with pleasure. Then he proceeded to tease me by slowly, and I mean *slowly*, thrusting in and out.

"Fuck me like you mean it, asshole." I snap.

"Clearly, I haven't been doing my job if my princess can talk." He chuckles before picking his pace up.

With a new rhythm set, I watch myself fall back on the mattress, and the camera goes back to recording where his cock thrusts in and out of me.

Watching as he fucks me has me captivated.

The slick slapping sound of him sliding in and out so quickly has me growing wet as I watch the recording. Each pulse of his hips has my pussy clenching with need as I sit in a puddle on my kitchen floor.

"Fuck. You feel so good." I hear myself moan from the phone speaker. "I love how you fill me up. I want you to cum inside me. Give me everything."

"Do you want me to fill you with cum. Make your pussy sloppy with my juices. Give you all my cum so I can make a baby inside you, Elsie?" He says, the video returning to my face as I look away. "Fuck yes... that's so... hot."

I remember the heat that formed in his eyes and the way he licked his lips as though just the thought of my secret desire was the hottest thing he'd ever heard.

"You want me to fuck you and fill you with my cum, don't you? Your pussy is so greedy for it. You want my cum in you?" He purrs, each phrase punctuated by another thrust. "Then beg."

"I don't beg." I snap, my tone serious.

"Oh yes, you will. You want me to fill you up with my cum? Then beg daddy for it." He growls.

Even now, hearing him call himself 'daddy' has my pussy clenching like a needy whore again.

"Tell me how you want me to use your tight little pussy, princess." He says.

"Fuck you." I snarl.

I watch his thrusts stop, and a pitiful whine of distress escapes my lips.

"Tell me how, princess." He pulls me up by my hair, forcing me to rest on my elbows again. He looks me straight in the eyes. "Tell daddy to use your pussy like the bitch in heat you are."

I remember the anger that surged through me and how determined I was to defy him.

Yet, I was desperate for it at the same time.

Despite endless flirting between us, we'd never slept together before this night. It was supposed to be a one-time thing for us.

The dynamic was volatile, each of us clamoring for dominance as we played. The give and take between us is almost as erotic as the sex itself. The heat and tension were intoxicating. It's something I never allowed myself before because I know how he is.

He's a player.

A true dragon to my unicorn.

He's a single man in the lifestyle who sleeps with, well... everyone. Plus, he'll fuck them in any way they ask for. No kink is off-limits.

While I may be single and bisexual, I'm more discerning with whom I play.

Which is why we never played before, but *fuck* did I want it that weekend.

I wanted everything.

And, drunk on orgasms, he finally broke my mind until I was genuinely begging.

I see on the screen when my sanity snaps.

I reach up to pull him into a kiss, and the video stops abruptly on the last frame, but the memory of that night continues.

The phone was quickly tossed to the side to free up his hands, one of which went to play with my clit while the other reached up to slide into my hair and tightly grip at the root as we kissed.

My skin grows hot as I remember how we fucked. Every cell in my body seems to vibrate with the memory of his touch on me, the heat between us, and the thrill that rolled through me.

It felt so good, and I was out of my mind with pleasure.

But then that key memory breaks through.

"*Fuck*. The condom broke." He says, pulling out of me and taking off the broken condom. "Hold on one second. I'll get another."

"No. Please don't stop." I cry, grabbing him by his now unsheathed cock and guiding him back into my pussy.

"Elsie."

"No. Not Elsie. Right now, I'm not her." I say breathlessly. "Fuck me raw. Give me your cock. Please... fill me up. I need it."

He leans down until our lips are just a breath apart.

"Tell me what you want, princess." He commands. "What you *really want*."

I remember hesitating, but the feeling of his tip just barely grazing my entrance had me desperate.

"Fucking fill me up with your cum. Please, I need it." I relent, falling back onto the mattress. "Breed me, Daddy."

The smile that breaks over his face is everything I need at that moment.

"That's it." He smirks, lining up his cock to enter me once more. "Daddy's gonna give his little princess everything she wants."

"Everything. Please." I groan.

"You want me to breed you?" He says, thrusting into me. "I know you do. You want me to fill you with my seed. Just a greedy cunt desperate to be filled up."

"Yes, give me your cum." I moan as his pace picks up. "Give me your seed. I want your baby."

Leaning down so his lips barely graze my ear, he whispers. "You're gonna look so good carrying my child. Your breasts full and round, softly draping over your swollen belly."

I let out a high-pitched whine. "Please. I want it."

"Shhh... Don't worry. Daddy's got you." He soothes, his hand coming to caress the side of my face.

Each of his thrusts drives me closer and closer to my climax. Energy buzzes through me each time I clench around his cock. A hurricane of pleasure builds in my entire body.

"Fuck I'm so close." I moan. "Give it to me, daddy."

He picks up his pace, our skin slapping together loudly.

"Fuck. I'm almost there, too." He groans.

"Daddy. Please!" I scream. "Please!"

"Gonna. Make you. My baby. Mama." He grunts with each thrust. "Gonna. Fill you. Up."

Marshall cries out as he cums. He shudders with each release, but he doesn't stop fucking me. Each thrust in and out squelches, proof of the cum he's filled me with.

The sound alone and the knowledge that he just gave me everything I needed sends me over the edge.

My orgasm crashes into me like a storm that knocks me out completely.

The feeling of Marshall pulling out brings me back to myself.

I start to pull myself up, but then his fingers slip through my slit to gather up the cum that's escaped my pussy. When he pushes his cum back into me, my head drops back, and my body shudders.

"Take it all, princess. Take daddy's cum like the dirty bitch you are." He murmurs before crawling up on the bed next to me.

He tugs me up so my whole body is laying on the mattress, encompassed by his massive frame. One of his arms props up my head like a pillow, but his free hand reaches down to my pussy.

Fingers rub at my lower lips, and every time that I feel a little bit of cum drip out of me, thick callused fingers push it back inside. After a few times, his fingers remain in me and gently stroke that sensitive spot in my pussy.

The soft strokes have my body tensing, readying for another orgasm.

This time, when it comes, the sensation is a soft wave of pleasure.

"Sleep, princess. Daddy's got you." He whispers, placing a kiss on my forehead. "I'll wake you up when we need to go."

After that, every sensation fades out except the warmth of him curled around me and his hand cupping my pussy.

The chime of the phone in my hand brings me back from the memories into my kitchen.

Fuck.

I'm gonna be a mom.

Someone is going to call me Mommy.

And this babies "daddy?"

"Daddy" was supposed to be role-play.

It was sexy, but just play.

But my goddess-damned uterus made it a reality.

I'm pregnant.

I'm going to be a mom.

And *Marshall Law* is going to be a dad.

3

ELSIE

March 7 — 9 Weeks 5 Days, Kumquat

Nausea is relentless today, and I want to murder everyone more than usual.

It's like my doctor's appointment triggered the symptoms everyone talks about having in their first trimester. Or maybe I was just ignoring the signs. But now, my body is overly sensitive, and my head is achy. However, it's the inability to keep food down and sensory overload that are killing me.

"Oliver!" I call out from my corner office. "Do we have more ginger ale?"

My overly chipper assistant with fashionable silver hair pops into my doorway with a hesitant expression on his face. "Morning sickness?"

I nod as much as I can without gagging.

"I'm sorry. Pregnancy is a bitch." He says with all the confidence of a man with three kids already.

Oliver has been with me for the past five years and has become like family.

So, when I came into the office this morning after my doctor's appointment yesterday, looking distraught and overwhelmed, Oliver dragged the news of my pregnancy out of me, and he's been fussing ever since.

It's sweet.

It also makes me want to scream.

"I suspected something when you did not return to the office yesterday and went radio silent. Chandler gave me these ginger chews last night." He says quickly as he rushes off to his desk. I hear him rustling around before his footsteps announce his return. "They're supposed to work wonders. Xe got the recommendation during our most recent pregnancy. The first two kids were a breeze. But, of course, the symptoms were awful this last time."

I try to smile in thanks, but the truth is that every act of kindness and support grates against my belief that I should be able to do this on my own.

That's what I had planned, after all.

"I don't know how you did it so young." I marvel as he hands me a can of ginger ale and a bag full of what looks like candies. "You're what, 30?"

"Yeah, but it was really our only option, given that xe's ten years older than me. It needed to happen sooner rather than later." He shrugs. "I was ready to start a family."

I crack open the can of ginger ale, taking a few slow sips between deep breaths to calm myself.

"I understand." I sigh, thinking of my struggles for the past two years. "Biology waits for no one."

"It was right for us. Our first child was a little bit of a surprise, but I was ecstatic when xe told me the news every time." Oliver says with a smile before he grows quiet. "When are you going to tell him?"

I sigh, regretting telling Oliver the truth about how I got pregnant versus rolling with the lie of using IUI. "I'm not sure how to."

"You'll have to do it sometime." He says gently. "And soon."

"I know." I straighten myself at my desk. "I'll do it this weekend. I just need some time to wrap my head around the idea."

"I get that." He says, a knowing silence growing between us.

"Did you send out the reports for tomorrow's Board meeting?" I ask, desperate to change the subject.

"Yes. I sent those out this morning. They are in your inbox." He says.

"Thank you, Oliver," I say calmly.

"Of course." He replies with a smile before leaving me to work.

Unfortunately, I couldn't give less of a fuck about the report for tomorrow's Board of Directors meeting. I try, I really do. But my eyes just scan the same phrase over and over, still not absorbing anything.

Finally, there's a knock at my door, and a friendly face appears in the entryway.

Selene Solis de Estrella and I met at The Playground Club about a year and a half ago. We hit it off as friends immediately.

However, it took about three months before I fully learned the extent of her background in technology development. Once I did, I stole her from her former employer and made her my Chief Technology Officer here at Coral Crude.

The petite woman with wavy brown locks and a round body and face, similar to my shorter version, always manages to brighten even my worst days.

They say, "don't work with friends", but she's one of the few people genuinely capable of making me feel anything close to joy.

She's infectiously cheerful.

"Alright, Señora Presidenta, time for lunch." *Madam President.* She says, casually strolling into my office. "Otherwise, you'll get hangry and turn poor Oliver into an ice sculpture with your freaky ice queen magic."

I scowl. "I'm not an ice queen."

"You don't really get a choice in what the staff calls you behind your back, Elsie." Selene giggles while fiddling with my perfectly arranged bookshelves.

"Do they really call me the ice queen?" I ask, rising to fix the mess she's made.

"Oh, don't take it personally. Everyone in the industry thinks of you that way. They're all terrified of you." Selene tosses all this out casually before turning to me with a wide grin. "It's what makes you a badass CEO and why absolutely no one fucks with you."

Seeing my stricken face, Selene's victorious smile drops.

"Oh, Presidenta. It's a good thing!" *President.* She says in a cheerful tone as she marches over to my pile of bags to grab my purse.

We've had this conversation several times now: how the world perceives me as cold and unfeeling. She's right, though. I can't help how others see or think of me.

"Plus, you have your friends from The Playground. You don't need the approval of others." She continues.

"They're club friends." I protest.

"Yeah. They're people who get you, have similar values to you, and don't judge you for who you are." Selene says reassuringly. "Though, I will say, whatever you and Marshall got up to a few weekends ago? It's made you... warmer or something. You're happier when you're well fucked."

I scoff, trying to hide my rising panic at the mention of Marshall. "I would hope so."

"It's true!" She cries. "Nothing like a good steamy fuck to thaw out the ice queen."

"No comment."

"Oh. You're definitely commenting at lunch. You've been holding out on me, and after whatever went down at my engagement party with our fuckboy, Marshall? I want the *tea*." She says, pushing me out the door in front of her. "So, we're going to lunch at that steak place with the filet mignon you love, and you're going to tell me all about your 'arrangement.' Right?"

"Fine. But no to the steak. I can't stand the smell right now." I acquiesce.

"Okay..." She says, drawing out the vowels. "But you're paying."

Her confident strides down the hall leave me hurrying to catch up with her.

"Well, that doesn't seem fair." I toss out when I meet her at the elevator.

"Life's not fair, Presidenta." She throws over her shoulder as we enter the lift. "It's your hot gossip tax. And it's time for you to *spill.*"

"Fine. But you have to promise to keep this to yourself." I tell her, but she just rolls her eyes at me. "I mean it, Selene."

Her brow furrows, and there's a moment of silence before she speaks. "Sure. I promise."

"Thank you." I sigh in relief.

Selene regales me with a few work-related topics on our drive over to the restaurant, but she mostly tells me about plans for her upcoming wedding. Soon enough, we're seated at one of our favorite places, but she wastes no time jumping into what she really wants to know once we've placed our orders.

"Spill." She commands, delicately laying her napkin in her lap. "What happened with Marshall?"

I hesitate, not sure how much I want to share with her right now.

I settle on a partial truth. "We slept together. That's all."

"Nope." She scolds as the waiter places our starter salads before us. "No holding out on me. I want the full details."

Forking a bunch of lettuce and shoving it in my mouth, I ignore her question for a minute.

"Elsie," Selene says, warning in her tone.

I slowly chew, and when I'm done, I take a sip of water.

Folding my hands in my lap, I look at her.

"I'm pregnant," I state.

"What? Oh! Congratulations!" She exclaims. "The last round of IUI worked?"

"Not quite..." I take a deep breath. "The weekend of your party..."

"Oh. My. Goddess." She gasps. "Marshall?"

I nod and reach for my fork to take another bite.

"Have you told him yet?" Selene asks.

"Not yet," I mumble around a bite of salmon.

"Shit. He's like, what? 29?" She says with a heavy sigh. "How do you think he'll react?"

"That's the problem... I don't know how he's going to react." I put down my fork. "But no matter what happens, I'm prepared to have this baby and raise them. Whether he wants to be involved or not."

"Well, whatever happens, Gunnar and I are here to support you." She goes quiet and then smiles at me. "I'm happy for you, Elsie. You're going to be a fantastic mother."

"Thank you," I reply with a grin.

"Now, chow down. You're eating for two!"

4

MARSHALL

March 9 — 10 Weeks, Lime

Elsie, splayed out before me, lying on her back with her legs spread open and inviting, is quite a sight to behold.

Though it's her stomach, swollen with my seed growing inside her, that has my heart pounding.

My fingers skim up the inside of her thighs, sending shivers through her body.

When I reach her center, I spread her lips open and take in the beautiful view of her pussy.

"Fuck. You're incredible." I murmur.

"Shut up and fuck me already, Marshall." She commands.

My cock swells at her authoritative tone, and I ready myself to enter her.

I skim my tip up and down her center, making her squirm in anticipation, but before I can thrust into her, I'm interrupted.

"What the fuck!" I cry, jolting up in bed and wiping water from my eyes.

Every night for weeks, I've had the same dream about Elsie Snow. In every one of them, she is heavily pregnant. Plus, I seduce her into taking my cock again and again until she's screaming my name every time.

But the cold water that just woke me from my dream isn't part of that fantasy.

"Oh, good. You're up." A cool voice says before mumbling under their breath. "Fucking finally."

Shaking the sleep from my eyes, I look over to the side of my bed to find a tiny woman glaring at me with murder in her eyes.

"Elsie?" I ask.

"Yes, asshole." She says, placing the offending empty glass on my makeshift nightstand.

Box. It's a box.

"You sleep like the fucking dead." She grumbles.

"No shit. I work on an oil rig that operates 24/7. Those things are loud." I say groggily while shifting to swing my legs over the side of my bed.

When Elsie's gaze shifts down, I realize my mistake.

I'm hard as fuck.

And having the subject of my dream standing before me in all her curvy glory is not helping.

She looks incredible, her full auburn curls framing her face perfectly to highlight the roundness of her rosy cheeks and pale complexion. She's dressed comfortably in leggings and an over-sized t-shirt, but it doesn't detract from her beauty.

Seeing her for the first time in weeks is making me light-headed and my cock harder than before.

I shift to try and cover my erection a little, but she gives me the courtesy of looking me in the face when she says. "Put on some clothes, and then we need to talk." Her voice is cold and unfeeling, but there's a slight wobble that makes me nervous.

"What? Why?" I ask, confused.

I haven't seen Elsie in weeks, at least 28 days, to be precise. I only got home from my last rotation on the rig on Sunday earlier this week and have been sleeping away the week. I haven't left the pool house Gunnar and Selene let me rent in days.

What could I have done to get her this worked up this early on a Saturday morning? Or is it afternoon?

"Because. I said so." She says, turning on her heel.

Before she can leave, I grasp her by her wrist and pull her into my body so her tiny frame nestles between my legs as I sit on the bed.

At 6' 5", I typically tower over her, but right now, we fit perfectly together, with her lips so close to my quickening pulse.

For a moment, she's rigid, but then her whole body melts into my embrace. I feel satisfied at the knowledge that she feels comfortable in my arms, and I relax as well.

"Marshall." She protests half-heartedly from in my arms.

"Elsie," I say slowly.

"Let me go." She sighs.

"Not until you tell me what's wrong," I tell her.

Being so close to me, I know she can feel how hard I am.

What she doesn't know is that it's for her.

For that simple kindness, I'm grateful.

"Talk to me, princess," I murmur in her ear.

The force with which she pushes me away startles me a little, but it's her seething expression that has me freezing in place.

"Shut it with the princess shit. I'm mad at you." She snaps, turning once again to leave the bedroom. "I'll be in the living room."

"I'm gonna take a shower," I call out as she leaves, which only earns me more muttered curses.

I chuckle at the sound of more mumbled cursing under her breath, but once she's gone, I do as she asks and head to my bathroom to shower and dress.

I take my time to shower and get ready to face the ferocious Elsie, trying to think of what could have pissed her off so much to get her to the point where she's breaking into my place and tossing cups of water on me.

Working on an offshore oil rig means working 28-day shifts, leaving me with very little reason to rent my own place. I used to live with my mother at my childhood home because I could not justify the cost of an apartment, I only used half the year.

But a year into dating, Selene and Gunnar bought a house together, and while we were only friends from the club at that point, they heard of my unfortunate living situation and offered to let me move into the pool house behind their new home about a year and a half ago.

The place is perfect for me, but it's not really home.

Home isn't really a place... it's people.

It's family.

So, for now, outside of my blood relatives who I'm close with, Selene and Gunnar are the closest thing I have to that dream.

In terms of a place to live, though, I only really need a fridge for takeout leftovers, a couch, and a television to watch my teams. There's a bed to sleep away my days and fuck away my nights. It even has a hot tub out back, which is the perfect way to get my multitude of guests naked.

So many good memories here.

Once I'm done getting ready, I walk into the kitchen to find the counter piled high with containers from my fridge, which stops me in my tracks.

Elsie is bent over, rooting through my freezer drawer, and it's the best memory I've ever had in this place.

"Elsie?" I ask, mirth in my voice.

She spins around. "Why don't you have ice cream? There's sorbet but no ice cream. Who the fuck doesn't have ice cream? Who even eats sorbet!"

"A man who's lactose intolerant?" I try with a laugh, rounding the counter to where she stands.

The glare she gives me stops me in my tracks.

"Any particular reason you've emptied my fridge?" I ask.

"You take for-fucking-ever to get ready, and I had a craving." She shrugs.

"So, you took everything out of my fridge?" I chuckle.

"No. I threw out half of it, though. It smelled awful, and I'm pretty sure there were a few blocks of cheese growing mold."

"Elsie, that's not..." I sigh, reaching over to grab a few containers and put them back in the fridge. "Let's try this again. You got hungry. So, you were looking for something to eat?"

She rolls her eyes at me in confirmation.

"What do you want if I don't have ice cream?" I ask simply, turning to the pantry to see what I may have there.

A sniffle has me stopping and turning back to Elsie.

"I don't know." She whines in a voice which I've never heard come from the small woman. "I can't... I'm just... Marshall, I'm falling apart."

"Oh, baby," I say, putting down a bag of bread on the counter.

This woman has no idea the power she has over me.

I've been absolutely enraptured by her for a year, but every flirtation and hint I threw her way was shrugged off. It wasn't until Selene and Gunnar's engagement party that I finally had my chance with her.

Since that magical night, I've done everything in my power to get her attention and really make an effort, but I was brushed off while I was in town. Which meant there was no real reason to try while I was gone for work.

I told myself when I got back that I would try again, I had to.

But first, I needed to sleep.

The universe seems to be on my side, though, if she's currently standing in my kitchen just waiting for me to comfort her, to show her how good I can be for her.

I try to pull her to me for the second time today, but she bats me off when I reach out.

"Don't baby me." She says indignantly. "I'm not your baby."

"Okay..." I say patiently. "Elsie, what's wrong?"

Tears start streaking down her cheeks, and I start to panic. This was not how I imagined our reunion going when I saw her again.

"Elsie. Talk to me. Why are you here?" I ask as calmly as I can manage.

If my mamá and sisters taught me anything, it's that a woman crying is never a good thing.

"I'm... Ugh." She says, wiping away her tears, clearly frustrated. "I'm hungry all the time, but half the time, I can't figure out what I want to eat. Then, when I figure it out, I cannot keep it down. I'm exhausted and moody, and everything hurts. I'm so fucking done, Marshall. So. Fucking. Done."

By the end of her tirade, the usual chill that Elsie speaks with is back, along with her commitment to looking at me like I've broken her favorite toy.

"Okay," I say, reaching up to grab a glass from the cabinet and fill it with ice water from the fridge. "Why don't you go sit down on the couch and get comfy. If you're hungry, then I'll make you something."

"But..." She starts.

"No. If you don't like it, then I'll just make something else." I say sternly.

"Fine." She pauses on her way to the living room couch. "No beef. I can't stand the smell."

"Got it. No beef." I chuckle.

Looking around, I grab the bread I had set down earlier and pop it onto a baking sheet. Then I go to the pantry to find ingredients for the only comfort food I know how to make and get to work. Ten minutes later, I'm pulling my creations out of the oven and putting them on a plate.

Walking into the living room, I find Elsie snuggled on the couch under the quilt my mamá had sewn.

I hold out the plate for Elsie as she unwraps herself from her blanket cocoon.

"Beans and toast?" She asks.

"Ah. Not quite." I laugh. "Molletes. Toast, refried beans, cheese, and salsa. My mamá made it all the time for us growing up."

"It smells delicious." She says softly. "Gimme."

The grabby hand motion she makes, combined with her hermit appearance under the quilt, makes me laugh, and I hand over the plate.

Sitting down on the coffee table before her, I watch as she takes her first bite.

When her eyes close and she moans in pleasure, my chest swells with pride. I don't know how to make much, but I know mis familias recipes by heart.

"Good?" I ask, already knowing the answer.

She groans with a nod of her head and dives back into devouring the dish before her.

After a few minutes, with only the sound of her adorable munching, I break the silence.

"You wanna tell me why you broke into my place, poured water on me, and cleaned out my fridge?"

She takes her time to finish her snack before speaking.

"First off." She clears her throat. "I didn't break in. Selene gave me a key when I asked for it."

"Alright. The other two statements are still true."

"You sleep deeper than a koala, Marshall. I tried everything else before resorting to cartoonish tactics. And your fridge is filthy." She says with a huff.

"Okay." I acquiesce, going back to my initially intended question. "Why are you here then?"

Elsie grows quiet, putting her plate to the side. Her gaze drops down to her hands, which are now flat against her knees.

The sight of her, still bundled in the quilt and looking as vulnerable as I've ever seen her, makes me ache to touch her.

Reaching out to grasp her hand, I plead. "Elsie, what's wrong?"

She lets out a deep sigh and straightens herself before looking me in the eyes.

"I need to tell you something, but you weren't answering your phone. Not that I would have told you over the phone. That would have been a bitch move." She finally says, mumbling the last of her words.

"Okay," I say slowly.

"You weren't answering. So, I tracked you down." She reasons.

"By breaking in."

"I got a key!" She snaps. "This is not a breaking and entering situation."

"So, you're not a burglar. Got it." I joke. "Then what are you?"

I love teasing her, seeing the furrow that forms on her brow when I do.

"I'm pregnant." She states cooly without breaking the connection between our gazes.

Everything slows down to a halt.

Pregnant.

Elsie is *pregnant.*

"Like with a baby?" I ask, stunned.

"Yes, Marshall. That's kind of what pregnant means." She huffs.

There's only one reason she would be here, right now, telling *me* this.

Selene's engagement party.

We've only been together the one time. She made it clear that it would only be once, too, not that I would have listened to that part after how perfect our night was.

"And it's mine?" I ask.

"Yes."

"Fuck." I say softly, glowing inside.

I'm gonna be a dad.

Someone's gonna call me Papá.

Fuck.

"Marshall?" I hear Elsie ask, but it feels far away.

I've always wanted kids. I just didn't think I'd be doing that now.

I'm only 29. I thought I had more time.

But this?

This is everything I want out of life.

The woman I've obsessed over for the past year is pregnant with *my* child.

A vision of Elsie, round with our baby and wearing a white dress as she walks down the aisle to me at our wedding flashes before me. Pictures of holidays and birthdays run through my thoughts. There are mundane moments of making messes in the kitchen and playing in the backyard under the hot Texas sun. I envision our little family growing and forming memories together.

With each thought racing through my mind, my heart lifts, and excitement builds.

Letting go of Elsie's hand, I stand abruptly and walk to my bedroom.

I need to pack.

There's no way I'm letting my future wife and mother of my children go a single day without me there to support her.

I've spent my adulthood as a bachelor.

Many would even describe me as a player.

A man whore.
But all that's over today.
Because now I'm a father.
A father.
Damn.

5

ELSIE

It took me a half hour to gather myself up from Marshall's couch before I realized that he wasn't coming back. I could hear him in the other room, but I couldn't bring myself to go and face him. Something kept me rooted to the spot.

When I finally managed to move, I found Selene on the back porch of their home. She tried to talk to me... tried to comfort me... but nothing got through. It was like she was talking through water. Everything sounded garbled and messy through the pain that was radiating through my body.

Finally, I peeled myself away from her, concern still painting her face, and got in my car to drive home.

All I could focus on was getting home, locking myself into my safe space, and never coming out.

I don't remember the drive or taking the elevator up to my apartment and unlocking the door.

But now, ensconced in my bedroom, I undress and head into the bathroom for yet another comfort shower. Standing outside the shower, I lock down my thoughts while staring expressionless at the water falling from my shower head.

I can't fall apart.

Not yet.

The steam building in the room helps me stay grounded enough to recognize when the shower is ready. Stepping in, I let the water cascade over my body, and my thoughts finally run free.

I don't know what I expected when I drove over there and demanded Selene and Gunnar's key to the pool house to confront Marshall.

Anger, maybe.

Confusion, sure.

Shock, absolutely.

But nothing?

Nothing almost hurts the most.

His expression went completely blank when I told him. There was absolutely no reaction, no emotion.

Then he left.

He left me sitting there, alone.

It took me thirty minutes to leave because I kept expecting him to come back and talk to me, to say *something*.

Instead, there was just a ruckus coming from his bedroom.

At that moment, I felt like the ice queen everyone accuses me of being. Everything in my body went cold and hard. Everything shut down.

There was no warm feeling of joy to share with him: no smiles or excitement.

He left.

He's not ready for this.

I'm ruining his life.

Only, it feels like mine is just starting, and I don't know how to handle the conflicting feelings.

Part of me is elated.

I'm going to be a mother!

But another portion of me is devastated at Marshall's reception of the news.

He's so much younger than me.

There's no way he's ready to be a dad.

This is so much responsibility, and I *know* him.

He's a womanizer.

Personizer?

What do you even call a man who sleeps with anyone who's interested?

Man whore?

If he wants to walk away from me and our baby, fine.

I don't need him.

I don't even want him.

I'll do this on my own.

Reassured by my conviction, I force my pruned hands to turn off the water. I climb out of the shower and wrap myself in a fluffy towel before making myself go through my hair care and skincare routine. But exhaustion sets in, and I can't bring myself to do anything more than dress in a nightgown before dragging myself into my bedroom to collapse, with wet hair and all, into my bed.

Laying there, sunlight shining through the windows, I start making plans in my head. The mental list of things to do and buy eventually gets long enough to where I start a list in the note app on my phone of everything I need to do.

Despite it being only noon, the task relaxes me enough that soon I'm drifting off to a deep, though restless, sleep.

When I wake up to the sound of banging, my bedroom is dark.

"The hell?" I mumble, dragging myself out of the comfort of my king-size bed.

Reaching under the bed, I pull out the gun safe, which I keep there, and press in the code. I pull out the small piece I keep there and check the empty barrel before clicking the magazine into place.

Maybe it's excessive, but it's not just me I'm protecting anymore.

So, I click off the safety and swipe the slide back to load the chamber.

When I open the bedroom door as quietly as I possibly can, I don't expect all the lights to be on.

Keeping close to the wall with my gun at the ready, like I was taught in my gun safety training, I make my way down the hall but halt when I spot the front door wide open only a few feet away.

No one should be able to get up here without the front desk giving them access. I've given them a strict list of people who are allowed free access to the penthouse elevator, and I wasn't expecting anyone today.

When I reach the end of the hall, I stop and take a deep breath, readying myself for whatever is around the corner.

As I turn the corner, I raise my gun and sweep the room quickly, looking for the intruder.

Only, instead of a burglar, I find Marshall surrounded by bags and boxes, looking delicious in a tight-fitting t-shirt, worn blue jeans, and his signature work boots.

His dark hair is messy around his face, highlighting the tight line of his jaw, covered in stubble. His brown eyes are alight with mirth at this whole bizarre situation.

"The hell?" I gasp, looking up at him.

"Oh, good!" Marshall says, turning in my direction. "You're up!"

Quickly, I lower my gun and release the bullet from its chamber before flicking the safety back on.

"The actual fuck, Marshall?" I shout. "I could have killed you!"

"Well, thank you for not doing that." He says, still smiling. "Now that you're here. Where should I put my stuff?"

"Your what?" I ask, bewildered. "What are you even doing here, Marshall?"

He steps around one of the boxes and takes a few strides to me, gently taking the gun out of my hand and setting it down on a nearby side table.

"Okay, that's better." He says with a smirk. "I knew you were a Texas girl, but I didn't realize you owned a gun."

"Guns. With an S. I hunt too during the seasons." I correct before shaking my head. "Stop changing the subject. Why are you *here?*"

He looks around at the bags and boxes that are around the room as though they answer my question, but I refuse to believe my eyes.

"I'm moving in." He says simply.

"The hell you are." I snarl. "I did not invite you into my home, Marshall. Get the fuck out."

He takes a step toward me, but I've already snatched the gun off the side table and started my march back to my bedroom before he can reach me.

"Elsie." He calls after me. "Come on. At least talk to me about this?"

I turn back to him. "Fuck no. Now get your shit out of my house."

"I tried calling!" He shouts down the hall.

"Don't care!" I shout back. "Get out!"

Shutting myself into my bedroom, I slump against the wall.

My heart is hammering in my chest. I am still in disbelief that Marshall not only managed to get *into* my apartment but also had the audacity to think he could just *move in.*

I lock the bedroom door, just in case, and crawl back into bed.

"Fucking, Marshall Law."

March 10 — 10 Weeks 1 Day, Lime

The next morning, I wake to a delicious smell wafting through the apartment.

Following my nose, I make my way to the kitchen to, once again, find Marshall Fucking Law standing there, making breakfast at six in the morning.

"MARSHALL!" I shout. "What the hell!"

He spins around, looking deliciously rumpled in his tight-fitting t-shirt, sweatpants, and bedhead.

"Morning!" He says cheerfully, ignoring my rage and returning to what he was doing at the stove.

"You're still here," I say in disbelief.

"Well, yeah. I found the guest room and slept there. Hope you don't mind. I made myself at home." He says, shrugging.

"I mind. I very much mind." I snap, my frustration with this man increasing with every passing second.

"Well, I tried calling you yesterday, but you didn't answer." He continues.

"So, you broke into my apartment?" I squeak, pacing toward him.

"Just returning the favor, princess." He jokes, making my scowl deepen. "The front desk person was really sweet and understanding. They helped me get everything up here last night."

"How did you get in? They don't keep keys to the individual units." I ask, mentally composing the email to building management about letting uninvited guests into the building.

"Selene gave me her key." He says simply.

Of course, she did.

I can't help but stand there, frozen in place, as the whole scenario plays out in my mind. How he turned on his charm and pled his case to Selene and, true romantic that she is, she caved and gave in to his bizarre plan.

In fairness, she did the same thing for me, but it feels invasive, nonetheless.

At least she's technically his landlord.

"Marshall. Be reasonable. You can't just move in with me." I say, shaking my head.

"I can, though." He says simply. "I don't have a lease to break. Moving is super easy for me. You have the space. What's the problem?"

"The problem is..." I sigh, frustrated. "It's..."

"Exactly." He says with a massive grin on his face.

I close my eyes, searching for patience. "But why? Why the fuck would you move in with me?"

This time, there's quiet before he responds, as though he's genuinely thinking through his answer.

When I finally bring myself to face him once again, he's standing there with a spatula in hand, looking down at me with the most deadpan expression I've ever witnessed him make.

"Because you're having my baby, and I'm not letting one day pass without me being there to support my family." He says, his voice completely serious.

"Your *family*?" I screech in disbelief.

"Yes. My family." He says, taking a few steps toward me and placing his hands on my shoulders. "Ahora eres mi familia, Elsie." *You are my family now, Elsie.*

It takes a minute for my brain to translate his words with my rusty college-level Spanish skills, but when they settle in, my jaw drops.

"You've lost your mind. You're not thinking clearly, Marshall."

"No. I've never been more clear-headed." He says, returning to the stove to check on whatever he's making.

I march up to him and poke him in the side. "You are *not* moving in with me."

His 6'5" frame towers over me, but I'm not afraid of him. If anything, I'm growing more impatient with each passing second.

"Yes. I am. You're not doing this on your own." He says softly with a glance down to my stomach.

My hands fly to cover my belly, protecting what I know is growing there.

"Fine. You want to be involved. Great!" I take a deep breath, trying to calm my racing heart. "But you don't need to live with me."

"You keep saying that, princess. But I'm already here. You're not getting rid of me. I'm not going anywhere." He says sweetly. "Now, sit. Breakfast is almost ready."

This man has absolutely lost his mind.

There's no way this is happening. There's no way this is real. It must be a dream, right?

I close my eyes and pinch myself, hoping I'll wake up from whatever the fuck this is, but when I open my eyes again, Marshall is still standing there.

"Sit," he repeats, gesturing to the dining room table, which has already been set with silverware, napkins, and glasses of juice and water.

"Right," I grumble, finally admitting defeat. "It smells delicious."

"Huevos rancheros." He smiles, turning from the stove back to the two plates he has laid out before plopping the fried eggs on top of the fried tortillas and refried beans. "I was going to deliver breakfast in bed, but you beat me to it."

"Where'd you get the stuff for all of this?" I ask.

"Ah. Yeah. You don't exactly keep a whole lot of fresh ingredients on hand," He chuckles. "But a buddy of mine's wife owns a local grocery and opened up for me early."

"Marshall. You don't even cook for yourself. What the hell are you doing?" I ask.

"I'm cooking for my family," he says simply, bringing the plate to me as I sit at the dining room table.

"You keep using that *word*," I stress the last syllable.

"What? Family?" He asks as he sits down next to me.

"Yes! That! Stop saying that." I scold.

"Elsie. You're the one who showed up to my place yesterday and told me you're pregnant. What did you expect was going to happen?" He says calmly. "You're having my kid. We're family now. That's how this works."

Panic rises in my chest every time he says that *word*. To me, it doesn't mean what he thinks it means.

Family is an illusion—a facade with no substance.

It's not something I want.

I just wanted a baby.

"It's really not, though," I say, picking up one of the tortillas laden with goodness and taking a bite. "Mhmm. Okay. That's good."

"I'm glad." He beams beside me before digging into his own food and talking through a mouthful. "You'll have to let me know what foods you're craving, and I'll make sure to keep those on hand."

"You've been here all of, what, eight hours?" I laugh, covering my mouth when a few crumbs fall out. "And now you're suddenly 'Susie Homemaker'?"

"Why not? I'm home for the next three weeks before I have to go back to the rig. Might as well make the most of my time." He says, leaning back and rubbing his hard stomach in satisfaction. "Good, right?"

"Yes. It's really good." I admit. "Normally, I can't eat in the mornings, but, yeah, this is good."

"Perfect. I'll call mi mamá and ask her for more recipes. I think this kid's gonna fit in just fine with the rest of the family. We'll have to introduce you to them soon. Maybe tonight's family dinner? I'll ask if I can bring a guest."

I nearly choke on my next bite at his words. "What?"

"I'll call mamá and see who's coming to dinner tonight. She should be up by now." He says, reaching for his phone. "We'll have to leave here by 4:30, though, to make it there before six and not be late."

"Marshall. Stop." I plead, placing my hand over his phone screen. "I am *not* meeting anyone today. Especially not your family."

"You'll have to meet them eventually. Might as well be now." He shrugs, picking up his plate and going to the sink. "Mamá is going to be so excited to hear about the baby."

"No!" I command, stopping him in his tracks. "We're not telling anyone about this. Not until at least the 12 week mark. And not until I'm ready."

He gives me a curious look before continuing slowly. "Okay... Then what *do* you want to do?"

"Right now, I just want to have a peaceful Sunday. Go to the farmers market, maybe. Get my nails done. Catch up on emails." I sigh.

"Okay. I'll put clothes on, and we can go."

"Go? Go where?" I ask, wide-eyed.

"Farmers market. Nails. Then home." He lists off, counting on his fingers as he goes.

"You're coming with me?" I ask, bewildered.

"Princess, for the next three weeks, I'm going to be stuck to you like a barnacle. You'll be sick of me by the time I leave for my next rotation." He smiles, turning to head to the guest bedroom.

"I already am..." I grumble.

6

ELSIE

March 14 — 10 Weeks 5 Days, Lime

Marshall wasn't kidding about the barnacle thing.

The first few days after he moved in on Sunday were cute, and his attentiveness was almost... nice? But now it's Thursday, and I'm pretty sure my assistant wants to strangle the man more than I do now.

"He has to go," Oliver says, storming into my office, nearly slamming the door behind him and cringing when it does. "Sorry."

Every day for the past week, Marshall has come into the office to be "helpful." Thus, my assistant's current look of frustration.

I sigh. "He's a lot."

"It was cute. It really was. And I do like sending him for coffee..."

"Which you won't let me have," I grumble, cutting him off.

"It's for your own good. You should have stopped a long time ago." He says, waving me off. "But the man is going to drive everyone to quit. He needs a real job."

"He *has* a real job. That's the problem." I sigh. "He leaves in 17 days. Then he's out of our hair for twenty-eight days."

"And when he's back? He goes back to following you around the office like a puppy dog?" Oliver whines, then dramatically collapses in one of the chairs in front of my desk. "I can't live like this."

"*You* can't live like this? The man literally sleeps across the hall from me now. He never leaves me *alone*." I say, my composure cracking. "I just want one god damned day away from this man, like it was before... you know."

Oliver doesn't miss my gesture to my stomach.

"He is a really good cook, though," Oliver admits. "The enchiladas he brought yesterday were to die for. I still need to say thank you for sending me home with a tray for my family."

"He won't stop feeding me," I smirk. "You think it's some kind of kink?"

"Nah, with how often that man put his hands on you and your belly? That man is more obsessed with you being knocked up than anything." Oliver says with a chuckle.

When my door swings open dramatically, I'm not even surprised to see a very furious-looking Selene standing in the doorway.

"He has to go." She says desperately.

"Ah. I'm so glad everyone is in agreement." I say.

"He's got my staff clinging to the end of their sanity. He asks *so many questions*." She complains.

Looking around the room at my two closest friends, I drop my head into my hands and begin to cry.

"Oh, my goddess. Babe. I'm so sorry." Selene starts, rounding my desk and kneeling beside me with a hand on my thigh.

"No." I cry. "It's not you. I'm just... overwhelmed and emotional."

"My partner did the same thing when xe was pregnant," Oliver says, grabbing for a tissue from the box on my desk. "It comes and goes."

"I just don't know what to do. He's driving me up a wall." I fret, trying to gather myself as I wipe my eyes with the tissue Oliver passes me. "Last night, he insisted on making dish after dish because either I couldn't stomach the idea of eating them or he would make something, and the smell made me gag."

"Oh. That's kind of sweet." Oliver coos.

"No. It's really not. He made a mess of my kitchen and gave me a headache with all his banging around." I gripe. "Then this morning, he woke up early and bought about forty different supplements he says I need to be taking. Now he's asking when my next doctor's appointment is because he has questions for her."

"Okay, the doctor thing is reasonable, you must admit." Selene contributes, to which I frown.

"Not when he wants to ask about whether or not it's safe for me to have sex." I scoff, thinking of the uncomfortable conversation we had driving into work this morning after he shoved his way into my car and refused to leave. "I want to scream."

"At least he's thinking about sex." Selene shrugs, standing up and going to the free chair next to Oliver. "I've heard once the morning sickness goes away that you become horny as hell."

"She's right," Oliver says with a far-off look and a smirk.

"I want to scream," I admit. "I want to run in the opposite direction. Just quit everything and escape to a country with no extradition treaty."

Selene and Oliver share a conspiratorial look, which makes me frown and wonder what they're up to.

"The man needs boundaries," Selene says with a devious smile.

"Clearly." Oliver agrees, a grin forming on his face as he watches Selene carefully.

"You should make a list of rules." Selene suggests, giving me a small shrug as though what she's suggesting isn't that big of a deal.

"Rules," I repeat, trying to follow the silent conversation going on between my two friends.

"Ooh. I like that idea," says Oliver. "The do's and don'ts of being together."

"We're not together," I interject sharply.

"Fine," Selene says in a soothing voice that's somewhat out of character for her animated personality. "In which case, think of it as like roommate rules then. That's what y'all are, right? Roommates? At least for the time being."

"I can live with that." I agree, slumping back in my chair.

"Then we make a list for him to review and agree to," Selene says.

"I'm loving this idea," Oliver says, standing and strolling out of my office. "I'm grabbing my computer. I'll take notes."

I sigh. "Y'all are ridiculous."

Only for the next hour, Selene, Oliver, and I work on creating a list of rules that Marshall must agree to in order to save my sanity.

When Marshall walks into my office promptly at five p.m., I silence my co-conspirators.

"I'll print off a copy of this for you to go over later," Oliver says as he rushes out of my office.

"Good luck!" Selene cheers as she leaves with Oliver, but her voice turns cold when she addresses the newcomer. "Marshall."

"Thank you," I yell after them as Marshall settles into one of the chairs that my friends just vacated.

Silence builds between Marshall and me, the only sound in the office being the clatter of my coral typewriter-style keyboard and the hum of the air conditioner blasting through the vents.

When Oliver returns to drop off the folder with our list of "rules" for Marshall, I thank him again as he exists.

"You know, Oliver and Selene are the only people here that I've seen you be outright kind to," Marshall says, finally breaking the silence. "You don't say thank you or please to anyone else in the building."

I look up at him sharply, trying to gauge his motivations.

"Your point being?" I question.

He shrugs. "You could stand to be a little nicer to your staff."

"My staff are here to do a job, Marshall. A job which I pay them handsomely for." I assert. "I shouldn't have to coddle them into feeling warm and fuzzy to do their job."

Silence passes between us before he speaks again, his voice gentle. "Did you know you made an intern cry after your finance meeting yesterday?"

My head whips over from my computer screen to look at him. "No."

"You asked her for her opinion on something in the meeting and shut her down when she responded." He says. "She left the meeting and cried in the bathroom for ten minutes."

"How do you know this?" I ask, my voice growing softer with each word.

"You have genderless bathrooms." He shrugs. "I waited for her in the lounge area by the door and checked in on her."

"You stalked my employee," I say, my voice hardening.

"No. I checked on her, which she seemed to appreciate." He replies more defensively.

"Not that it's your business, but everyone who works for me is treated exceptionally well here. They are all asked to create a flexible schedule of thirty hours a week, either working remotely, in person or some combination thereof. They all receive full benefits and six weeks of vacation time. There are six months of paid parental leave for every employee who is expanding their family, whether they've been working here for four months or four years. Interns receive very similar treatment, including the option of either being paid for their work or being offered course credit through their universities." I snap, frustration growing with each syllable uttered. "My team is treated well and compensated more than fairly. There's no reason for them to be crying in bathrooms."

"That doesn't mean that they feel emotionally safe and secure in their work environment." He says, holding his ground against me despite my growing annoyance. "Not everyone handles your sharp edges well, Elsie. Sometimes, people need a leader to be soft. They need to see you be vulnerable in order to feel comfortable doing the same in their work."

"Are you saying I'm a bad leader?" I ask defensively.

"No. Not at all." He sighs, shaking his head in exasperation. "I'm sorry. I just mean to help."

"Well, stop helping. It's not needed." I say through gritted teeth.

"Elsie! Responding to other people's needs is like 90 percent of being a parent." He says, glancing down at my still-typical curvy belly. "You're going to have to adapt at some point."

I look down at my body. I know change is coming and that things will have to shift when the baby comes. But that's an issue for later, and I don't need to worry about that right now.

"I have time," I murmur.

"Change doesn't happen overnight." He says.

"It does when you become a parent," I reply with a little too much sharpness. "I was preparing to do this on my own from the beginning, Marshall. There's no reason for that plan to change."

His eyes grow wide, and his face falls like I've genuinely hurt him.

"Except that I'm here. I'm here and asking to be a part of this, Elsie." He says, getting up from where he was sitting on my couch to come stand beside me at my desk.

With the gentlest of touches to my chin, he lifts my face to meet his own piercing brown gaze.

"I want this, Elsie. Don't deny me the chance to be a part of my child's life."

His voice is so tender, and the look he's giving me is so open and honest that I can't push down all the tears that want to come up.

Stuffing the emotions down, I shake free from his delicate touch and reach for the folder Oliver left on my desk.

"Here," I say, my voice a little too shaken for my taste. "Read and sign."

7

———

MARSHALL

lsie thrusts the folder in my direction without a glance and shifts back to her computer screen to continue working.

I take it from her desk making my way back to my seat, and collapse into it before opening the folder to examine its contents.

Of everything I could have thought it would be, what I find was not on the list.

"What is this?" I ask, looking down at the sheet of paper before me.

"Read it, and you'll find out," Elsie says, rolling her eyes and avoiding looking at me.

"It says 'Roommate Rules.'" I say, scanning the heading of the page again. "Elsie, what is this?"

"Exactly what it says they are." She snaps, turning to face me from behind the safety of her desk. "If you're going to barge into my life, camp out in my apartment, and interrupt every facet of my life, then you're going to do it with at least some respect for my life and how you're disrupting it."

My jaw drops in shock.

I know having me move in and be around all the time has been an adjustment, but this seems like taking things a little far.

"So, we need a formal agreement?" I ask, still taken aback by the whole idea.

"Yes." She says shortly.

"Elsie," I say with a sigh. "Do you really think this is necessary?"

"I do." She says, trying for a bit more patience. "Read and sign, Marshall."

The list isn't long, but I have to re-read each line to really wrap my head around what she's asking me for.

I can feel Elsie's eyes on me as I read, and I glance up a few times only to catch her looking away.

"It says I'm not allowed to eat anything you're unable to eat?" I ask, fully facing her this time.

"Yes. No sushi. No lunch meat. No coffee. Et cetera." She reasons with a roll of her eyes. "If I'm going to put up with you being around for the next seven months, then I'm not going to put up with you taunting me with food I can't eat."

"Okay," I reply slowly, drawing out the vowels. "That seems fair enough."

Gonna be a lot longer than seven months, though.

My eyes go back to the page in front of me and read through the rest of her "rules." None of which sound entirely unreasonable.

The document reads like a full-on lease. It starts with a breakdown of the agreement term—seven months—and my monthly rent, along with the breakdown of my contribution to each month's utilities and groceries.

<u>Article II: The Apartment Rules</u> are what have my eyebrows raised. It covers everything, including smoking, alcohol, *illegal activities*, parties/ gatherings/ celebrations, guests, and quiet hours.

She's even outlined things about laundry, cleaning routines, and schedules.

Article III: Decorum includes rules about not touching the thermostat, the food thing, and no shoes on in the apartment. Also, no gum?

But my eyes snag on the last rule and lock in.

"Sex at any time?" I ask.

"Yes. Free use, carte blanche." She says dismissively before mumbling. "It wasn't my idea."

Her's or not, the idea of having her body pressed against mine again, my cock snuggly fit in her pussy, has my whole-body heating.

"Tell me what that means *to you*," I say, looking to her for clarification.

I know what free use is and how it *can* work between partners, but I've also watched enough awful porn to know what *other people* think it is.

"It's a kink," She answers slowly, and I try to keep my expression neutral as she continues. "Essentially, either of us can request sex at any time, and the other party cannot say no."

Images of me fucking Elsie in every room of her apartment flash through my mind, driving my need for her higher.

Just the thought of how blissful these next months could be has my cock hardening beneath my jeans.

"So, *either* of us can request sex at any time? That's what you're proposing," I repeat back to her.

"That is what's outlined." She sighs, clearly done with my line of questioning. "Selene and Oliver insisted I include it. They say I'll be needy later in my pregnancy, and I should set a clear boundary around sex now."

Honestly, not the worst idea considering I don't know how long I'd be able to keep myself from riling her up just so that she'll fuck me again.

"Of course, they helped you with this." I chuckle before my thoughts grow contemplative.

Do I want to sleep with Elsie again?

Yes. Fucking hell, yes.

But do I want it to be because I demand it of her?

No.

I know she sees this as a short-term situation where I'm staying with her through the pregnancy. Then, well, I guess she has some bizarre vision in her head that I can't wrap my head around. Because in my mind, I'm not leaving.

Elsie and the baby she's carrying are my future now. They're my family.

You don't leave family.

I know what it's like to grow up without a father. I would never put my own child through that.

So, no. I won't be taking advantage of a clause that says I can take her whenever I want.

No. She has to want it just as much as me, need me just as much as I already need her.

She has to *ask*.

After a few more moments of silent consideration, my mind is made up.

"I can't agree to that part. The rest is fine, but that has to change." I explain firmly.

Like a meerkat, Elsie pops up from her chair behind her desk and rounds it before stopping before me.

She's a woman who's used to getting her way. I can imagine having me push back on a rule she probably imagined was something I would want would frustrate the hell out of her.

Maybe even more irritating than having me lurk around the office all week, which is strictly prohibited per the agreement now.

"I'm offering you unlimited sex, and you're saying no?" She asks, her voice pitching up at the end.

"Correct," I reply, standing as I speak so I'm looking down at her.

"Why?" She asks with a glare up at me.

"I want to renegotiate," I say firmly. "I'll agree to everything else, but this one rule changes."

I take her chin between my fingers and hold her firmly in place as I lean down.

"What are your terms then?" She huffs with chipmunk cheeks, and I smile.

"On one condition. *You're* the only one who can request sex." I pause. "And I have to ask permission to touch you. But you have to say it... out loud."

"What?" She asks, seemingly confused at my request.

"You heard me. You have to ask me for sex verbally." I repeat coolly.

"That's absurd. You're turning down unlimited sex?" She questions.

"Not at all. I'm totally on board for unlimited sex." I move my face inches closer to hers, just a breath away from her lips, brushing my own. "But you're going to ask for it every time. Not me."

"Why?" She says breathlessly.

"Because if I were given the option for unlimited sex at *my* request, I'd have you tied down to a bed 24/7 and fuck you full of my cum every chance I got."

8

ELSIE

March 23 — 12 Weeks, Plum

Since I gave him our new roommate rules, Marshall and I have been playing house quite successfully.

He's finally exited the office completely, which has my whole staff letting out a sigh of relief. He has found other ways to occupy himself during the day.

Despite having a cleaning crew come to the house once a week, my home has never been cleaner than since Marshall moved in. I'm pretty sure he's pulled every tchotchke off my shelves to dust, and he re-alphabetized my books by genre, then author's last name, all while keeping the series together and in the correct order.

He even put up a whiteboard on the fridge next to my pregnancy calendar and has been keeping track of the baby's growth. Every day, he marks the day on the calendar, and each time I hit a new week, I wake up to find another awful drawing of a fruit or vegetable alongside the phrase "Baby is the size of a...."

He's put hair claw clips in every bathroom so that when the

nausea takes over, he has one on hand to pull my hair back with, and he even wears hair ties on his wrist now.

There's dinner on the table waiting for me when I get home every night from work. Every dish of which takes my current food preferences into account.

I know he's been spending time with friends during the day, but I've never seen him go out like a single twenty-nine-year-old bachelor is supposed to do.

Not even on the weekends.

However, when I'm home, I become his whole focus.

This morning is no different.

"Good morning!" Marshall says when I appear in the kitchen at 6 a.m. on the dot, as is my routine.

"Morning," I grumble.

"Which sounds better, huevos rancheros or breakfast tacos?" He asks, turning around to heat up the cast iron skillet for our breakfast.

"Tacos. Always tacos." I reply, smiling softly at his consideration, to wait to start breakfast and ask my preference.

"Good. That's what I was hoping." He says, smiling to himself. "Do you think you can stomach chorizo?"

"Ooh. Yes. Gimme all the spicy." I groan.

In the past few days, I've been craving all sorts of spicy foods, but for some reason, it's hard to admit that to Marshall and just ask for the things I want.

It's that way with a lot of things with him.

"¿A mi princesa le gustan las cosas picantes? Anotado." *My princess likes things spicy? Noted.* He says with joy in his tone.

"You think you're being so clever speaking Spanish around me. While I might be rusty now, I'll have you know I aced all of my Spanish courses in college and did a study abroad in Spain for a semester," I say, my tone growing slightly too defensive.

"I'm not trying to be clever." He says, turning around to grab an onion from the basket on the island for the tacos. "Lo estoy haciendo para que la bebé también lo sepa." *I'm doing it so the baby knows it, also.*

"Oh," I say sheepishly, glancing down at my stomach where my hands are now resting. "Okay."

"I'd like all of my kids to speak Spanish. I think it would be nice for them to be able to speak fluently with my family and especially my grandparents, who only speak limited English." I shrug, going back to preparing our breakfast.

I'd never given much thought to Marshall's family before.

I know very little about the man who's now living with me, actually.

Sure, he barged his way into my life purely because of the new life in my belly, but that doesn't mean I should treat him like a stranger, right?

We have slept together, after all.

"Right. Sorry." I mutter.

"No need to apologize. There's a lot we still have to learn about each other." He says simply.

He's right, though.

While part of me wants to maintain a distance from him, another craves to know more about him and his life, including his family.

Family, who will soon also belong to our baby.

A thought that has me shuddering.

"So, what's the plan for today?" He asks when the room grows quiet.

"Mostly just work..."

"It's Saturday, though." He says with a raised eyebrow as he chops vegetables.

"I know, but work doesn't stop just because it's a weekend." I sigh, thinking of the to-do list I still have to get through. "Though, I was thinking..."

"What are you thinking?" He asks, switching to whisking the eggs for our tacos in a bowl while the chorizo cooks in the pan.

"You've been really... good... this week," I say carefully.

"Good?" He asks hesitantly.

"Yeah. You took the list, and you kind of ran with it." I say with a light laugh. "You even cleaned out the fridge of everything expired and anything I'm not supposed to eat, just in case."

"I'm not letting you get poisoned by expired food if I have anything to say about it." He says, his voice growing serious.

"I'm just saying I appreciate you making the adjustments I requested."

He whips around. "Are you saying... thank you?"

"Well..."

"You are!" He drops the tortillas in his hand and rounds the island to take my face in his hands. "Say it. Say, 'Thank you, Marshall.'"

"Thank you, Marshall," I grumble.

"Oh, hell yes. Mark the day. March 23. Elsie Snow said thank you to me!" He laughs, giving me a kiss on the cheek before returning to making our breakfast. "So, what's my reward?"

The moment is so candid it catches me off guard, and my hand goes to the place where he kissed me, marveling at the warm feeling it left in my chest.

"Reward?" I ask after a moment.

"Yeah. I get a reward, right?" He chuckles. "Bribery will get you everywhere, princess."

I roll my eyes at the endearment.

Which, unfortunately, is becoming less and less irritating each time he uses it.

"Fine. I was thinking we could go to the club this weekend." I say, confidence coming back into my voice and posture as I remember myself. "Today marks twelve weeks, and I am almost in the second trimester."

"I know." He says, nodding to the pregnancy calendar he marks off each day. "La bebe tiene el tamaño de una ciruela ahora." *The baby is the size of a plum now.*

"Yeah, well... I thought we could celebrate a bit and go to the club." I suggest.

"I did notice that the nausea and whatnot seems to have gone away. It seems like la pequeña ciruela azucarada is giving you less of a hard time now." *The little sugar plum.* He shrugs and tries to hide his goofy grin before returning to making breakfast, but I catch it just before he turns. "I'm game for a weekend at The Playground, though."

"Good," I say with finality.

Reluctant as it may be, I've realized Oliver and Selene are right about the horniness which showed up around the time my morning sickness stopped earlier this week.

He has been an excellent trophy... something, the perfect boy toy. So, I fully plan on playing with him this weekend while we're at the club to curb some of this need that appears every time I see him in his gray sweats or coming back from a run without his shirt on.

Those are my favorite mornings, seeing him shirtless and glistening with sweat. The man is absolutely gorgeous with his tanned skin and ocean-themed tattoos on his right arm.

He said I have to ask for what I need, especially when I need to be fucked. And, while I've been tempted several times to jump him this week, I could never bring myself to do it.

The Playground Club is neutral ground, though, and it's intended to be used for meaningless sex at that.

The Playground Club and Resort is a swingers resort and BDSM club an hour outside of Houston that caters to patrons with particular lifestyle interests. People come from around the country to stay at the resort for several days, or even weeks, and attend the club in the evenings. Those who are primarily local chose to only come for a night or two and enjoy the club atmosphere.

It is a getaway from the mundane of daily life and a retreat from the expectations of society for many who come to visit, including myself.

Though my friend group adopted me only a year ago, I found the club long before then, visiting for a long time just to watch others navigate the lifestyle club.

"You said you had to do some work?" Marshall asks, putting my breakfast tacos down before me.

"Yeah," I say, shaking myself from my thoughts.

"Why don't you spend the morning doing that, and I'll pack our bags for the weekend." He suggests.

"You'd do that for me?" I ask, shocked that he would want to do something so silly for me. "I can pack my bag, you know."

"I know, but you have other things to do, and I didn't make any plans otherwise." He explains, which makes me feel better about asking him to do this for me.

"Then, yeah. That would actually be really nice to have that off my plate." I say.

"Consider it done then." He smiles, settling down at the breakfast table with me to eat.

Breakfast goes by with a pleasant quiet between us, and when we finish, I go into my office to get work done while he does... whatever he does during the day.

It all has a very homey domestic feeling, which is both a little shocking and... pleasant?

9

ELSIE

I closed my laptop around noon for lunch, and with all of our things ready to go, Marshall loaded us up in his truck shortly after to drive out to The Playground.

The resort is a beautiful structure that flows seamlessly with the Texas landscape of tall grasses and sprawling trees. Every facet of the campus was carefully thought out for the benefit of its patrons. Knowing the owners—the Morgan polycule—is all very deliberate.

The staff quickly checked us in, and soon enough, we are entering the rooms I had booked for Marshall and me.

As you enter the top-floor suite, you pass a small kitchen with all the amenities you would need to stay for long periods of time, as some people do. The room then opens to plush couches placed in a U shape in front of a massive television screen. Beyond the media area is a balcony looking out across the whole resort, including the club, which is situated directly across from us.

Knowing I wasn't quite ready for the intimacy that comes with sharing a bed, I booked us a suite with two bedrooms, each with California king beds. The suites are intended for guests with larger groups like those in polycules, but I thought it was necessary for us to have separate sleeping accommodations.

When I finished work today, I was too tired to think, much less pack a bag.

Pregnancy is a bitch on your energy levels like that.

So, I was so glad that, at the time, Marshall already did everything for me, but I'm now severely regretting that decision.

"Marshall!" I yell from the primary bedroom of our suite.

"What! What?" He asks frantically as he enters the bedroom.

I'm frowning in front of the suitcase he packed for me.

"What in the hell did you pack?" I snap.

"What are you talking about?" He says, stopping in his tracks in the doorway.

"Marshall," I growl. "There's nothing here but skimpy lingerie and bikini bathing suits!"

"I'm failing to see the problem here." He questions, looking around at the items I've pulled out of the bag.

"The problem is I'm fat, Marshall. I can't wear any of this!" I say, frustrated beyond measure. "Where did you even find this stuff?"

I love my fat body, but that doesn't mean I don't have insecurities or that I don't dress to my level of comfort, even in body-positive spaces like the club.

"First off, your body is fucking incredible, and I don't want you ever talking negatively about it like that again." He says with a slight growl in his voice.

"Fat isn't a bad word, Marshall. It's just an accurate description of my body." I say a little too curtly. "I'm not using it to talk down about myself. I'm reclaiming the word. Got it?"

"Fine, but I don't have to like it." He grumbles before getting back to my original question. "Second. Some came from your closet, but I went out and got the rest because I couldn't find anything that worked for the club."

I groan, holding up a sheer, stretchy mesh bodycon dress with rhinestones. "And you didn't bother to ask where I keep all my club wear in the apartment?"

"I was just trying to be helpful." He says before taking the dress from me and setting it back on the bed. He takes my hand and stroking the inside of my wrist. "And you're going to look fucking incredible in all of it."

I take in a deep breath, unprepared for the fire of desire in his eyes.

But this is my fault, after all.

I should know better than to depend on other people for anything.

Including something as simple as packing a suitcase.

"It was very sweet of you to pack everything for me this morning." I sigh, knowing he was only trying to help. "It's on me for not checking to see what you packed before we left."

He sits down on the only empty portion of the bed, then curls our fingers together before tugging me between his legs.

"I'm sorry." He says softly.

"Goddess. You're too hard to stay mad at when you look at me like that." I say when I look up at him. "It's not a big deal. I'm just... not used to dressing like this."

He looks around at the bikinis, lingerie, and dresses I've thrown out on the bed as though trying to find a solution to the problem he created.

"Do you not like them?" He asks, giving my hand a squeeze.

"They're pretty," I say slowly. "I just don't normally wear such revealing or form-fitting clothes when I come out here."

"Isn't that kind of the point?"

I shrug. "For some people, probably."

He hesitates. "Elsie, why do you come to the club?"

"What?" I ask, not sure where he's going with this.

"Why do you come to The Playground? Why'd you start coming last year?" He asks, more confident in his question now.

I start to pull back but soften when he shifts his hold on my hand to rub small circles on my inner wrist.

Thinking it through, I try to decide how honest I want to be with him.

Do I tell him everything?

After a moment, I figure the man is going to be around for the next eighteen years for this kid. He might as well know how fucked up I am.

"My father and I went no-contact four years ago." I start.

"The club only opened three years ago, though." He questions.

"If you would let me finish..." I say impatiently.

"I dove into work when I stopped talking to him. He's really the only family I have—my mom was gone shortly after I was born." I say.

"Elsie, I'm so sorry." He says, true sadness in his eyes.

"It's okay. I've had a long time to adjust to that loss." I shrug. "But Father was different. He was always working his agenda. We never had a good relationship, but it was nice to have *someone*. You know?"

He nods but doesn't interrupt me again.

"I kind of lost it after a while and threw myself into dating, thinking that I could just replace the emptiness with someone else rather than dealing with my issues." I continue. "One of the girls I dated for a while invited me to an event downtown. It was one of the brunches that happens every month."

I think back to how out of place I felt at first when I was there, but how everything changed when I started talking to people.

It wasn't like my work relationships, where everyone *wanted something* from you. It all felt genuine. People were actually interested in me as a person.

"I didn't know it was a lifestyle event. I didn't even know what the lifestyle was then, but everyone kept talking about this club that just opened up."

I pull away, taking each of the garments I'd thrown onto the bed, and begin folding them to go back into the packing cubes Marshall put everything in.

"It sounded almost magical. A place where I was free from judgment. Some place where I could let go and not worry about what others thought of me or my interests."

"You wanted the freedom." He adds.

I turn to him, remembering the lightness I felt the first time I walked into the club. "Yes. I wanted the weight off my shoulders for once."

"Did you find it?"

"Kind of? I came as a lurker for the longest time." She looks at me with a smirk on her face. "I found Selene and Bex and the rest of the group a year ago, but actually, I'd been going to the club as a patron for a little over two years."

"Really?" He says, genuinely shocked.

"Yeah. For the longest time, I would come and grab a soda at the bar and watch." I shrug, pulling out my toiletries and unzipping the bag. "I just wanted to see what it was like... and for a little bit, I got to let go and lose myself in the club atmosphere and the energy of everyone around me."

"So, what brought you into the group?" He asks.

"Selene." I smile. "She found me in a corner watching a scene between Alvie and Bex. Next thing I know, I'm being tied in a rope harness."

I can't help but notice how Marshall shifts at the mention of me tied up and how he blocks off my body so I can't see but instead can feel his hard cock.

"I spent the rest of the night with the group and then just never really left. Finding the group felt like... Well, I found my community, my people, with them." I shrug before reaching to move the suitcase off the bed, but he immediately pushes my hands aside.

"Tell me where you want it," he says, and I point to the bench across from the bed.

"I can do things on my own, you know," I say quietly.

"You shouldn't have to." He smirks, placing the nearly empty suitcase down and turning around to face me. "You're a princess, remember?"

A laugh escapes from my lips, and his grin only grows at the sound.

"No." I remind him. "I'm a fucking queen."

10

———

MARSHALL

Only assholes in untested shiny armor fight a dragon.

Dragons are protective of their valuables. Don't fuck with them or their stuff.

As a philandering single man in the lifestyle, there's not a lot I say no to.

I enjoy sex. I enjoy people. I enjoy sex with those people.

I fuck hot wives and vixens while their stags watch. I make cuckolds cower in corners. I'll fuck you if you're single or not.

As long as there's enthusiastic consent and everyone's enjoying themselves, I'm game.

There are no attachments and no obligations.

I liked my single dragon status.

I owned it.

But now that's changing, and the protective impulses I used to have toward my friends are coming out tenfold now that Elsie's become my family.

She's convinced herself that I'm going to be a nuisance in her life and a failure as a father, but I'm determined to prove her wrong.

I want this.

Was I anticipating my life to change in a matter of a few words? Not really.

But here we are, and I couldn't be more on board.

I've always wanted a big family, just like the one I grew up in. I had a good childhood, and I'm determined to make sure that my children have the same love and stability.

My biggest concern, though, is that Elsie will be resistant to having me around.

I know how she values her independence.

She doesn't need a savior or a protector.

She's no damsel in distress.

She's a queen.

Elsie insisted that we go about our night as though nothing had changed. She doesn't want anyone to know about the baby yet, and despite the fact that our entire relationship has changed in a matter of weeks, I'm still just a friend.

Hence why, I've been watching her from the corner of The Club, where I sit next to my friends Zuri, the founder of an adult toy company, and Ivy, one of the club's volunteer employees.

The two-story club itself stands separate from the resort, but its distinct design draws attention from anywhere you stand on the grounds.

Inside the club, every inch has been thoughtfully designed to elicit desire from the members who patronize it.

The lobby is practically an art gallery, each wall adorned with paintings of sensual moments in every style of design and perspective. Bird cages, the inspiration for the club's distinct logo, hang from the ceiling and act as chandeliers to light the lobby.

Though it's inside that really draws people in.

When you enter, the space opens to reveal a central dance floor around which everything else revolves. The second floor of the club, where the majority of the playrooms and BDSM equipment are, looks down on the dance floor, providing the perfect opportunity to watch as people dance and drink the night away. There, everything is on display.

There are small nooks and crannies throughout the club, too, as well as alcoves to escape to with your partner—or not your partner—for a quick tryst.

The first floor, though, is mostly seating for people to gather and mingle. There is a bar at the back where patrons can retrieve a setup with ice, cups, and mixers for the evening.

Right now, my attention is entirely on the man standing a little too close to Elsie at the bar, and it's testing every boundary I have not to storm over and demand he back the fuck away from her.

Watching my queen from across the club being hit on by this sleazebag has my hackles raised.

The dipshit hunting after my baby mama is begging for a fist in his face.

"You gonna step in?" Zuri asks as she follows my gaze across the club.

"She's fine," I say, knowing Elsie would kill me if I intervened.

"Smart move." Ivy chimes in, sipping on the drink in her customized tumbler. "Elsie can take care of herself."

"Sure, she can." Zuri agrees. "I'm not worried about Elsie. It's the guy who doesn't know what's coming."

I glance back over at the interaction happening across the room and wince when the man puts his hand on Elsie's hip.

"Oh. He's so dead." Ivy giggles tipsily, which gets me moving.

Time passes in slow motion as I watch Elsie glance down at the man's hand on her. Thankfully, I'm already across the room and meeting them where they stand at the club's central bar before she can do anything about it.

"Problem here?" I interrupt, wrapping Elsie in my arms and pulling her back protectively against my chest.

"Nope. Not at all." The man says, meeting my eyes with his unimpressed look.

"I've got it, Marshall." My ice princess says coolly.

Leaning down, I whisper in her ear. "You can't fight him, Elsie."

When she turns to look at me with her brilliant ice-blue eyes, I freeze. "I know that. Let me. Handle. This."

I loosen my grip around her waist, but I don't fully let her go in case she decides to pounce and rip out his heart.

"Marius, right?" She says, her voice going subzero.

"Marcus." He corrects.

"Right, whatever." She continues with a roll of her eyes. "If I wanted you to touch me, then I would invite you to do so. But seeing as I have less interest in that than I do in remembering your name, I suggest you leave."

I suppress a smile when the man's jaw drops fully.

"Fine." He says, turning on his heel before mumbling under his breath. "Frigid bitch."

When he's fully retreated, Elsie turns her cold glare on me and shoves a pointed finger in my chest.

"Don't fucking do that again." She scolds. "I don't need you to save me, Marshall."

Despite being a whole foot and a half shorter than me, Elsie exudes power like the badass CEO she is.

That said, at 4' 11", she's still adorable, especially since her auburn curls are out of control after dancing and shaking her perfectly round ass all night.

"Marshall. Tell me you're not going to do it again." She commands.

I hesitate, and she gives me a deadly look that gets my lips moving.

"I promise not to intervene next time," I say carefully.

"Good. Now. You're coming with me." Elsie says, grabbing me by my collared shirt and dragging me in the direction of the private bedrooms. "And I'm fucking you senseless until I'm no longer pissed off."

"Yes, my queen." I laugh as she drags me along. "Use me as your personal dildo."

"Shut up, toy." She says with a grin.

Toy.

The endearment sends a shiver down my spine.

I've been called many things by partners, but never *that*.

With anyone else, I might have an issue with a term like toy, but with Elsie, it feels natural.

If being her plaything is what she needs from me, then that's what I'll be for her.

If this is how I get close to her, show her I'm not going anywhere, then I'm in.

Elsie pulls me through the club, and I can't help but beam with the small claim she exerts by wrapping her hand around mine as we go.

We are stopped on occasion to talk to acquaintances and friends. Though the impatience in Elsie's jaw, like she really does want this, wants me, gives me a thrill like no other.

Zuri and Ivy give me a knowing look as we pass them to go up the stairs to the second-floor playrooms, and I wink back at their smirks.

Even though our friend group might not know what's going on with Elsie and me, they likely have an idea.

The second floor of the club, where all of the play areas are set up, wraps around the balcony that looks down onto the dance floor below. It is split into two areas.

We come up the stairs that lead to an area with a St. Andrew's Cross, spanking bench, and hard point set up in the center for rope suspension scenes. Couches wrap around the space, with plenty of seating for a crowd to gather and watch whoever is being put on the equipment for a scene. On the mirror side, there's a similar set-up with a voyeur bed at the center of the space for public play.

Elsie drags me through the throng of people who have gathered to watch our friends, Alvie and Bex, put on a show on the cross. Elsie glances into a few of the rooms, only to find them occupied with people already fucking, but she keeps searching until we get to the final bedroom in the row.

We walk into the empty room, and Elsie quickly closes the door behind us, locking it with a click.

"Strip." She commands.

11

ELSIE

There's something about tonight that has me feeling bold. Having Marshall come up behind me and wrap me in his arms to protect me was both aggravating and comforting.

And hot.

Maybe it's outdated, but having a partner come to your rescue still sends a shiver down my spine.

Plus, I've hit the point in my pregnancy where morning sickness is no longer an issue, but instead, that daily problem is replaced by another.

One which makes me extremely horny.

The dreams started a few nights ago, visions of me and Marshall together, naked. Every one of them feels more vivid than the last, and everyone leaves me worked up and needy.

Tonight, I plan on doing something about it.

Hence, dragging Marshall through the club to find an empty bedroom where I can make all those dreams come true.

The room is simple but beautiful, with wainscotting on the walls, all painted a deep plum color. Every room is a little different, but we've luckily snuck our way into one with one of the industrial four-poster beds, built for tying or hooking up restraints and a myriad of other playtime aids.

I look around, see what the room has to offer, and see the dresser, where sheets and towels, along with other self-care items like wipes and water, are stored.

Nothing catches my eye that I might want to use tonight, though; I want this simple and fucking dirty.

"I said strip," I repeat, annoyance growing.

"Yes, ma'am."

"Queen." I correct. "Tonight, I'm your ruler, your queen."

"Yes, my queen." He says with a smirk. "Should I kneel as well?"

"Not yet. First, I want you naked." I say, smiling up at him before taking a step back to enjoy the view.

Marshall takes his time undressing. He starts by, ever so practically, taking off his boots and socks before he lifts his shirt off in one smooth movement in that sexy way that men do.

His naked chest is a marvel. All of his muscles are on display, toned from years of hard labor. His tattoos are less visible in the dim lighting of the room, but their black ink beautifully contrasts his tan skin.

Then he reaches for the button on his pants and slowly undoes it. He lets the jeans fall open at his hips but makes no move to pull them down and reveal what I really want to see.

"You want me, Elsie?"

I glare at him for breaking the moment by calling me by my first name.

"Take what you want, my queen." He corrects, but his next words light me on fire. "I'm yours to use."

A shiver rolls down my spine at the idea of using him for my pleasure. Having him underneath me while I ride his face, his cock.

"Off," I say through panting breaths.

"As you command." He teases back.

Hooking his thumbs under the waistband of his briefs, he draws the remainder of his clothing down and off his legs and tosses them to the side.

"Much better," I say coolly.

"You like what you see?" He asks, less teasing and more like he's looking for validation.

I look up into his face, and even in the dim lighting of the bedroom, I can see the earnestness in his expression.

This man cares what I think of him, which is a terrifying thought to have. And a terrible power to hold.

There's an ongoing internal battle between my two conflicting needs: my need for independence and my need for him.

My body craves him, but the tiny voice inside of me says that my soul does as well.

But right now isn't the time to think about how souls intertwine. It's time to focus on the physical instead.

The man before me is a sight to take in, his muscular thighs toned and tanned just like the rest of his body. The small trail of dark hair which leads down to the part of him I desire most right now, his cock.

Memories of how well he fills me spring to mind, and my pussy clenches at the promise of pleasure to come, and come and come, and come.

"My queen?" He asks, a little more tenderness in his voice than before like he's waiting for a biting remark to come and hurt him.

But I could never do that to him.

Not this man.

"Yes." I breathe out, letting my hands move forward to rest on his abs and trace the curves of each one. "I like it very much."

One of Marshall's hands comes to wrap around my own, and he looks down at me with such sincerity when he speaks. "What do you want, my queen?"

I hesitate for a moment, knowing nothing will happen tonight or ever if I don't explicitly ask for it from him. But there's a mental barrier to asking for what I need, one that I'm not fully prepared to face.

So, instead of asking for the intimacy I crave, I settle for the physical that I need.

"Get on the bed and lie down on your back." He raises a dark eyebrow at me. "I'm going to ride your face until I come, then ride your cock until you do."

"Fuck." He moans, his head dropping back. "You're wicked with your words, woman."

When he doesn't move quickly enough, I grab him by his dick and stroke him up and down his length. At my touch, his pupils blow wide, and I can see fireworks in his eyes.

"And your touch." He groans out.

I love that I know what he likes and how to coax him to his edge.

One time together, or many depending on how you tally our night at Selene's engagement party, taught me enough to know when he's nearing his finish. And I memorized it well enough to know when to stop.

My gaze flicks between his cock and his face as I stroke him, loving the sight of both while I do. His face is open, lost in the pleasure of my touch, while his cock twitches in my hand as I stroke him.

"On the bed," I whisper as I release his cock and push him away from me by the hip.

"Yes, my queen." He murmurs.

Quickly, he climbs on the bed but looks back at me for further instructions.

"On your back for me, toy," I instruct, which gets him to flip over and lay sprawled out on the bed.

When he's settled, I climb up on the bed and make my way up his body to straddle his legs.

When I find a comfortable position on my knees, I take his cock in hand once more and lean down to kiss the tip.

The smallest of touches has his hips bucking up, already anticipating and needing me and my cunt.

"Not yet, toy." I croon. "First, I'm going to play with you."

I lean down and take the tip of his cock into my mouth. My sucking around his head causes a gasp to escape from his lips, and I relish in the shiver of pride it sends down my spine.

Pulling off his cock with a pop, I then blow a steady stream of air onto his now glistening tip, making him groan once again. Then, I dive in, taking his cock into my mouth fully.

I love giving blow jobs, and the rush of taking control of someone's pleasure puts me on a high I can't explain. I love taking him down my throat and sucking along his length as I back off. Each time I swallow him, he makes small sounds that encourage me to keep going. Every withdrawal has him begging for more.

I may be on my knees for him, but he's not the one in control right now.

I am.

After a few minutes, I can tell he's holding back. He's dug his fingers into the sheets, trying his best not to reach for my head and take control. But he's unable to control the little thrusts of his hips that drive his cock deeper down my throat until I'm gagging on him.

"Please." He whimpers, but I don't relent.

I keep going with my ministrations and bob up and down his length, swallowing him whole and pulling off him in a steady rhythm. My tongue swirls around his head, teasing him each time I give him a break from the tightness of my throat.

"Please, my queen." He tries again, his voice more desperate this time.

This time, when I pull back, I let my teeth lightly graze against his shaft and head until I've fully released him.

"Let's see if you're as good with your tongue as I am, then. Shall we?" I smirk.

"Yes." He sighs. "Please, I need to taste you."

I can already tell how wet I am just from giving him a blow job, my thighs sticky as they rub together while I crawl up his body.

When I reach his shoulders, I stand up so I can position myself over his face and begin to lower myself.

"If you need to breathe, just tap my leg three times," I tell him.

"I won't, my queen." He pants, his gaze fixated on my cunt as I lower myself to my knees. "Use me as your throne."

I smile. "My pleasure."

"As it should be." He says, grasping my hips and pulling me down.

Before I'm even fully settled on his face, his tongue is already reaching for my pussy to lick through my center. The feeling of his rough tongue on my sensitive folds already has me moaning in pleasure, and I wiggle to settle myself comfortably on his face as he begins to eat me out.

When his tongue finds my opening, his nose finds itself in the perfect position right by my clit. A zap of energy shoots through my body at the contact, and I lift ever so slightly in shock.

Marshall takes a quick breath, but just as fast, he's already pulling me down to bury himself in my cunt once again. He uses his tongue to lick at and thrust into my channel, driving my need higher with each movement.

Soon enough, I'm grinding against his face. His tongue is in my pussy, and his nose hits my clit with each rock of my hips. Every ounce of his attention is entirely devoted to my pleasure, which keeps climbing with each second.

His fingers dig into my flesh hard enough to leave bruises, and I know he's likely in need of air.

But I'm so close, so close, to my release that I don't care.

He's mine to use for my pleasure, and I intend on dragging every second out of it that I can.

I keep going, my hips moving at a more desperate pace than before as I feel the peak of my orgasm approaching. I bear down on him, my hands flying to the headboard to keep me upright as I grind into his face.

By the way, his legs are bouncing beneath me, I know he's desperate for air. But he hasn't tapped out, so I keep going.

Then, he licks up from my core and presses the flat of his tongue up on my clit, and I crash.

Electricity rolls through me, frying every nerve in my body and making me cry out. The orgasm feels like it rolls on forever as I continue to grind against his tongue, which he holds in place for me.

I release the headboard and fall forward, the shocks of energy still making my body shudder in a pleasure that borders on pain.

Marshall is beneath me, sucking in air as fast as he can before letting his breath out again so he can try and fill his lungs.

As my orgasm is starting to fade, I push myself up using the headboard and shakily walk down the side of the bed with the help of the bar above me.

When I let go, I fall to my knees, my pussy perfectly lined up with where his cock stands at attention, and begin to rock against it.

Marshall cries out through his desperate gasps of air, and his hips buck up into me, causing his cock to bury between my folds and press against my clit that's hidden between my full lower lips.

I rock against him as his hips buck, and on occasion, his tip brushes against my entrance, making my need to be filled even more prominent in my mind.

Unable to pull myself upright, I slide up his body slightly and grind back down again so his tip finds my opening and slips in this time.

"Fuck!" Marshall screams as I let out a sigh of relief.

What feels like heaven to me must be a torturous hell for him, but he doesn't ask me to stop. He doesn't use the safe word we agreed upon many months ago.

Instead, I push back on his cock, and he thrusts his hips up, helping drive his length further into me.

The fullness is overwhelming every one of my senses. My eyes fall closed, and all sound tunes out as all of my focus trains on the pleasure of having him inside of me.

Gathering my strength, I push myself up using his muscular chest so I can impale myself further on his length. I can't bring myself to lift my hips yet, but I am able to rock my hips in a pattern that helps open me up to take in more of him.

Marshall is beneath me, noises escaping from his lips that don't sound like they belong to him. He squirms and writhes on the bed as I ride him, but he still doesn't ask me to stop. His hands finally release their death grip on the mattress and fly to my hips, drawing me up so I'm hovering above him with his cock only half-way in.

There's no relief on his face, though.

Instead, he quickly adjusts his position, digging his feet firmly into the mattress and thrusting up with his hips so he fills me completely again.

His abs ripple and tighten under my touch, shocking me into moving them so I'm holding myself up on the mattress instead of him.

Where his fingers dig into my thick thighs, I'll indeed have bruises, but I don't care at all. I want them, need them even.

Each thrust into me somehow feels deeper than the last. His cock is at the perfect angle to rub against my front wall where I'm most sensitive, and the sensation has another orgasm building in me once again.

Soon, his thrusts grow erratic, though no less harsh or pleasurable.

"Fuck." He pants out between strokes. "I'm going to come, my queen. Please, can I come?"

His tone is high and pleading, making my body melt into him.

"I need to give you my cum. I need to fill you up. Give you everything." He begs. "Let me cum inside you. Let me... I need to... Fuck!"

His whole face is pinched with the pain of holding back his orgasm as he forces himself into me deeper and harder than before.

"Need to give you my cum." He groans through gritted, grinding teeth. "Breed you. Breed. Fuck! Breed you."

My orgasm is close but still so far away. So, I help him by reaching down to rub my clit and get myself there.

One of his hands reaches out to grip my breast to the point of pain as the other knocks away my fingers from my clit and replaces them with his own. His fingers mirror my own pace I had set, but he presses firmer into my clit.

"Gonna have my baby. Be my baby mama." He forces out just as I'm nearing my peak. "Please. Come. Let me come."

I throw my head back as my orgasm rushes at me. It's slower this time, less forceful, but somehow more powerful, and I scream, clawing at Marshall's chest.

"Please." He sobs as my walls flutter around him. "Gonna be a mama. My mama. My... *Mine.*"

The growl in his voice, the sheer possessiveness to his words, sends another sudden orgasm through my body, and I collapse against him.

"Come for me, daddy." I pant out as his erratic thrusts slam into me. "Come for Mama."

His breath stops, and he crunches up with a twisted look on his face.

Then I feel it, the flood of cum inside me and dripping down my thighs.

His hips fall down, but mine follow with them to stay impaled on his cock. His arms wrap around me and pull me down, so I fall with him as he relaxes into the mattress.

A breath whooshes rapidly in and out of our lungs, and we search for every ounce of oxygen in the room.

Every time my walls flutter around him, he sighs in contentment.

We lay there like that for a while, just taking in air and feeling the heat of our bodies together.

Every bone in my body feels like melted goo. I couldn't move from where I'm wrapped in his arms if I wanted to.

The joke's on me because I don't.

I don't want to move.

I'm exactly where I should be.

12

———

MARSHALL

April 1 — Second Trimester — 13 Weeks 2 Days, Lemon

"Get your ass in gear, pretty boy! Boat's gonna leave without ya." My rig boss calls out.

He's an ass, and I can't wait until he retires. However, he keeps the crew in line mostly because he puts the fear of the Goddess in our 60-person crew.

Which you have to respect.

But 'pretty boy' drives me up a wall and down the stairs.

The only person on earth I let call me names are the people I'm fucking. That's it.

Womanizer.

Player.

Playboy.

Ladies' man.

Daddy.

Toy.

Now, Elsie Snow is the only one I want to call me anything. She can call me however she likes. I'll still fuck her 'til I take my last breath.

Which only makes going back to work after eight days of incredible sex even more impossible.

Since our night at the club, Elsie's pussy has kept my dick busy every free moment in her day. We've fucked in every room of the apartment when she's home, in her office when I brought her lunch one day, and in the backseat of my truck on a side street when we were headed to the grocery store. She's even taken to letting me sleep in her bed because it means easier access to my cock.

The words 'I need you.' get my dick standing at attention faster than a bullet out of the barrel of a gun.

That woman's cunt has me by the balls, and she knows it.

"Pretty boy! You payin' attention?" The boss yells.

"Fuckin' hell. I'm comin', ya tool!"

"Not for 28 days, you aren't, pretty boy." He laughs as I approach him, which only makes me want to punch him in the face more. "Sky's not clear enough for a 'copter to get us out there. Workboat's gonna take us this time."

"I know. I got the email, too." I roll my eyes.

"Pretty boy can read? I'm shocked." He laughs but seems to recognize my sour mood and changes his tone. "Just givin' you a hard time, kid. Com' 'n. Grab ya shit and get on board before Cap blows a line. 90 minutes to departure. Got it?"

"Sure thing," I grumble, grabbing my bags from the back of my truck.

We make our way onboard the boat, which will take us on a 16-hour ride to drop off the crew shift change and supplies for the rig. It's God awful early, and I don't want to be here—I didn't even get to say goodbye to Elsie because she was still asleep—but it's part of the gig.

The ship is massive, with all the room for cargo, but the cabins they give us to bunk in are smaller than a horse stall. I can touch both walls standing in the center of the room.

It doesn't take long for me to make my way through the ship and find my cabin. Once settled in, I collapse on the bed to pass out for a quick nap before we ship off, and someone comes to find me and give me a task to do.

I settle into the bed, and relaxing comes surprisingly quickly despite the ship's noise.

Just as I am drifting off - BANG - BANG

A loud banging on my cabin door wakes me.

Much to my annoyance, the banging doesn't stop, and I struggle out of bed.

"I'm coming!" I grumble, pulling open the door leading to the hall.

When I open the door, I'm greeted by the sight of a grumpy-looking Captain and...

"Elsie?" I ask.

"Hello." She says with a little wave.

I look to her right at the other woman standing before me.

"Captain," I say tentatively.

"She yours?" The Captain asks with a frown on her face.

"Uh. Yeah." I stutter at the intimidating woman.

"Well, she's quite persistent. Demanded to be let on board and threatened every crew member I sent down to deal with her until I came to handle it myself." Cap says, glancing over at Elsie with a look of almost... respect? "I like her."

"Thank you," Elsie says, her voice confident at the Captain's acceptance.

"That said... whatever your business is?" Cap snaps, turning on the heel of her boot. "Wrap your shit up quickly. Then get off my ship."

"Thank you, Captain," Elsie says.

"You're welcome!" The Captain calls back, then turns over her shoulder with a small smile. "And congratulations."

I look after the retreating woman, stunned. "What does she mean, congratulations?"

"I told her." Elsie shrugs, shouldering her way into my cabin. "Well... maybe there was a little fib involved."

"Told her what exactly?" I ask.

"The baby." She says simply. "No one would let me on board. I think she originally came down to tell me to fuck off, but I asked for a moment of her time and told her."

"You said you fibbed, though..."

When she bites her lip, I have to resist the urge to pluck it free and replace the snap of her teeth with my own.

"Well... I kind of told her a little story about how I suspected and just had an appointment to confirm I'm pregnant." She pauses. "So, I asked to come and see you because I didn't want to wait a month until you're home, and I didn't want to tell you over video chat while you're on the rig."

"Elsie Snow... did you *beg for me*?" I ask, my voice lilting up at the end.

Her brow furrows in a way that makes her look less menacing and more adorable than anything.

"Oh, don't look so shocked," she says, turning to face me as I stand in the doorway of my tiny cabin. I really did need to see you, so I did what I had to and got on board.

I eye her suspiciously, knowing there's more to the story.

"I feel like you did something more than just tell her you're pregnant," I say skeptically.

Elsie looks at me with a twinkle in her ice-blue eyes.

She's always beautiful, but there's something about seeing her display genuine joy and mirth, or in this case, a healthy mischievousness, that makes her even more stunning than she usually is.

"I may have also bribed her..." She says with a smirk.

"Bribed?"

"Yes." She states.

"Bribed, *how*?" I ask, perplexed.

Elsie shrugs and pushes into the cabin with me so I can close the door behind her.

"She's wearing an engagement ring but no wedding band." She shrugs. "I simply offered to pay for her honeymoon as a thank you."

My jaw drops. "You *what*?"

"You heard me." She says, plopping herself down on the bed next to us and waving off my shock. "Moving on. I probably don't have much time before they throw me overboard."

"Right." I sigh, still astonished she's here at all. "What did you need to tell me so desperately that you couldn't just call?"

"Not tell you." She says, setting down and opening up the large tote she had thrown over her shoulder. "Give you."

"Give me," I repeat.

"Yes."

Reaching into her bag, she pulls out a small stuffed animal.

"A dragon," I say, completely confused but taking the stuffed animal from her outstretched hand anyway.

"Yes."

"You brought me a dragon."

"Press the paw." She says with a rare smile, her voice gentler than usual.

I find that one of the paws has a heart-shaped pad instead of a circle like the other. Shifting the soft toy in my hand, I press down on the paw.

From the dragon comes a soft, rhythmic murmur that has me freezing in place. My gaze shoots up to Elsie, who has a broad smile on her face.

"Is this what I think it is?" I ask.

"Depends on what you think it is." She says, her smile shifting to a soft grin.

"That's my little girl's heartbeat," I reply.

"Marshall." She scolds. "We don't know that it's a girl."

"I do," I say confidently, looking down at the dragon again. "That's the heartbeat. El latido de mi pequeña ciruela azucarada." *My little sugar plum's heartbeat.*

"Yes," Elsie says softly. "I thought you would want something from that appointment to remember them by. Since you're going to miss the next one."

"Yeah. I..." I choke up, holding back the tears that want to come up. "Thank you."

"You're gonna be gone a lot during my pregnancy." Her voice turns more distant. "You'll miss a lot."

I nod, thinking of the milestones and moments I'll be gone for. Doctor's appointments and pregnancy symptoms. First kicks and sleepless nights.

For the first time, I realize how hard this is going to be.

I like my job, and plenty of people on rigs have families, but I don't think I ever thought about how hard it would be to be away from them for so much of the year.

"I wanted you to have something of them to keep with you." She says. "A little reminder for you."

For the first time since I started working on rigs, I don't want to leave.

"Thank you, Elsie," I say softly, trying not to choke up. "This means a lot."

"You're welcome."

I put the dragon on the bed by my pillow and reach for Elsie's hand.

"Let's get you home before someone actually does try to throw you overboard, okay?"

"Yeah. Of course." She says, gathering her bag and tossing it over her shoulder again.

Together, we walk through the ship in silence. When we reach the ramp for her to exit, I squeeze her hand and pull her into me so she's looking up at me.

"I'm going to miss you, I think," I murmur.

"Me... I..." She stops herself, and her gaze drops from my own. "I know."

"Elsie. It's okay to say you're going to miss me."

"Please, don't. Don't make this hard." She interrupts. "Just let me leave, and I'll see you in 28 days."

"Okay. Okay." I say, pushing a lock of hair that's escaped back behind her ear.

We stand there for a moment, just taking each other in, and I'm grateful when she doesn't flinch away as I lean down to place a kiss on her forehead.

"28 days," I promise.

"28 days." She repeats.

Then she turns to walk down the ramp back to shore. I wait until she's solidly on land, and when she turns back, I give her a little wave of goodbye.

She doesn't return the gesture, but that's okay.

When I return to my cabin, I pick up the dragon she gave me and press the paw.

The little murmured heartbeat fills the space, and a smile forms on my lips.

"28 days, pequeña ciruela. I'll be back for you and your mom in 28 days."

13

ELSIE

April 2 — 13 Weeks 3 Days, Lemon

Elsie,

Made it to the rig and got settled in. Just wanted to let you know I arrived safely.

Reception is non-existent out here, so we mostly email to keep in touch with people. Occasionally, depending on my schedule, I'm able to do video calls. I'll let you know next time. I think I can make one work so we can catch up.

Marshall

P.S. 26 days until I'm back.

April 3 — 13 Weeks 4 Days, Lemon

Elsie,

Hope you're doing well.

Getting back into the swing of things is always a bitch. So is sleeping on a rig. Your apartment is always so peaceful, and here, it's just loud all the time. The food is alright, but I miss cooking for you.

Are you keeping up with your vitamins? I hope the pill containers I put them in help.

I hope work is going well. Let me know if there's a good time we can do a video call. My shift is 8 to 8, so I'm free to talk in the evenings. I hope that isn't too late for you. I read that pregnancy requires more sleep than normal.

Marshall

P.S. 25 days.

April 4 — 13 Weeks 5 Days, Lemon

E, (Hope you don't mind me calling you E in these...)

The guys noticed the dragon yesterday and have been teasing me about it relentlessly. They keep asking if I need a fucking night light too.

Still... it's worth it. I love having our little girl's heartbeat with me. I hope she's doing well.

Let me know when you have some time. Would love to call and talk.

M

P.S. 24 days.

April 5 — 13 Weeks 6 Days, Lemon

E,

Everything is good here. Boring, but good. Rig work is long and hard, but I like the physicality of it. It's hard to explain.

Oliver sent me an email asking about my schedule when I'm back but wouldn't tell me why. Are you planning something?

I would love to see your face. Let me know if we can do a call.

M

P.S. 23 days.

April 6 — 14 Weeks, Nectarine

E,

Our baby girl is the size of a nectarine today. How are you feeling?

I hope everything's okay. You've got me a little worried out here.

Just an email back would be great if you're too busy for a call.

M

P.S. 22 days.

April 7 — 14 Weeks 1 Day, Nectarine

Gunnar,

Elsie hasn't answered a single email I've sent her since I left, which is weird considering how attached she is to her email.

Can you or Selene stop by and check on her? I'm starting to worry.

Thanks,

M

April 8 — 14 Weeks 2 Days, Nectarine

Every time my phone buzzes with another email, I jump.

I know I *should* respond to the messages from Marshall, but I can't bring myself to reply.

I open them, read them, and immediately delete them.

They just bring up too many memories.

A single postcard mailed from a foreign country while my father was on a business trip for weeks back when he was just a regular attorney.

Phone calls mere minutes before my school activities, letting me know my father's flight got delayed or he was stuck in traffic coming back from Austin and he wasn't going to make it in time.

The box of pre-signed birthday cards I found when I was a teen because my father could never make it home for my birthday for this reason or another.

Flowers and gross boxes of chocolates meant it was one of my graduations from high school, college, and my master's program.

Emails with links to articles about my achievements with notes about what I should work on next.

My father was never a parent to me—and this is the one thing I am determined to change. He never knew how to show up. He just never could.

He provided for me, but that's not the same as parenting me. My nannies, sitters, and tutors did that for him.

This? With Marshall?

The emails are too much, too close to all of those wounds I thought I healed a long time ago.

Every email reminds me that he will eventually leave and will not be back.

Then I'll be on my own.

Again.

Which is fine. It really is. I'm prepared for that eventuality. It was my plan all along, after all.

But there's a part of me that craves the feeling I had when he was here.

Like a weighted blanket settling over me, there's a calm reassurance about having him around, much as I loathe to admit it.

So, instead of answering his daily emails, I've thrown myself into work.

I've taken to working from home, and I've informed the front desk that I don't want visitors. I don't need anyone stopping by.

I tell myself it's not to avoid anyone per se. It's more like a measure to ensure I'm focused throughout the day.

Oliver has already filtered through the emails I respond to, which helps me avoid unnecessary tasks, but my to-do list grows longer with each one I open.

That is why I haven't responded to Marshall's pleas for attention.

Not because I'm scared.

I'm sitting in my office, reviewing another report for a meeting tomorrow, when my doorbell rings.

"The fuck?" I say, and then the pounding starts.

"Elsie!" A deep voice comes down the hall as I approach my front door. "Open up!"

Tapping on the screen beside the door, an image of Gunnar, dressed in combat attire, appears.

"Elsie! I know you're there." Gunnar says a little quieter. "Let me in, or I'm forcing my way in."

"He wouldn't dare," I mutter.

"One." He counts. "Two."

"Fuck." I curse, reaching for the door handle.

"Three." He says, just as I swing the door open. "Oh. Good."

Gunnar looks smug, which I hate.

"What are you doing here?"

"What does it look like?" He shrugs, his massive frame towering over me. "I'm here to check on you."

"So, you threaten to break into my apartment?" I squeak.

"You weren't opening up." He says blandly. "You gonna let me in, darlin'?"

"Ugh. Fine." I say, stepping to the side to let the blonde Viking of a man inside. "How did you get up here, anyway? The front desk was supposed to shut down the penthouse elevator. Only I have a key to that."

He gestures over his shoulder to where the elevator doors are, wide open.

"Not the first elevator shaft I've climbed up." He chuckles. "Might be the tallest one yet, though."

"You did *what*?" I ask, mouth agape.

"No big deal." Suddenly, he looks a little uncomfortable. "Maybe just don't tell Selene?"

"If I'm keeping secrets from my best friend, then you'd better hurry up and tell me what the hell you're doing here," I demand, turning to go back inside and letting Gunnar follow behind me to the kitchen. When I turn around, Gunnar looks at me with genuine concern.

"I already told you that part." He says softly. "Checkin' on you."

"Why?" I demand with a little too much bite.

He sighs. "Because Marshall said you haven't responded to any of his emails, and he's worryin' about you."

"Well, tell Marshall to mind his own business." I snap defensively.

Gunnar gives me a look that says he's not putting up with my icy demeanor today.

"You *are* his business, Elsie." He reminds me. "You're literally having his kid. He's gonna be involved much more than just makin' your breakfast every day."

For the first time, I realize that I've made a mistake.

I could have kept this to myself, kept Marshall out of all of it. Now, it's not just me and the baby, but all three of us.

"He's going to want to be a part of all of it, isn't he?" I say, realization dawning.

"Part of what?" Gunnar asks. "Mind if I grab some water. That was kind of a workout."

In a daze, I go to the cabinet, pull out a glass, walk to the fridge and fill it with water, and hand it to Gunnar. Then, on autopilot, I find myself walking over and sinking into the couch.

"Elsie?" Gunnar asks, coming around the couch and sitting across from me on the coffee table. "Elsie, when was the last time you took a break?"

"I took a nap after my meeting earlier," I reply, my tone flat.

"No. Like a real break. A vacation even." He pushes.

"I don't..."

"Don't give me that bull about not needing a break. Selene tries to pull that shit on me every week, but it's not gonna work." He says, cutting me off.

"Fine." I huff and admit. "I haven't had a real vacation since before I started Crude Coral."

"You should consider it." He says, reaching out and putting his massive hand on my knee. "Take Marshall and go to The Playground for a few weeks. Get to know each other."

I look up at him and only find genuine concern in his gaze.

Selene is my best friend, but I never really thought too much about my relationship with Gunnar. He's just her fiancé.

Right now, though, I realize he cares quite a lot about me, more than I would have presumed previously.

"Get to know him." Gunnar continues. "If you don't want to be with him, like in a relationship, that's fine. But figure out how you can work together. You're gonna have to eventually."

Silence fills the room as Gunnar sits with me while I process.

Deep down, I know he's right.

I chose this. I chose to bring Marshall in on all of this.

I could have not told him anything and gone through with this on my own.

The guilt of keeping that kind of a secret and eventually having to lie to my child about their father might have crushed me, though. I would have caved eventually. But that never crossed my mind in the first place.

He deserved to know. He deserves to be a part of this and deserves the chance to be a dad.

I'm keeping that opportunity from him.

"Okay." I acquiesce, and hope shines in Gunnar's eyes. "I'll make the time."

"I don't think you'll regret this one, Elsie. Marshall's one of the good ones." He says, giving my knee a squeeze.

"I know," I say simply.

14

MARSHALL

April 9 — 14 Weeks 3 Days, Nectarine

Marshall,

I've made arrangements for us to spend a week at The Playground when you get back. We check in on May 4 and return home on May 12.

The baby is good but giving me the worst heartburn.

Stay safe.

Elsie

April 10 — 14 Weeks 4 Days, Nectarine

E,

TUMS. All my searches say TUMS will help with the heartburn.

Looking forward to a week at The Playground. While we're out there, we should go see my family. They're only an hour away from the resort.

M

P.S. 17 days until I'm home.

April 12 — 14 Weeks 6 Days, Nectarine

Marshall,

You want me to meet your family? Doesn't that seem a little soon? I am still not sure I am ready to meet the family.

The TUMS are working. Well, they work when I pop them like candy. Thank you.

Elsie

April 13 — 15 Weeks, Apple

E,

Today marks 15 weeks. The baby is the size of an apple now.

No. I don't think it's too soon. We should probably tell them about the baby soon anyway. They're going to be so excited.

P.S. 14 days until I'm back.

April 16 — 15 Weeks 3 Days, Apple

Marshall,

How do you always know that stuff?

And that's fine. We can visit your family. Just let me know what day, so I don't make other plans.

Elsie

April 17 — 15 Weeks 4 Days, Apple

E,

I downloaded an app that keeps track for me. I check it every morning when I wake up. It's fun. <u>Download it.</u>

Mamá said May 5 would be a good day to come. They're having the annual Cinco de Mayo celebration with all the extended family, too, so you'll get to meet everyone all at once.

I know you're going to balk and say it's a terrible idea, but I promise I'll hold your hand the whole time. And if it becomes too much, we use the 'I'm pregnant and tired' excuse.

M

P.S. 10 days.

April 17 — 15 Weeks 4 Days, Apple

Marshall
You're right. It is a terrible idea. We might as well do it now, though.
Elsie

April 19 — 15 Weeks 6 Days, Apple

E,

Can I tell mamá about the baby? Or do you want to wait until you meet her?

M

P.S. 8 days.

April 21 — 16 Weeks 1 Day, Avocado

Marshall,

I think I'd prefer if we tell her in person if that's alright.
Also, everything is set for our vacation.
Elsie

April 22 — 16 Weeks 2 Days, Avocado

E,

Yeah. Of course, that's alright. It's your choice who we tell and when.
Did you get us separate rooms this time? Or are we still pretending that I don't sleep in your bed every night anyway?

M

P.S. 5 days.

April 24 — 16 Weeks 4 Days, Avocado

Marshall,

I booked us one room.
Elsie

April 25 — 16 Weeks 5 Days, Avocado

E,

>*Good girl.*
>*M*
>*P.S. 2 days.*

April 26 — 16 Weeks 5 Days, Avocado

Marshall,

>*Just something to look forward to when you're home.*
>*Elsie*
>*Attachments:_*For_Fun.mp3.*

I'M SEQUESTERED QUIETLY in my room on the rig, staring at my computer screen and the most recent email from Elsie.

I'm trying to build up the courage to open the audio file she sent.

There's no telling what it contains, but based on her message, I'm hopeful.

I click on the file, and it opens in my computer's player. Curiosity takes over, prompting me to press play on the file.

"Umm... Hi." Elsie's voice comes through my computer speaker. "I've never done something like this before. But... I thought... well, it doesn't matter what I thought."

There's silence before she speaks again, softer this time. "Zuri gave me a prototype of her newest toy. She dropped it off last week, but I haven't used it yet."

My eyebrows shoot up.

Zuri Valentine is the founder of an adult toy company. Her toys are the best on the market, and she's a badass in her own right.

"But I've wanted to." She whispers. "I've been so horny. It's brutal, Marshall."

There's some jostling of the phone while she sets it down.

"I hope you enjoy this." She says, and I can hear her smile through the speakers.

There's a buzzing noise that starts low and slow. Then Elsie gasps.

I imagine her placing the toy on her clit, sending vibrations through her whole body and shocking her system. How she'd take the toy and run it up and down her center, working herself up until she's wet.

"Fuck." She whispers over the sound of the toy. "That feels incredible."

Rustling tells me she's getting comfortable in her bed before continuing.

"I'm so wet, Marshall." She says. "Fuck, I wish you were here. I've missed your cock so much."

"I've missed you too, princess," I murmur in response, knowing I mean more than just her body. "So much."

The sigh she lets out has me hardening in my jeans, and I palm my cock through the fabric, trying to get it to calm down.

It would be wrong to masturbate to her recording, wouldn't it?

But this is why she sent it to me, right?

Then she moans, and there's no holding myself back.

Quickly, I unbutton my pants and pull out my fully erect cock, and palm it.

I groan in unison with Elsie as I tighten my grip around myself.

"Daddy." She pants out.

"Princess," I reply.

The little sounds Elsie lets out have me adjusting my grip and increasing my pace.

"Fuck, princess," I say to no one. "I wish I was there."

She sighs over the vibration of the toy. "I'm imagining that this toy is your cock, daddy."

"Yes, princess."

There's rustling once again, Elsie adjusting the position of the phone again.

A slick sound comes through the speaker alongside her moan.

"Fuck. You feel so good." She groans. "I fucking love your cock."

Running my fingers over my tip, I gather my precum to use as lube and resume stroking myself.

I can hear how Elsie plunges the toy in and out of herself, how wet and ready she is to be well fucked.

"It's been so long since I've been properly fucked." She whines. "I need you, daddy."

"You have me, princess," I promise.

The sound of her fucking herself with the toy is intoxicating. Every sound she makes has my need for her building, a need which can only be satisfied by the feeling of her cunt around my cock.

But she's not here. So, my fist will have to do.

When she groans next, I tighten my grip around my cock.

"I'm so close, daddy." She pants out. "Fuck me harder, please."

The sound of her plunging the toy into her pussy speeds up, and her moans get louder.

"Come on, princess. Come for daddy." I whisper.

"Daddy." She whines. "Daddy, please! Please. Please!"

I can see the vision in my head of how wet she is as she fucks herself, and it has me climbing to my peak alongside her.

"Daddy, I'm gonna come." She pants out.

"Come for me, princess. You can do it."

Her scream penetrates my room, and suddenly, I'm there, careening over the edge alongside her.

My orgasm feels like it extends forever, and my heavy breaths match the sound of Elsie's gasps for air as well.

"That was so perfect, princess," I murmur.

The only sound in my room is her heavy breathing coming through my computer speakers.

"Fuck, Marshall." She sighs. "That was fantastic."

There's a few more seconds of silence where I just listen to her breathe.

"I hope you enjoyed that." She says, then the recording stops.

I look down at my hand, covered in my cum, and grab for the box of tissues within reaching distance to clean myself up.

That was more than I could have hoped for.

I can't wait until I get to replace that toy with my cock.

April 27 — 16 Weeks 5 Days, Avocado

E,

Fuck. That was incredible. You're so fucking sexy. Thanks for the surprise.

And you're bringing that toy with you to The Playground. I want to see you make those noises in person next time.

M

P.S. 1 day until you get to ride this cock again. See you tomorrow.

15

ELSIE

May 5 — 18 Weeks 1 Day, Artichoke

Marshall arrived home on the night of the 28th. Having him there was a weight off my shoulders.

I hadn't fully realized what a stressor it was to have him away, but having him back eased a tension in my shoulders that had been accumulating for the past 28 days.

It wasn't my intention to take his first day home as a full day off and spend it rolling around in bed with him, but that's what ended up happening. Then, while during the day I've been desperately trying to get ahead on work, in the evenings, it's been just us and a multitude of orgasms. I'm pretty sure he's fucked me on every surface in my apartment. Yet, it still doesn't feel like enough sometimes.

I crave the man constantly.

We arrived at The Playground on Saturday to find the entire place brimming with science fiction lovers celebrating May the Fourth with full costumes and regalia. Several of the resort's patrons invited us to join in on their festivities, but we quickly absconded to our room.

Unfortunately, the realization of my impending meet and greet with Marshall's family today has my nerves in knots, and not even a good dicking down this morning was able to solve the anxiousness that's taken residence in my stomach.

I shouldn't be nervous. They're just people, after all, not monsters. But something has my stomach churning in a way I haven't experienced since my first trimester.

The drive from The Playground to Marshall's family home only takes us an hour, but it's an hour of me twisted up in nerves.

The problem isn't Marshall or his family... it's *me*. I'm the problem.

Cinco de Mayo is a big deal in his family, so it only made sense that we join for the celebration, especially since his abuelos flew in for the weekend as well. The idea of meeting his entire extended family in one go isn't helping my nerves, though.

"¡Hijo mío!" *My son!* A warm voice cries as Marshall helps lift me down out of his massive truck. "¡Él está aquí! Finalmente." *He's here! Finally.*

"Hola mamá." *Hi mom.* Marshall says with a smile as he turns to embrace the woman charging toward him. "Mamá. This is Elsie."

He turns to me with his mom wrapped under his arm as though to hold her back and keep her from jumping me.

"Preciosa niña. Ella es bonita. Ella me dará unos nietos bonitos." *Precious girl. She's pretty. She'll give me pretty grandbabies.* The woman rambles off.

"Ella habla español, mamá." *She speaks Spanish, Mom.* Marshall chuckles, and the woman's eyes widen before her expression goes bland.

"I'd say it in English, too, mija." *Darling.* The woman says with a smile. "You're gorgeous."

"Thank you, Mrs. Law. It's really nice to meet you." I smile, holding out my hand in greeting.

"Oh! No need for handshakes here, mija. Hugs are for family." She says, shaking off Marshall's hold and coming over to embrace me tightly. "And you can call me Mamá if you like."

Warmth spreads through my chest at the casual acceptance of me into her family unit, an acceptance I wasn't anticipating considering my relationship with her son.

"Inside! Inside! I have food in the works, and I don't want your younger cousins to get their grubby hands into my pork filling. It will be all gone before I even get a chance to fill the tamales." She rushes out, ushering us into the house.

The inside of the ranch-style home is gorgeously decorated in bright colors and art. Every piece that hangs on the walls or lives on a shelf has an air of sentimentality, which has always been severely lacking in my own home.

"You have a beautiful house," I say as Marshall's mother ushers me through the house and into the kitchen.

"Thank you!" She says cheerfully with a small smile and a shrug. "It's home."

The kitchen she leads me into smells incredible of spices and sauces that make my mouth water. Every surface is covered in pots and pans filled with dishes and ingredients that smell like heaven and I groan at the smell.

"A woman with a stomach. I love her." Mamá smiles. "Now, Marshall. Go say hi to your sisters and cousins. Elsie can stay in here with me and say hello when people come in for snacks. Now shoo!"

Marshall gives me a nervous glance before bending down to give his mom, who's only a few inches taller than me, a kiss on the cheek and retreating from the kitchen.

"Now. I have you for about an hour until you're going to want to lay down, aren't you?" She asks, making my eyebrows rise. "How far along are you?"

"How'd you?" I start before she laughs cheerfully.

"You're already cupping your belly, mija." She gives me a wink. "A good sign of a protective mother-to-be."

"I didn't realize," I say softly. "I thought I was hiding it better."

"Why?" She asks, her expression one of shock. "Babies are a beautiful thing. Nothing to hide at all, mija."

"We just haven't told a lot of people. Not much reason to. It's a little weird to have people guess." I shrug.

"Well, you're going to have a lot of excited guesses today." She says with a smile. "Now. Let's get you an apron, and you can tell me about yourself while we wait for people to stop in."

Marshall's mom is a comforting presence. I spend the next hour telling her my story as various family members come in and out of the kitchen to say hello and grab food and drinks. The whole time, there's laughter and joy in the air, which I've never experienced before at a family gathering.

My family events were always businesslike, formal lunches or dinners. They were gatherings for the purpose of checking off a box on a list of requirements rather than an opportunity to spend time with people you love.

Love.

That's the feeling that's been floating in the air since I arrived. Every fiber in my being takes in the feeling of comfort and safety that this home and these people provide.

Marshall pops in to check on us several times throughout the hour, but between being plied with delicious traditional snacks and the childhood stories of him I'm getting out of his mom, I couldn't be more content.

"Marshall has been asking for recipes." His mother says at one point. "Is he cooking for you?"

I nod.

"Good boy." She smiles. "I always told him that when it was time to introduce someone to the family, first, they needed to be introduced to our food."

We've been working on filling the corn husks lined with masa with the pork filling to make tamales, and the rhythmic work allows us to fall into a comfortable silence before she speaks again.

"Food is the language of families. It's how traditions are passed down and how legacies are built." She says finally. "That's how I met Marshall's papa. I was here for school, cooking in our dorms much like this, and this tall white boy wandered into the communal kitchen looking for whatever was making the hall smell so good."

"You won him over with his stomach?" I chuckle.

"Maybe. I like to think that community is built around the kitchen table. Cooking gave Paul and I a way to talk, a common language." She looks up at me with stars in her eyes. "He proposed to me by making every dish I ever taught him, you know."

"He did?" I smile, thinking of how precious that moment must have been. "That's so sweet."

"I would have said yes either way, but the fact that he took the time to show me he saw me as I am? It meant the world." She says with a fond smile.

"Is he here today?" I ask. "I haven't met him yet."

Her expression grows dark and haunted. "Paul died when Marshall was eight." She says somberly.

"Oh, I'm so sorry. I didn't know." I say regretfully.

"That man was Marshall's whole world," Mamá says with a small smile. "He's the baby of the six children and the only boy. I think it affected him the most out of all of them."

We work in silence for a while before she speaks again.

"I think this is what I was hoping for with Marshall. I never knew who he would end up with. But I always told him that they were all welcome at our table no matter who he brought home."

"You know about Marshall being pansexual?" I ask, a little surprised.

"Of course." She chuckles. "Marshall is always interested in people, not their labels. But I'm glad it's you. I'm glad you're the one he's brought home."

"Am I the first?" I ask, genuinely curious.

"And the last." She says with a finality that sends goosebumps down my skin. "You're good together. I can tell."

"Thank you," I say, wiping my masa covered hands on my apron. "I'm glad he has such a supportive family."

"You, mija." She interrupts. "You have us too now."

Tears well in my eyes at the proclamation, damn pregnancy hormones.

"Oh, mija. I didn't mean to upset you." Mamá says, rushing over to me and taking me by the hands. "I just want you to know you're always welcome here."

I chuckle with water in my eyes. "Sorry. Just my hormones acting up."

"I think it's time for you to rest. I'll take you to Marshall's room and tell him where you are." She says all business as she cleans herself up.

As we pass through the hallways of the home, the family stops us at every turn to say hello or wish Marshall and me well, and the overwhelming feeling of acceptance is almost too much to handle without tears.

By the time we reach the side of the H-shaped house with the bedrooms, I'm exhausted physically and emotionally.

"Here you go," Mamá says, opening the door to one of the bedrooms at the front of the house. "I'll send Marshall to check on you in a few minutes. Just make yourself comfortable. Extra blankets are in the closet."

She closes the door behind her when she leaves, and I take a good look around the room.

Marshall's childhood bedroom is a shrine to his accomplishments. Every wall is covered with trophies and ribbons for various sports and academic achievements. What I wasn't expecting was all the art on the walls, among posters of sports icons and favorite bands.

A knock on the door draws me out of my observations.

"Hey." Marshall's head pokes in the doorway. "Can I come in?"

"Yeah, of course." I chuckle. "It's your room."

"Sure. But you deserve privacy if you need it." He shrugs as he closes the door behind him. "I know my family can be a lot."

"They're wonderful." He gives me a skeptical look. "Really. I like them, especially your mom."

"Mamá is the best." He says with a genuine smile. "It's been too long since I've seen her."

"We can come visit more if you'd like." My hands go to cup my stomach where our child grows. "Maybe she can come stay with us when the baby comes."

"Really?" He says, his eyebrows high on his face. "You'd want that?"

"Sure." I shrug. "It would be nice to have... people."

He's before me in two strides and wrapping me in his arms.

"Thank you, Elsie." He whispers into my hair. "Thank you."

"Of course, Marshall."

We stand there together like that for a while, rocking back and forth in the silence of his room while muffled noise from the festivities outside filters through the walls.

"I should probably get back. Mamá said you need to rest, though," he says, stepping back from me but not letting go.

I nod, but a tug in my chest tells me I shouldn't let him go.

When his hands leave my body, the impulse becomes too much to ignore. "Stay."

Marshall glances back at me over his shoulder with a quizzical look.

"I want you to stay," I say softly. "Just for a little while."

"Okay. I'll stay." He says simply. "Anything you want, princess."

16

ELSIE

P*rincess.*

Suddenly, I'm not tired, and the last thing on my mind is a nap.

Now I'm needy. Needy for him.

"Daddy," I whisper, our gazes connecting with storms of desire in our eyes.

"Does my princess need something?" He asks me in a deep rumble, making my pussy clench.

"I need you to take your clothes off." I breathe out. "Now."

His smirk smolders hot with a flame of desire that matches my own. "As my princess wishes."

In one swift movement, he pulls off his tight gray t-shirt, revealing his bare chest to me.

I take in his body, taught and toned by the hard labor he does for work and all of the tattoos that cover him.

All of the art on his body is detailed to the point of realism. The octopus on his right hand is always visible, but I didn't quite realize the art snaked all the way up his arm, creating a complete scene of ocean life on his arm, starting at his shoulder. On his left bicep is a beautiful depiction of a dragon.

When he moves to unbutton his jeans, I step up to him and stop the movement, guiding his hands to his sides.

"I want to explore you," I say reverently, my hands moving up to trace over his hardened muscles and intricate tattoos. For the first time it doesn't feel as frantic so I take a moment to appreciate the tattoos and his body. "These are beautiful. How long have you had them?"

"I started my full sleeve years ago when I got my first job on a rig at eighteen. Found an artist who liked ocean shit, and we worked on it for about two solid years. The other I had done a year ago." He says, his gaze never leaving my face.

"Because you're a dragon?" I chuckle.

"Kind of? It's not really a dragon. More dragon-esque." He replies, his face contorted as he thinks of how to explain it. "A couple of years ago, I took a long break between rig jobs. I went back to Mexico to visit mis abuelos for a summer, and while I was there, Abuela took me to the markets with her." *My grandparents. Grandma.* He says, his brown eyes glittering with mirth. "We would walk past these shops with all these colorfully painted Alebrijes."

The unfamiliar word has me frowning.

"It's a type of folk art, and they're all sorts of magical and fantastical creatures: leopards with talons and wings, birds with snake-like tails, and whatnot." He smiles and reaches to smooth out my furrowed brow with his thumb. "They're painted in these beautiful colorful patterns. No two Alebrijes are alike. Everyone is different and unique."

"Just like you," I say.

"Sort of." He says, much more serious now. "Abuela is a very religious woman, goes to her parish every Sunday without fail and confession twice a week. The whole nine yards. But she's also a spiritual woman."

"Isn't it the same thing?" I ask.

"Not always. Religion is one thing; belief in the spiritual is another." He shrugs. "Abuela believes that we have guardian angels, spirit guides, or protectors. There was one time when we were walking through a market, and she stopped dead in her tracks. I thought she was having a heart attack or something because she just froze in place and clutched her chest."

His expression grows worried, like he's reliving the memory in this very moment.

"Then she turns to the man in the shop doorway and starts speaking to him so quickly I couldn't keep up. But basically, she argued with this man for ten minutes over whatever had her so worked up. The man eventually gave up and motioned for her to follow him."

He shakes his head with a smile at the memory.

"When she comes out, she hands me this bag and says, 'Este es vuestro futuro, Orejotas. Tómalo. Atesoralo. No te sueltes.' and keeps walking down through the market like nothing big had happened."

"I don't understand," I say, shaking my head.

"What do you mean?"

"No, I literally don't understand. I can't translate in my head."

"This is your future, Marshall. Take it. Treasure it. Don't let go."

"Okay. That word definitely doesn't mean Marshall." I smile. "Pretty sure she called you ears."

"Nope. Marshall. Nothing big about my ears at all." He laughs.

"What was in the bag?" I ask.

"Eight little carvings. A dragon, a horse, and six smaller animals." He shrugs. "They're on the shelf."

"These? They're beautiful." I say, turning to the desk by his bed and picking up one of the smaller figurines in awe.

"Yeah. So last year, I brought the dragon with me to my artist, and we came up with this design." He shrugs the shoulder with the intricately designed dragon.

"It looks so real." I brush my fingers along the design. "But I see the inspiration now. The little designs on the dragon's scales. The way his eyes are shaped." I pause. "Did you ever figure out what they mean?"

His face grows contemplative. "I've had guesses throughout the years, but I don't think any of them were right."

"So, what does it mean to you? The dragon, I mean." I ask.

"I think it represents me in a way. And in another, I like to think of it as my guide, my guardian angel." He reaches to cup my face with his right hand. "The world offers us many opportunities to become who we want to be, Elsie. We're pieces of everything. Our past, our present, our future. It all makes us who we are." He takes a steadying breath. "But it does give us a choice. In our present and our future. We always have a choice for better, for *more*."

"Right now, the only thing I want *more* of is your cock." I smirk.

"Your wish is my command." He says, reaching down to unbuckle his jeans and shuck off his boots and clothes.

A naked Marshall is a sight to behold, and I can't help but let my jaw drop in awe as I take in his body.

"Someone's slacking." He smirks, motioning to my fully clothed form.

He takes a step toward me, his hard cock bobbing with the movement, and I scramble to undress out of my sundress.

"What do you say, princess? You want to take Daddy's cock like a good girl?" He rumbles, sending a shiver up my spine. "Is that what you want? Tell me, princess."

"I need you, Daddy," I murmur. "But what about..."

He cuts me off with a powerful kiss. His lips press against my own with a blistering heat between us that could burn the world to the ground.

Every touch of his skin against mine fans the flame of my desire and need.

"Say it." He growls into my lips. "You have to ask for it, Elsie."

"Please, Daddy. Fuck me." I pant out between kisses. "I need you to fuck me."

I reach down and wrap my small hand around his cock, causing a small groan to escape his lips.

"How do you want my cock, princess? You want me to fuck you slow and soft or hard and fast?" He purrs into my ear.

"Hard. Fast." I pant out.

"Good girl."

His hands come to my hips, and he pulls me in, giving me another searing kiss before spinning me around and nudging me toward the quilt-covered bed.

"On your knees." He growls.

Quickly, I crawl on the bed, positioning myself so I'm on my hands and knees, pussy on full display for Marshall where he stands.

"Like this, Daddy?" I ask playfully, looking over my shoulder at his perfect form.

"Just like that, princess." He smirks. "Now, stay quiet, or the others will hear."

I prop myself up and turn to him more fully. "Let them."

A raging fire burst to flame behind his eyes at my challenge. All softness from earlier is gone, and all that remains is a primal desire between us.

Marshall's hands on my ass are like a brand, claiming me with his touch. He strokes his palms over my round ass, giving it a light squeeze.

"You look so perfect for me like this." He says reverently, moving one hand to run his fingers between my folds. "Already so wet for me. All for me."

Our eyes are locked together as he brings his fingers up to his lips and licks off my flavor.

"Divine." He whispers.

His hands drop back to my ass, and he lines himself up with

my center. With a single thrust, he buries himself inside me. His thick cock filling me up completely and making me moan loudly.

"Good girl. Let them hear how good your Daddy makes you feel, princess." He says, pulling out and pushing back in slowly to give me time to adjust to his size. "Cry out and tell them just how good you are for me."

"So good." I moan. "More. I need more."

"As the princess wishes." He says with a sharp thrust.

His hips slam into me at a frantic pace. His tempo quick enough to have me building to climax in no time.

I'm constantly horny these days, and our sex is so hot and regular at this point to where he knows my body nearly as well as I do.

But his words, his *words* are what have me careening toward bliss.

"I'm gonna fill you up, princess. My cock and cum are yours." He grunts out. "Gonna fill you with my seed and have you walk around with it dripping down your thighs for the rest of the day."

"Daddy," I whine, needing what he says to be true.

I want his claim and his cum. There's a part of me terrified to be so completely owned by him, to be publicly his like this even if we're the only ones who know.

But another part of me knows this is exactly what I want.

"Give it to me, daddy." I groan.

Marshall reaches around and finds my clit with ease and pinching it between his fingers. The sharp sensation has me biting down on the palm of my hand to contain my scream.

The shock that rolls through my body has me trembling through my release. Every wave of my orgasm is somehow more powerful than the last, but Marshall doesn't relent.

He keeps his pace pounding in and out of me, making the bed squeak and groan underneath us until his breath is ragged.

I'm gripping tightly to the bed, trying not to be pushed off the other side, when I feel his pace falter.

"So close." He moans. "Take it. Take my cum like the good princess you are."

"Yes, Daddy." I groan.

Warmth floods my body as he comes and releases inside of me. His cum trickles out of my cunt and down my thighs as he pulls out, sending a shiver through my body once again.

I collapse into the bed, spent from only a few minutes of a good hard fuck.

Marshall helps maneuver me so I'm entirely on the bed before sitting beside me and pulling the blanket at the foot of the bed up around my shoulders.

"You good?" He asks a slight hesitation in his voice.

"Mhmm." I nod, my thoughts already fuzzy from pleasure.

He chuckles. "I'm gonna go downstairs while you rest." He gives me a kiss on the forehead. "Thank you for letting me take care of you."

I'm already drifting off to sleep as I hear him getting dressed, and I'm out like a light before he's even able to close the door fully.

"Sleep well, princess. Dream of good things." He whispers.

17

MARSHALL

May 7 — 18 Weeks 3 Days, Artichoke

According to Oliver and Selene, whenever asked, Elsie will insist she doesn't need a break or any kind of pampering.

But in the time I've spent getting to know her, I think that couldn't be further from the truth. Visiting my family made that more apparent than ever.

Elsie wants to be seen and appreciated.

She wants to be known and loved by those around her.

Her biggest barrier is accepting the love and care that is so readily offered to her.

So today, we're doing something about that.

Today is all about spoiling her.

I would never be able to convince her to take a baby moon, but I can push her into doing this.

The Playground Resort has a gorgeous spa retreat on its grounds. When you arrive, it looks like you're entering a cave oasis, and there's a small water feature that adds to the ambiance. The interior of the space is just as luxurious feeling as the price tag on their services would make you think it would be.

"Mr. Law and Ms. Snow. Welcome in!" The cheerful front desk girl says. "I've got you scheduled for a couples massage and facials as well, correct?"

"Yes." I reply, a little shocked that the staff already know who we are without giving them our names. "How did you know it was us?"

"Oh. Ms. Selene called ahead for you both to confirm everything. She told us to be on the lookout for a gorgeous redhead and her tattooed partner." The girl giggles. "She speaks very highly of you both."

"Ms. Selene." I shake my head, smiling. "Of course she did."

"That woman doesn't trust you as far as she can throw you, Marshall." Elsie teases, and it is so good to see her smile at me again that I'd take any kind of humiliation Selene wants to throw my way.

"One day, she'll come to trust me. You have." I say with a shrug and immediately regret it when I see how Elsie tenses up.

Turning back to the young woman checking us in, she hands us some paperwork, and we go to the plush couches to fill it out.

"Why do they need medical history?" I ask, staring at the lengthy questionnaire.

"You've never done this before, have you?" Elsie chuckles at my bewilderedness. "They need to make sure none of the treatments or products they use are going to have a reaction. Like if you're taking acne medication, they can't use certain chemical exfoliants in your facial. Then, if you have physical limitations, pain, or nerve damage in certain areas, they'll want to know that for your massage."

"I guess that makes sense," I mumble.

"You'll be thanking them later. Promise." She says with a reassuring pat on my knee.

Forgetting about the paperwork momentarily, I study Elsie as she fills out her form, biting her lip as she does.

I want to pull that lip out and bite down on it myself. I want to pull her close and kiss her with every ounce of lust I have for her.

I need her viscerally, but I know if I tried to force anything, she would panic and flee.

This is the long game now. I've rushed her and pushed her every step of this pregnancy, and to a certain extent, she's let me, but now it's time for me to be patient and let her come to me.

She needs to come to this realization in her own time.

There's nothing I can do to speed that process up.

So, for now, I'll study the slope of her button nose and the tiny freckles that peak out from under her lightly applied foundation. I take in how the light bouncing off the water fixture's falling streams makes the red in her hair stand out.

Elsie is the most beautiful person I've ever seen.

She holds herself with such quiet confidence that the world around her just seems inferior. She has a strength that I do not possess and can only hope that our daughter will have as well. She's magnificent.

She's my queen.

"Marshall. Focus." She snaps when she catches me looking, but there's a small smile on her face, which tells me she's not too upset about me staring.

"Right. Sorry." I apologize and go back to working on the paperwork before me.

When we're finished, I take our clipboards up to the front and let the woman know we're ready.

A few minutes later, we're being led back through the hallways of the spa and into the room where our massages are then left alone.

Elsie's been unusually quiet since we went to visit my family. Something changed on Sunday, and I'm not quite sure what.

This week has been really good for us, though. The sex between us has always been incredible, but it feels like there's a new intimacy between us that wasn't there before.

"I'm glad we got to visit my family while we're out here," I say, hoping she'll open up to me about the change I've noticed since then.

Instead, with her back to me as she undresses, she tenses before replying. "Yeah. It was really nice meeting them."

"Everything okay?" I ask tentatively.

"Yeah. All good." She says, turning to give me a small smile as I strip off my shirt.

I've never known Elsie to hesitate on anything. She walks through life with enviable confidence at all times. But right now, it's like she's almost afraid.

"Why didn't you tell me about your dad?" She finally asks, freezing me in place.

"I just... I don't talk about my dad a lot." I sigh, coming around the massage table to be closer to her. "He was my idol growing up. It's just... hard."

Even dressed in a terrycloth robe, you can see the soft curve of Elsie's stomach beneath the drape of the garment. My hands go to rest on her belly, and I pull her into me, rubbing my hand over where her body is now firm and slightly showing her pregnancy.

"It's why I want this so much," I say, marveling at her body and the child that grows in her womb. "I don't want my baby girl growing up without her papa."

Elsie smiles and reaches up to cup my face. "I don't want that either."

A knock on the door interrupts our moment, and Elsie pulls away from me, turning back to her table as the two masseuses enter the room.

The next ninety minutes are ones of bliss. I've never had a massage before, but it's incredible.

It sounds like Elsie is also enjoying herself by the small moans she lets out as the woman working on her body presses into her various tight muscles.

Unfortunately, it does mean that by the end of the massage, I'm fucking hard for her and ready to fuck those same little moans of pleasure out of her. Thankfully, my masseuse doesn't say anything about my massive hard-on.

When the two leave us, I'm immediately up and off the table.

"Marshall?" Elsie asks, a slight fear in her eyes at my predatory movement toward her.

Grasping her face between my hands, I pull her into an intense kiss. I love how she melts into the kiss, which quickly turns desperate and passionate.

Pulling her up into my arms and setting her down on the table, I spread her legs wide for me.

"Tell me you want this, Elsie. Because I fucking *need* you." I pant out, leaning into her space and nipping at her ear.

I let my tongue circle the sensitive point on her pulse before traveling down her neck and collarbone with small kisses and bites.

"Fuck, Marshall." She moans. "They're going to be back any minute."

"I don't fucking care." I bite down on her neck, and she moans. "I need to bury my cock deep in your pussy and fuck you till you're collapsing on this table."

"Fuck." Elsie groans out. "Yes. I want that, too."

Without any hesitation, I take my cock in hand and guide it to her entrance. My thrust in is hard and fast, causing her to cry out and let anyone outside know what we're up to.

"You're gonna get us banned if you keep that up, princess."

"I don't care." She pants out. "Just fuck me, Marshall. I need to come."

"Not Marshall. Right now, I'm your Daddy."

Fire lights in her eyes and she pushes up on her elbows to take my lips in a searing kiss.

"Fast, Daddy." She begs. "I need it fast."

"As you wish," I smirk.

My thrusts grow rapidly, and her walls flutter around me with each push into her.

Her body is so sensitive now that it only takes a few minutes to get her close. Her expression changes, and I know she's at her edge. So, I reach down and thumb her clit in a circular motion, just how she likes it.

"Fuck!" She shrieks, and then she's coming around my cock.

Shortly after, electricity shoots up my spine, and I'm following her off the cliff of pleasure, filling her with my cum.

Holding myself over her, I try to gather my breath as she collapses back onto the table.

I start to pull out of her slowly, but she grabs me by the hips.

"Stop. Just." She pants out. "Stay with me."

There's a need, an emotional one, not physical, in her expression, which has me gathering her up in my arms and holding her close.

In my arms, she relaxes, my cock still buried in her pussy.

After a few minutes, there's a light knock at the door, reminding us of where we are.

We pull apart, and both let out a simultaneous laugh. I finally pull out of Elsie, making her pout, and hand her the robe she draped over her chair.

When she stands, my cum drips down her thighs. I marvel at the sight of my release on her skin. Following my impulse, I reach over to gather the cum on my fingers and bring it to her lips.

"Open," I command, and she follows instructions.

I place my fingers covered in cum in her mouth, and without prompting, she sucks them clean.

"Good girl." I purr before pushing my fingers deeper down her throat. "Later, my cock is going to be buried so deep down this throat that you're going to choke on my cum."

Elsie's eyes fill with heat. "Yes, Daddy."

We both finish dressing quickly, but when we open the door to leave, our two masseuses are standing there, the woman bright red and the man with a smirk on his face.

The woman quickly passes by us to enter the room as we exited, but as I pass the man, he holds out his fist for me to bump.

"Nice." He whispers, and I can't help but chuckle to myself.

Elsie scurries away, mentioning something about showering off before our next treatment, and I settle into a soft lounge chair with a smile to wait for her to return.

Yeah, this was precisely the kind of pampering we both needed.

18

ELSIE

May 11 — 19 Weeks, Mango

There are whispers throughout the club.

Everyone is wondering: is she pregnant or fat?

Well, I'm both.

So, they can all go fuck off.

The stares I'm getting from everyone bring out Marshall's protective side, though, and every possessive touch sends warmth through my body.

Turns out, coming to The Playground for the week was an excellent idea for both of us. I needed the break more than I'm willing to admit.

The time together has been enjoyable, but right now, I'm enjoying having Marshall's whole attention a lot more than I maybe should.

All night, he's hovered around me.

The last time we came to the club, no one knew about my pregnancy. We were still just friends who'd slept together once.

This time, it's clear the rumor mill has been active with how people glance at us as we sit in our normal area with friends.

"People are staring," I whisper to Marshall over the music of the club. "I don't like it."

"I kind of do." He teases back at me. "I like them knowing you're mine."

"I'm not yours, Marshall," I say, rolling my eyes.

"You keep saying that." He leans to whisper in my ear. "But I don't believe you."

A shiver runs down my spine at his words and the heat of his breath against my pulse.

"Marshall." I breathe, pushing him back halfheartedly on the chest. "People are watching."

It's early enough in the night to where the curiosity of the crowd hasn't broken decorum yet. But I can see them wanting to come up and ask questions.

Marshall is one of The Playground's most infamous single members, with emphasis on the *single*. Seeing him with me, how he touches me like I mean more to him than one night or even one week of fun, is drawing the attention of more than one regular in the crowd. Add a suspected pregnancy, and our coupling is headline news in the lifestyle community now.

"Elsie!" A sultry voice comes to shake me from my fear.

"Zuri?" I say, turning to face the gorgeous Black woman.

Zuri is a longtime friend of both Marshall and me. She's also the badass founder of my favorite toy brand, Onyx Obsession.

"Hey, love." She says, her voice smooth and bright.

Zuri is a classic beauty; her deep umber skin is covered in a light layer of shimmering glitter, and her makeup is done in bright neon colors. Her locks are adorned with matching neon beads, and her lacey bodysuit is the same neon color palette.

"Any chance you could get your man to help me haul some stuff upstairs?" She asks.

"My man?" I ask, confused.

"Marshall?" She nods over to Marshall who's standing beside

me and chuckles. "Oh, please don't tell me you're pretending this isn't a thing."

I glance over my shoulder at Marshall, who's beaming down at me annoyingly.

"Fine. Yes." I admit. "We're... involved."

"Together," Marshall interjects.

"Together or whatever, can you help me lug my stuff upstairs from my truck?" She asks. "I'm running late."

Marshall steps around me and starts to walk toward the front lobby of the club. "Of course."

The pair turn to go outside, leaving me alone.

Suddenly, I'm exposed.

Marshall settled us at one of the tables in a back corner, but despite being away from the center of everything, it still feels like everyone's eyes are on me.

I sit there, slowly sipping on my tumbler of water, before I'm saved by Ivy strolling up to my table.

"Daddy left you here on your own?" She asks.

"What?" I reply, startled by her question despite watching her approach.

She plops down and wraps her arm around my shoulders. "Marshall. Your daddy. Your baby daddy."

My eyes grow wide. "What?"

"Oh, please don't lie to me." Ivy sighs. "Selene may have let it slip that you were pregnant, but it's Marshall's kid, isn't it?"

I hesitate, looking at Ivy carefully. "Yeah. The baby is ours."

"Oh good!" Ivy cheers. "I knew y'all would work out."

"What?"

"We've all been cheering you both on since Selene's engagement party. I think y'all are cute." She continues as though she hasn't just brought my whole world to a screeching halt.

Just then, Zuri returns through the main doors with Marshall at her heels, carting two large trunks on a trolley. As they pass, Marshall looks over at me and motions for me to follow them.

I stand by Zuri at the base of the stairs, watching Marshall pick up the first trunk and haul it up to the floor of the playroom.

"Isn't there an elevator you could have used?" I ask her.

"Yeah, but it's far more entertaining to watch him flex and carry shit upstairs," Zuri says, and she turns to admire Marshall in his tight blue jeans as he carries the heavy trunk.

There's a flare of jealousy when I witness how she watches him, the lust that appears there.

I know Marshall is attractive.

More than that, he's fucking *hot*.

But having Zuri ogle him so openly has my hackles rising.

"What's in the trunks?" I ask, hoping to distract her from Marshall's ass.

"Oh! It's my newest product. We haven't launched them yet. This is an exclusive first look." She says.

Marshall appears at the top of the stairs and begins jogging down. The way his muscles ripple with each step has me drooling.

He picks up the second trunk, repeating the process as we both watch him in silence.

"Yeah. You snagged a good one, girl." Zuri says.

"Oh. He's not mine." I say adamantly.

When Marshall comes back downstairs, there's a massive smile on his face, and when our gazes connect, there are stars in his eyes.

"You sure about that?" Zuri murmurs, drawing my attention away from Marshall.

"Alright," Marshall says when he stands before us, clapping his hands together. "What's next?"

Zuri and I look at each other briefly, her giving me a knowing look.

"Want to help me unpack everything? I'll let you pick out

something as a thank you." She says with a smirk, never breaking eye contact with me.

"Yeah. Of course." Marshall replies.

When I look back at him, he's still smiling at me. There's a look in his gaze that says there's trouble on the horizon.

As we turn to go upstairs, Marshall puts his hand on the small of my back, sending warmth through me. Just the slightest of touches has my body heating up, and I can already feel the need building for him.

Pregnancy is a wild ride, but the constant desire and horniness I've been feeling recently is so over the top.

The whole way up, Marshall keeps his hands on me, making sure I don't trip and fall.

Stairs are a bitch when you're pregnant.

Zuri already has the trunks open when we reach the top, and there are tables set up with black tablecloths.

"So, what is all of this?" I ask, approaching the trunk and picking up one of the packages inside.

"Most of it is our most popular products, like our vibes and dildos." She explains, beginning to pull out different products. "But the new stuff is in the other trunk. Go ahead."

I shuffle over to the trunk and open it to find a collection of sleek black and purple packages.

"We're finally expanding to male pleasure," Zuri says with a smile, clearly proud of her work. "So, we've been spending the past year developing cock sleeves, rings, and anal toys specifically for men."

I've always loved how passionate Zuri is about her work and how sex-positive and body-positive her company is. Seeing her rave about her new line makes my heart light up.

"Anything I should add to my toy bag?" Marshall jokes.

Instead of laughing along, she very seriously strides over to the trunk and pulls out a box. "Joke if you like, but toys are your friend, Marshall. Try this out, and tell me it isn't some of the best sex you've ever had."

Marshall doesn't take the box. So, I reach over and take it from Zuri's outstretched hand.

The packaging has the image of a sleek black cock ring on it.

"It vibrates?" I ask, reading the description.

"Yup." She says with a smirk. "Remote controlled."

"Oh. That's something I could have fun with." I smile deviously at the box in my hand.

"If only you had someone to use it with," Zuri chuckles. "And we were conveniently at a venue where you could escape and test it out."

I look up at her, and there's mischief in her eyes when our gaze connects.

"They come fully charged." She murmurs. "And the battery lasts for two hours."

My eyebrows raise at her insinuation, and I glance over at Marshall, who's unpacking the other trunk.

"Even if he's not *yours*, he is a fun plaything." She says with a wink.

I look back at Marshall, and when I look back at Zuri, she gives me a look of insistence.

Marshall has his back turned to me when I walk over to him, and I wrap my arms around his waist. I let my hands travel up under his shirt to feel his firm body.

One of his hands comes to cup my own, and there's a moment of connection between us that's far too intimate and sweet for where we are.

I move my hand down and cup his cock through his jeans, giving it a squeeze.

"I want to try something," I murmur to him.

He turns in my arms, pressing me against him firmly.

"Oh?" He asks, leaning down to look me in the eye. "And what would that be, princess?"

"I want you to wear one of Zuri's cock rings while you fuck me, *toy*," I reply, emphasizing the last word.

He takes in a sharp breath, and his gaze turns smoldering.

"Whatever you want, my Queen." He murmurs, leaning down to give me a kiss on the cheek.

I grab his hand and drag him over to where the second trunk lays open, grabbing the box from before.

"Now?" He asks, his voice lilting up in surprise.

I spin on him and narrow my eyes. "Yes. Now."

Tugging him by the hand, I proceed to drag Marshall through.

"Have fun, you two!" Zuri calls after us with a chuckle.

19

MARSHALL

Elsie closes the door behind us when we reach one of the private bedrooms and leans against it.

"Off." She commands, glancing down at my quickly thickening cock.

I move quickly to follow her instructions.

I love it when she's like this. I love it when she takes command over me.

When she uses me.

Most of the time, she tells me I'm going to fuck her, and I happily oblige. But when she gets like this, it's truly like I have no choice, and I revel in the feeling of complete lack of control.

Her gaze is heated as I strip off my boots, socks, and shirt before reaching for the button of my jeans.

When I look up at Elsie, her gaze is heated, and there's a need adding a flush to her skin.

Slowing my movements, I unbutton my jeans and push them down along with my briefs, releasing my hard cock.

"Is this what you want, my queen?" I ask when I have my clothes off. "Naked and bared to you?"

"Yes." She breathes out.

She fingers my tip, making me groan.

When she looks up at me, there's lust in her eyes, but there's also a need that doesn't seem to be physical. It's more than she's willing to admit, but her gaze tells me everything I need to know.

She needs me.

She *wants* me.

I lean down, taking her lips with my own as she strokes me to my full length.

The kiss is delicate and sweet, slow and sensual. Everything in the moment focuses on her. Just her.

Quickly, the kiss turns more heated as we melt into each other.

She bites down on my lip as we kiss, and I emit a whine.

"I love when you make those noises." She murmurs against my lips, both of us breathing heavily now. "I love it when you let me see how much you need this."

"Yes." She gives my cock a firm squeeze, making me moan. "Fuck. I need you."

"Yes. You do." She smiles. "But first, you're going to put on this cock ring, and then I'm going to suck you off."

She hands me a box and starts to move down to get on her knees, but I stop her before she can lower herself, and she gives me a questioning look.

I look around the room. Spotting the pillow in the center of the bed, I grab it and put it on the ground before.

"Ah." She lets out a chuckle. "Good idea. My knees hurt after last time."

She starts to kneel, and I take her by the elbows, helping lower her to the ground carefully.

When she's situated, she pauses to just look at my cock. There's an awe in her gaze that I always love seeing when she looks at me.

I'm proud of my body, but having her look at me and worship it has a whole different form of gratification humming through me.

She nods at the cock rings box, where I set it down on the bed, and I snap to reach for it.

Tearing open the packaging, I pull out the cock ring and a remote.

"It vibrates?" I ask, glancing down at her.

"Yes." She says with a smirk. "Now give me the remote."

"Fuck." I groan.

I hand her the remote and go to place the ring around the base of my quickly hardening cock.

The ring slips on with only slight resistance, with me already being half hard. I adjust the ring so the bulky top is above my cock, so that, hopefully, when I fuck Elsie, the vibrations of the ring hit against her clit.

When I'm finished, Elsie gives me a devious look.

Circling my cock with her fingers at the base, she leans in to take me in her mouth. Instead of taking just my tip into her mouth, though, she swallows the majority of my cock down her throat.

Holding herself there for a minute, she gags on my cock and lets out the most beautiful groan.

When she begins to pull back, her lips are wrapped around me and suctioning on my cock as she goes. The sensation has me groaning and my head dropping back in pleasure.

"Fuck, Queen." I groan.

Reaching for her, I thread my fingers through her hair and grasp at the base. She glances up at me from beneath me in warning, but I have no plans of controlling her movements. I solely want to touch her, to feel her underneath the tips of my fingers, and show her how much I desire her.

She continues to suck me off, causing me to make those sounds she loves so much.

Then she clicks on the cock ring, and it's like my whole body is electrocuted. The sensation overwhelms me, and when it becomes too much, I give her a tap on the shoulder and push her back slightly, gasping for breath.

"I..." I gasp. "Too much. Too much."

"Oh?" She asks with a raised eyebrow and a challenge in her eyes. "Maybe you won't be able to hold off long enough to fuck me then."

She reaches for my cock again, but I push back gently against her shoulder.

"Fuck that. I need to be inside you. *Now.*" I growl, leaning down to help her up from the floor where she kneels.

When she's standing, I pick her up, and her legs wrap around my waist.

"Oh!" She says in surprise. "Put me down. I'm too heavy."

"You're not." I protest. "I've got you."

I turn to the bed and gently lay her down on the mattress.

When she's settled, I take in her body.

She really is glowing at this point in her pregnancy. The radiance I've always seen from her has grown exponentially.

I trail my fingers over the stretch marks, which are light purple streaks on her stomach, taking them in reverently. Everything about her in this state has me feral.

I've always thought Elsie is a gorgeous woman, but seeing her grow with our child in her womb makes her even more so.

"You're incredible," I murmur, letting my hands roam over her belly and up to her breast.

Climbing onto the bed with her, I hover over her.

"Fucking incredible," I murmur, giving her a kiss on the lips. "I love seeing you like this."

"Like what?" She asks.

"Like a fucking fertility Goddess," I say in awe. "And I can't believe you're *mine*. It's an honor, my Queen."

She sucks in a breath at my words, and I give her another kiss, hotter and heavier this time.

Her hands come up to thread her fingers through my hair, and when she grips at the base of my head, I groan.

"Now, fuck me, toy." She growls into my lips, upping the vibration of the cock ring to a higher setting.

"Fuuuck." I moan and then pull myself together. "With pleasure."

I pull myself up onto my knees and smile down at her.

I take deep breaths, trying not to cum with how the cock ring vibrates around my shaft, and line myself up with her pussy.

Her cunt is already wet for me, and I run the head of my cock through her slick folds. A tingle shoots up my spine at the contact.

"Do you know how much I love fucking you?" I groan as I push the tip inside her and stop when she lets out a sigh of relief. "Your pussy is fucking heaven."

Elsie leans up on her elbows and smirks. "Well, then, what are you waiting for? Fuck me like you mean it."

"Oh, I'll fuck you. I'm gonna make you feel so good you'll black out from the pleasure." I purr, pushing a little further into her.

She sighs and falls back onto the bed.

When I thrust into her fully, she moans loud enough to be heard outside of our private room, and I smirk, knowing that everyone upstairs knows we're in here.

"You like that? Do you like how I fill you up? How I stretch you out?" I ask, reaching down to thumb her clit to encourage her to relax around me. "I fucking love how tight you are. How it doesn't matter how often we fuck, you're always tight and ready for me."

My Queen is so desperate for me that she begins rocking her hips, trying to get me to move.

"Patience, my Queen," I murmur. "I want to try something."

With the cock ring still vibrating around the base, I push just a little further into her and grind my hips so the toy presses into her clit.

At the contact, Elsie shrieks, a noise I've never heard before from her.

"Fuck!" I cry when she clamps down on me.

I can feel her trying to get me to move, to fuck her at the even pace I know she loves, but she has me locked in place, and I'm unable to move.

"Elsie." I pant out, breathless from the sensational overwhelm of her pussy clamped around my cock.

I manage to pull back just enough to relieve some of the pressure of the vibrator off her clit, and she relaxes enough to allow me to pull out of her slowly.

My pace is slow as I begin to fuck her. The strokes are a steady rhythm, and with each thrust, I press my hips in so the toy is forced up against her sensitive nub once more.

Every time the toy comes in contact with her clit, Elsie cries out, and her body begins to shake.

Usually, Elsie loves hard and fast, but right now, her body is responding to the combination of the vibrator and my cock in a way I've never seen before.

She's writhing beneath me, both trying to escape the sensations and get closer at the same time.

"That's it, my Queen," I murmur as her back bows, pushing her stomach out to be even more prominent.

"More." She whines. "More. I need more."

"You're the one with the remote." I tease and immediately regret my snark as the cock rings vibrations grow stronger. "Holy. Fuck."

The next grind of my hips into her has her crashing over the edge, and I'm quick to follow behind.

I collapse forward but hold myself up to hover over her and watch as the shock of her orgasm morphs her face into one of absolute bliss.

She's so beautiful when she comes, and the knowledge that I helped her get there is definitely a boost to my ego.

I start to pull out, but she grabs me by the hips to stop me.

"Flip us over so you're on your back, but don't pull out." She commands, still breathless from her orgasm. "I want to ride you with this ring on your cock until you're soft, and I've come a dozen more times."

My eyes widen at her brazen words, but immediately I'm lifting her up and positioning myself so she can easily ride my cock.

I'm still hard within her, but I know it's only a matter of time until I'm entirely soft, like she says.

I may be 29, but my refractory period isn't *that* superhuman.

She lowers the vibrations of the ring back down and leans over me with her hands by my face so she can grind herself into the toy while still riding me.

The moans and groans she lets out as she moves have me snapping my attention to her face. Her eyes are closed as she focuses on her pleasure.

Smiling, I reach up to push her hair back out of her face and lean up to kiss her.

"I can feel my cum leaking out of you all over me," I tell her. "You're such a good little cum slut, taking everything I give you."

"Yes. That." She groans against my lips, and her pussy tightens around me, clearly aroused by my words. "Tell me more. Talk me through my orgasm."

"As you wish, my Queen," I smirk, giving her another kiss before continuing. "Your cunt feels so incredible around me. It's like being suffocated by your pussy."

She begins to shake again.

"Filling you with my cum is the most pleasure I've ever had with anyone," I say. "Breeding you is my new obsession. I want to spend every day fucking you full of me until you're pregnant again. I'm going to keep you knocked up as often as I can."

That's what sends her over the edge, and my heart swells at the thought that maybe she wants that, too.

She shakes uncontrollably, but she keeps moving her hips to grind against the toy, and I continue to whisper into her ears.

Time passes, and I lose count of the number of times she's come around me and how many additional loads of cum I've deposited in her. It's enough to now be painful each time, but I hold back my cries, knowing she needs this.

Whatever my Queen wants, she gets.

When the toy dies, I'm fully soft at this point. Elsie collapses against me before rolling off onto her side, letting my cock slip out of her.

"Fucking hell." She gasps, heaving for breath.

"Yeah. Zuri knows what she's doing." I chuckle, matching her breathlessness.

"Yeah." Elsie sighs.

We lay there on the bed in silence, trying to catch our breath, but when I turn to look at Elsie, her eyes are closed, and she's fully asleep.

I let out a laugh, but it doesn't even disturb her slumber.

I would be proud of wearing her out, but I know that was all her.

Getting up, I glance around to locate my jeans, then hobble over to pull them on. I don't bother putting on my briefs, knowing the tightness would only aggravate my already over-sensitized cock, but even the denim of my looser jeans is nearly enough to have me wincing.

I slip out of the room and find Ivy standing right outside the door, watching an ongoing scene on the voyeur bed.

"Hey. Would you mind making sure no one goes in? I need to grab Elsie's bag and change of clothes." I ask her.

"Yeah, of course," Ivy replies.

"Thanks."

"Sounded like y'all had fun." She calls after me.

"Sure did," I say, waving over my shoulder to go downstairs and grab our stuff.

I gather everything up downstairs and quickly make my way back to Elsie, thanking Ivy at the door when I pass her to go inside the room.

Elsie is now curled in an adorable ball on the bed, but she looks a little chilled.

I set down our bags to dig through hers to find her street clothes, a simple loose cotton dress, and walk over to try and wake her.

When I shake her shoulder a bit, and she doesn't move, I sigh, knowing I'll have to get her dressed and carry her through the club and back to our room.

I quickly dress her and stuff all of our belongings in her over-sized bag, including our new toy and its accessories, before opening the door again to find Ivy.

"Hey. Would you mind carrying our bag so I can take Elsie back to our room?" I ask her quietly so as not to disturb the orgy currently occurring on the public play bed.

"Is she okay?" Ivy asks, concern marring her elegant features.

"She's perfect. Just fell asleep." I chuckle.

"Oh." She smiles. "Yeah, of course. I can put it behind the check-in desk, and you can pick it up tomorrow if you want."

"That would be perfect."

I go back inside the room and pick up Elsie in a bridal carry, and she automatically wraps her arms around my neck and snuggles into my chest.

Ivy is standing in the doorway with a look of awe and a little jealousy.

"She's a lucky woman to have you." She whispers, going over to grab our bag.

"No." I look down at Elsie and give her a kiss on her hair, which has her smiling in her sleep. "I'm a lucky man to have her."

20

ELSIE

May 31 — 22 Weeks, Papaya

Monday, Marshall left for work again, and the past five days have been brutal.

The two weeks before, though? Absolute heaven.

Something changed between us during our vacation at The Playground. Maybe it was meeting his family, or it could be all the sex. The part that stands out the most is our night at the club and me riding Marshall's cock until I passed out, literally.

I woke up the next morning surrounded by his warmth and had never felt so peaceful. So *good*.

He makes me feel good.

Marshall, despite my best attempts, has become a place of comfort for me.

For the past two weeks before he left, I've lived in a state of genuine contentment and happiness. Even Oliver has made comments, much to my chagrin.

All good things come to an end, though, and Marshall left once more.

Since then, my anxiety has been sky-high, right alongside my blood pressure.

Evidently, the solution to my woes, though, is brunch, according to my friends who've dragged me out of the office on a Friday morning.

The audacity of taking a pregnant woman to a bar that serves brunch with bottomless mimosas should, quite frankly, be a crime.

Nonetheless, Selene, Naomi, Zuri, and Ivy somehow convinced me to leave the safety of my home office and ditch my responsibilities in exchange for a few hours with girlfriends, breakfast food, and *water*.

The bar we frequent for brunch is nice enough, with excellent food and drinks.

I'm sipping on my water that was dropped off at our table when our usual waiter comes over to greet us.

"Good morning, ladies. Welcome back. How are we this afternoon?" They ask.

The look around the table is less than cheery.

"I think we need food and drinks." Selene chuckles, trying to lighten the mood.

"Of course." The waiter says, shifting on their feet. "The usuals for the table?"

Everyone else nods their heads in confirmation.

"Um... Can I do breakfast tacos instead?" I request.

"And a bottle of hot sauce on the side." Zuri chuckles at me. "What? Like we all haven't noticed, your cravings lean toward a particular spice level during this pregnancy."

"Of course." The waiter replies with a glance down at my now heavily protruding stomach.

"I get that you're white, but like, babe, you down spicy food like it's vanilla ice cream these days," Zuri says with a broad smile. "I think it has something to do with a certain someone who's been cooking for you for the past few months."

I shake my head and reach to unfold my silverware from its cloth napkin.

Selene eyes me suspiciously but lets me avoid commenting by changing the subject.

"Alright. Y'all bitches catch me up." She says, clapping her hands. "Zuri, I wanna hear about the new line. Elsie, I know how work is. I want baby updates. Nay gets a pass today, but I expect participation at a minimum. Got it?"

"Yes, captain," Nay says with a mock salute, her face not moving from its delicately held-together neutral expression.

I've heard from Selene that the woman has been going through trouble in paradise with the couple she's dating, and it's been brutal on her.

"Zuri. Kick us off. Work update, please, and thank you." Selene commands with a smile.

With a sigh, Zuri starts telling us about the security threats her company has been receiving and how she's now working with the security firm owned by Gunnar and Emir. Emir is also on my Board of Directors and a mentor. Gunnar and Emir are working on increasing security at the building and upping safety protocols for their internal systems as well.

"I met his husband, Derek, the other day when I was leaving their offices," Zuri mentions with what I think is a blush under her deep umber skin.

"Oh?" I ask, curious as to what would make our Zuri smile like that.

"It was a classic rom-com run-in. Spilled coffee and everything." She explains with a chuckle. "He was sweet about it, though."

"Based on that blush blooming in your cheeks, it was far more than just a run-in." Selene jokes, but Zuri's expression only seems to confirm Selene's suspicions.

"He's cute," Zuri admits. "They're a cute couple."

"Cute?" Selene questions. "Cute doesn't cut it, babe. They're hot as hell."

"Fine. They're hot." Zuri acquiesces.

"Who is this?" Naomi asks. She is the newest addition to our friend group since she moved to the city after quitting her doctorate program in Dallas.

"Emir and Derek Bonner. Emir is the other founder of the security company Gunnar works for." Selene explains, turning to engage Naomi in the conversation more. "Derek is…"

"Oh my god. He's the bisexual linebacker, right?" Naomi gasps. "He's an icon."

"Yes. That he is." Selene smiles at her friend, likely just pleased to see her friend excited over something once again.

"That's so cool," Naomi says with a little more light in her eyes.

"You should see Derek shirtless, though. I've seen him working out with Emir in their corporate gym. Phew." Selene says, fanning her face. "I don't understand why they had him in all those clothes for the magazine article he was in."

Zuri laughs alongside Selene, and they have both me and Naomi grinning.

"The two of them together though?" Selene continues. "Oh, would that be a marriage bed I'd like to be a part of. Don't tell Gunnar."

"Selene!" Zuri scoffs with a deepening blush.

"What? They're hot." Selene shrugs.

"Yeah. But they're not even in the lifestyle. They're Gunnar's business partners. They're not kinky." Zuri pushes back.

"Oh, Zuri. Everyone's a little bit kinky." Selene says offhandedly. "They've never batted an eye at any of the shit that Gunnar tells them. I doubt they're as vanilla as you think."

"Then why haven't they come to the club? I'm sure Gunnar has invited them." I question. "The Playground is run by a queer polycule. If anyone's going to create a space where two gay men feel comfortable, it should be the Morgans, right?"

"Bisexual and queer." Zuri corrects.

"What?" I ask, turning to her.

"Bi and queer. Emir is queer, and Derek is bisexual. They're not gay." She explains further. "Well... they are, but they aren't."

"Okay, fine. We're all a little bit fruity." I chuckle. "My own bisexual ass included in that."

"Now you're getting it," Selene says with a smile.

"Okay. They're hot." Zuri admits. "Nothing's going to happen though."

"But you're interested," Selene says with a raised eyebrow.

"That doesn't mean they're interested in me." Zuri protests.

"That doesn't mean they're *not* interested in you either, Zuri." I point out. "Polyamory is becoming more and more popular. You have no idea what their relationship dynamic is."

"And what about you and Marshall?" Selene says, seizing the opportunity to steer the conversation in a direction that fulfills her curiosity. "What's y'all's relationship dynamic like these days?"

I look away from her piercing stare. "I don't know what you're talking about."

"Oh, you are an absolute fibber. You know exactly what I'm talking about." Selene insists. "Something's changed between y'all. Spill."

When I look up at the girls, each of them has an entirely too eager and focused expression on their faces. They look like they need a good tea-spilling session almost just as much as I have this gnawing feeling that I need to word-vomit all my thoughts and feelings to them.

"Fine." I sigh halfheartedly. "Marshall and I are... figuring things out."

I spend the next hour filling in the trio on everything that's gone down between Marshall and me. All of the moments of joy and tension and everything in between. They ask questions as I go and interject freely with their thoughts and opinions.

By the time I've sufficiently caught them up, I'm breathless from talking so much, and after drinking so much water to keep my mouth from going dry while I spilled, I desperately need to pee with how the baby is pressing down on my bladder.

"You're squirming like you need to escape." Selene chuckles.

"I just need to use the ladies' room," I say, already pushing myself up from the table. "I'll be right back."

"I'll come with you. Girls go in pairs. Buddy system." Naomi jokes, her demeanor much more cheerful now than when she first sat down at the table an hour ago.

"You know we're fully going to scheme shit while you're gone, right?" Zuri asks with a smile as we both leave the table.

"I expect nothing less," I say, returning her grin.

Naomi and I make our way through the bar to the restroom, and she kindly waits for me when it takes me longer to finish up in the bathroom than her.

Walking back to our table, we pass the bar, and something catches my eye on one of the TVs placed above the shelves of alcohol, making me stop in my tracks.

BREAKING NEWS: Texas Supreme Court rejects challenge to state's abortion law over medical exceptions

But it's the man on the screen that truly has my attention.

When the banner scrolls to its next caption and confirms my fear, my heart drops out of my chest.

NOW: NewsNow LIVE with Texas Attorney General Charles Snow on the court ruling.

My father.

I knew I'd never be able to avoid him completely.

But still... that fucking man. His presence is everywhere.

Waddling up to the bar with Naomi close behind, I get the attention of the bartender.

"Can you turn up the volume on that TV?" I ask them, and they give me a nod.

It's busy despite it being a weekday, but when the TV is loud enough to hear the sound, it's like all the noise falls away, and all I can hear is my father's voice.

"Joining us now is the man behind this monumental decision, Texas Attorney General Charles Snow." The news anchor says, turning to address the other man on screen. "Attorney General Snow, thank you for joining us."

"Thank you for having me." My father says with a smile that would look genuine and charming to anyone but me.

I should walk away. I don't need to listen to his lies. He's not here. I'm not trapped. I can leave.

But something keeps me rooted to the spot.

"Elsie?" I feel Naomi addressed me more than I hear her. "You, okay?"

I want to reassure her that I'm good, but I can't bring myself to speak. Breathing is hard enough as it is, and the world feels like it caves in as I watch my father casually talk on screen with the news anchor about the most recent ruling on the state abortion ban.

"This is a case that hits close to home, isn't it Attorney General?" The anchor asks.

"Yes. Very much so." My father says, his face dropping into a mask of false sorrow. "My wife, God rest her soul, passed shortly after giving birth to our daughter."

The anchor gives him a sympathetic look that sends rage through me.

I know how calculating my father is and how every word and expression is carefully measured to get the desired response from his audience. I can see straight through him, but everyone else falls for his performance every time.

"There were medical complications toward the end of her pregnancy. The doctor let us know there was a high likelihood that the complications would impact her during labor and delivery, and there was a high risk for loss of life, either hers or our daughter's. The medical team we worked with at that time strongly encouraged terminating the pregnancy. But..." He has fake tears in his eyes, and his voice is choked. "My wife told me and the doctors that if anything happened, the only priority would be to save our daughter. She wanted our baby girl to live."

"What do you say to those people who argue that a woman should be able to make that choice for herself? Like your wife did?" The anchor asks, thinking they're going to get my father to admit he's pro-choice after that experience.

But no.

The asshole stays true to his controlling ways.

"I would say the same thing my wife said to me before she passed away. That bringing life into this world is the most important thing a woman can ever hope to do." Father says, seemingly gathering his composure again and returning from whatever sad distant memory he conjures anytime he needs to emote.

"So, you maintain your goals align with the anti-abortion movement." The anchor prompts.

"While the sacrifice is significant, our future depends on our children, on the next generation." My father says. "My daughter is the most important person in my life. I love her more than anything. My wife's sacrifice only solidifies that belief for me."

"Fuck you," I say, my voice growing louder with each phrase. "Fuck you. Fuck you. Fuck you! You fucking asshole!"

"Elsie!" Naomi says in shock before turning to where our friends sit a few tables away.

I'm drawing attention now, with my heaving sobs and tears streaking down my face.

Logically, I know there are so many false narratives that he's spinning right now, but the hurt is just the same.

My hands go to my belly, cupping where my baby grows protectively.

"Selene..." Naomi says frantically, causing Selene to shoot up from her chair and come over.

One glance from her up to the screen to the tragedy I'm witnessing is all she needs to understand the situation.

"Zuri," Selene says to the woman who's joined us at the bar. "Can you cover the bill? We're gonna take Elsie home."

"Yeah, of course," Zuri says as Selene wraps an arm around my shoulder to lead me out of the building.

"I'll grab our bags and meet you at the car," Naomi says, rushing back to the table.

My whole body is shaking as Selene walks me through the bar, the whole way feeling like my own personal funeral march.

Naomi has already re-joined us by the time we make it to my car, and she automatically hops in the driver's seat.

"I'm fine. I can drive." I protest.

"No." She says calmly. "You're not fine. You shouldn't be driving, and Gunnar would kill us if we let Selene drive."

"One little wreck, and suddenly, you're not trusted to drive by anyone," Selene grumbles, drawing a watery smile out of me. "Now, let's get you home and into comfy clothes."

Shame flows through me, knowing my friends have seen me at my absolute worst.

"Don't do that," Naomi says, intuitively sensing how I'm feeling. "Wipe that look off your face. There's nothing to be ashamed of here. You're allowed to experience your emotions and process them any way you see fit. We will sit with you through them. Then, you get to decide what to do next. Okay?"

I chuckle through my tears. "You're gonna be a great therapist, Naomi."

"And you're going to be an incredible mother, Elsie," Selene says reassuringly.

I attempt to smile at her. Thankful for my friends. For the fact that they know me well enough to know my fears and assuage them, even if just a little.

The whole drive home, though, there's an unidentifiable tightness in my chest.

A longing.

It's not until I'm dressed in pajamas and laying in my king-sized bed, cuddled by my closest friends, that I realize why.

It's him.

Marshall.

He's the one I want here right now.

I want *his* comfort and reassurance.

I need *him* to tell me everything is going to be okay.

But he's not here.

And even as I'm surrounded by people I logically know love me, I still feel alone.

Because, ultimately, that's what we all are.

On our own.

I need to get used to that.

Again.

21

ELSIE

June 2 — 22 Weeks 2 Days, Papaya

When Marshall is away, we pretty exclusively communicate through email. It's the easiest way for us to keep up with each other. Unfortunately, the cell signal isn't good enough out where he is in the Gulf for phone or video calls.

We aren't able to go back and forth every day, but we respond to each other within 24 hours most of the time.

Only, I can't bring myself to physically pick up my phone right now, much less respond to an email.

Seeing my father on TV triggered the release of all the memories and feelings associated with him. All of the emptiness, loneliness, neglect, and abuse rushed to the forefront of my mind. And since then, I've just been numbly going through my days.

I'm sure Gunnar or Selene told Marshall about what happened, but despite how desperately I want his comfort, I can't bare to bring myself to tell him everything.

I can't do it because I'd break down. There's no chance of getting around it.

And if I'm going to break down, then I want him *here*.

In general, I want him here, in our home, with me.

Every day that passes while he's away has my chest aching for him to return.

The longing I felt for him while laying in bed being comforted by my friends has only compounded with each hour that's passed.

It feels crushing.

I'm sitting in the kitchen, trying to choke down some fruit, when my phone buzzes on the counter where it's remained plugged in for the past few days.

I know it's him that he's reaching out again.

But this time, I resist the urge to retreat back to my bed and walk over to grab my phone and face the music.

June 2 — 22 Weeks 2 Days, Papaya

E,

I haven't heard from you in a few days. Everything okay?
M
P.S. 21 days until I'm home.

HIS RESPONSE HITS SOMEWHERE deep in my chest, a place more tender than I care to admit.

So, I keep my distance by keeping my reply short.

June 2 — 22 Weeks 2 Days, Papaya

I'm fine.
Elsie

· · ·

WITHIN MINUTES, another email comes through, making my heart plummet.

June 2 — 22 Weeks 2 Days, Papaya

No, even I'm not naive enough to fall for that. I have five sisters.

If you're saying you're fine, then everything is definitely not fine.

Gunnar says Selene told him about something that happened on Friday? At your brunch with the girls?

Elsie, what happened? Are you okay?

M

TOO WORKED up to give him any kind of meaningful response, I turn my phone off and go back to bed.

Days pass, and I know Marshall hasn't given up his mission to check on me, as people have now started showing up at my doorstep.

First, he sent Oliver, who camped out in the lobby for over six hours before I finally let him come up to see me. But only because he left and came back with my favorite takeout.

Then Selene and Gunnar came by. After my last experience with having Gunnar show up at my door via the elevator shaft, I let them in immediately. Which then meant I proceeded to push them out of my home as quickly as I possibly could. It was a feat unto itself with how overbearing they were the whole time.

Today, when the front desk calls up, it's Zuri who's downstairs.

Too exhausted to do anything other than cave, I drag myself out of bed and to the front door to let her in.

Before I even get the chance to open the door fully, Zuri is already pushing into my entryway.

"You've us all scared shitless, Elsie," Zuri says sternly. "What the hell are you doing, woman?"

"Marshall sent you," I conclude.

"No shit he sent me, he's worried! We all are!" She continues her desperation to get through to me, making her voice climb with each sentence. "You've gone completely MIA, Elsie. This isn't how you treat people."

"I know," I mumble.

"Then *do* something about it." She says emphatically. "Talk to him. Us. A therapist. Talk to fucking *anyone*."

"I can't," I say listlessly as I shuffle over to plop myself on the couch. "I just. I can't."

"Girl. You have to do something." She insists.

"I know." I sigh.

"You can't keep going like this."

"I know," I repeat.

"Think of..."

I cut her off. "I said I fucking know, Zuri."

Silence rings through the whole apartment as I try to catch my breath after snapping at my friend.

"I'm sorry," I say.

"I know." She says with a small smirk. "Things are tense. I know you're not okay, and that's okay. But we have to do something to get out of your slump."

"Okay."

"Okay?"

"Yes. Okay." I capitulate.

"Where's your phone?" Zuri asks, glancing around.

"Dead."

"That explains a lot." She groans before refocusing. "Computer then. If I accomplish one thing while I'm here, it's going to be responding to that man's fucking emails."

"It's in the office." I bemoan. "It's probably dead too."

"You haven't been working?" Zuri asks, her dark eyebrows raised in surprise.

"No..." I admit.

"That's..." She ponders for a moment. "Almost impressive? If the circumstances were different, I mean."

I let out a chuckle, more like a huff, in agreement.

"I'm grabbing both, and whichever is charged enough first to send an email from is the one we're using." She says in an authoritative tone.

Turns out my computer wins the contest, and within seconds of the screen lighting up, Zuri is thrusting it in my direction to type in my password.

"Thank you." She chimes when I give her back the computer.

I watch her as she clicks around to open my email inbox and find the emails from Marshall.

"Do you want me to read them to you?" She asks, her eyes wide, probably because of the sheer number of emails in my inbox from him.

I don't even need to look to know he flooded it with messages. I just know.

"No. Just respond to the most recent one for me?" I ask her.

"Yeah. Sure. Secretary Zuri Valentine at your service." She says with a genuine smile.

It takes me a while to choke out the words, but I do manage to dictate a reply for her, and she clicks send when she's done.

June 5 — 22 Weeks 5 Days, Papaya

Marshall,

Yes, something happened. But I'm handling it. I don't need you butting your way into my business. Let it go.

Elsie

· · ·

WE PROBABLY WOULD HAVE SAT in silence for a while if only my inbox hadn't pinged almost immediately with a reply.

June 5 — 22 Weeks 5 Days, Papaya

You are *my business, Elsie.*
Please don't shut me out like this.
M
18 days

ZURI'S VOICE is even and nonjudgmental when she reads me the message, but her face is full of pity.

Instead of trying to muster the energy to send another response, Zuri lets me off the hook for a little while, and we order delivery for two before curling up on the couch to watch something on TV.

My now charged phone sits on the coffee table before us, surrounded by takeout boxes, but I still jump when the screen lights up, and it pings with a new email.

The food, company, and comfort shows were just starting to pull me out of my dark headspace, but all I needed to bring back those feelings fit perfectly in the email preview notification on my phone screen.

June 5 — 22 Weeks 5 Days, Papaya

I'll let you have until Monday, then. Then I need you to talk to me. If you don't, I'll call Mamá.
M
17 days

· · ·

10:59 P.M. ON MONDAY, I'm restless and awake when my phone, which I've kept charged this time to stay in touch with my keepers, pings with a new email.

June 10 — 23 Weeks 3 Days, Grapefruit

Elsie. Talk to me.
   M
   13 days

FRUSTRATION AND ANGER BOIL UP, and I tap out a sharp reply. Hoping I can stop things in their tracks.

June 11 — 23 Weeks 4 Days, Grapefruit

Stop it with your fucking countdown. I'll see you when you're home.
   Elsie

June 11 — 23 Weeks 4 Days, Grapefruit

Okay. No countdown, but you have to talk to me.
   I've arranged with my crew boss to do a video call at 8 p.m. tomorrow. It might be a little spotty because we don't have the best reception, but it's something.
   I need to see you, make sure you're okay.
   M

June 11 — 23 Weeks 4 Days, Grapefruit

Fine. See you tomorrow.

. . .

I HATE the part of me that feels butterflies float up at the prospect of seeing Marshall again. I've spent all this time trying to isolate myself and re-acclimate myself to being alone, and the reminder of how much I want him, *need him*, is brutal and devastating to my ego.

Even worse, the knowledge is evidently precisely what I need in order to fall asleep.

22

ELSIE

June 12 — 23 Weeks 5 Days, Grapefruit

All day, my stomach has been in knots, waiting for this call with Marshall, so much so that it reminds me of my days of morning sickness.

By the time 7:30 p.m. rolls around, I'm already sitting at my desk in front of my computer with the video call active, waiting for Marshall to join.

The minutes tick by, and I feel like I'm going to be sick.

When the standby screen finally changes, I'm suddenly looking at a clearly exhausted Marshall.

"Hey." He says, his smile reaching his eyes.

"Hey," I say, letting out a breath I didn't know I was holding.

Things quickly turn awkward, but Marshall saves me by asking about the baby, and I give him all the little updates from the past 12 days that he's been gone.

"Sounds like the baby's going to have quite the personality." He chuckles before growing quiet. "Elsie..."

"Yeah?" I ask when he doesn't continue.

"Elsie. What happened? How are you? Really." He asks, his eyes full of concern. "I've been really fucking worried, Elsie."

"It's nothing," I say.

"No. It isn't nothing if it sends you into a spiral like this and has you isolating from everyone." He says sternly, almost like he's scolding me.

But then his expression turns back to the gentle, kind man I know.

"You can tell me." He says softly.

I bite my lip, considering how deep into things I should go.

"My father's an asshole." I start. "He wasn't physically abusive or anything, but there was a lot of other... stuff."

He nods encouragingly.

"He wasn't a great parent. He was head of the household for sure, but not any kind of guardian or role model for me." I start to get lost in the memories once more but pull myself back. "He treated me fine for the most part. Like, I had a happy childhood. I went to camps and played in tennis tournaments at the country club. The nannies who took care of me when he was gone were kind. There are happy memories there, but he only seemed to be present when he needed to take me places with him, fancy events, and stuff. To be seen as a family man."

Marshall's face is bright with his smile as I recount the better times of my childhood, but there is also concern in his eyes.

"But there was other stuff that wasn't so great, like him not being there for those tournaments and school events." I shrug. "Our relationship got so toxic that I'm now no-contact with him. So, when I saw something while we were at brunch, it triggered those less happy memories and feelings. I was..."

"Scared." He offers when I don't continue, but I scowl at him.

"Not scared. I'm not scared." I protest. "I just couldn't handle it. With everything going on," I glance down and place my hands on my round belly. "It was just too much. And you're not here. So, there wasn't anything you could have done anyway. I was handling it to the best of my ability."

"But you still weren't handling it well." He points out. "You tried to do that alone, and it didn't work. So, what can I do to help? How can I fix this?"

"You can't. It just is, Marshall." I sigh.

"Elsie. *I* was scared. Scared to death when you stopped responding to me." He says with a slight shake of his head. "If there's something I can do to make sure this doesn't happen again, I'll do it. Just tell me what you need."

"I..." I hesitate.

"Name it, Elsie." He says, his jaw tight with conviction.

"I want you to quit." I blurt out.

Marshall goes so still that I think the video feed froze, but then he shakes his head, and I realize he was literally frozen by shock.

"What?" He asks, completely caught off-guard.

"I want you to quit your job," I say more slowly but no less passionate.

"Elsie. What does that have to do with any of this? I can't just..."

"No." I cut him off. "You absolutely can quit. I make more than enough to take care of us for the rest of our lives."

"Our lives?" He says, a light sparking in his eyes, which makes me cringe at my word choice.

"You know what I mean." I huff. "Just that you wouldn't have to worry about money if you wanted to take a break and find another career."

"Elsie..." He says, his voice is soft.

"Hear me out. You could do whatever you want. Take up woodworking or go back to school and get another degree. Literally anything. I'll support you."

"Are you bribing me?" He asks with a smirk.

"No," I reply, shrinking back a little. "More like begging you."

Marshall goes quiet for a moment, and I hold my breath while he thinks.

"Why?"

"Why what?"

"Why is this so important to you?" He insists.

"Because. Your job is dangerous. I don't want you getting hurt." I reason.

"But you've known that this whole time." He says, cocking his head to the side. "What changed? Why now?"

"Nothing's changed." I snap, suddenly feeling like a cornered animal.

"Something's changed. Something happened." He says surely. "If I'm going to consider this? If this is a deal breaker, then I deserve to know why it's so important to you."

"Because..." I try.

"Elsie." He warns.

"Because I don't want my baby sitting on the porch steps wondering when their dad is going to decide they're important enough to show up finally!" I throw the words at him like daggers.

Only I'm not expecting them to hurt *me* so much when they land dead center in his chest.

His expression falls instantly.

The only sound coming from my computer speaker is the background noise from the rig Marshall's on that filters through the thick walls of the room.

"Is that..." He tries again. "Is that what you think is going to happen?"

I stay silent.

"Elsie. I know what it's like not to have a dad around. I get that. But What are you really afraid of?" He says gently. "I'm not going anywhere. I told you, *keep telling you*, I'm in. All in."

"I..." I choke on the rest of my words, seeing the earnestness on his face.

"You're not alone in this. I won't let you do this by yourself. I..." He shakes his head. "You mean a lot to me, and I really value my relationship with you."

"What are you saying?" I ask.

"You're, I can't believe I'm saying this, but you sound scared, Elsie. And if there's anything I can do to take away that fear, then let me know." He explains.

But I still have no reply for him.

"What do you need from me? How can I help?" He presses.

"Quit," I whisper.

"I can't." He replies softly.

Silence extends between us, and at this moment, I fully feel the miles between us.

He's so far away.

So distant.

"I don't know how to fix this." He says.

"Me either."

"Why don't we start..." He straightens up in the chair he's sitting in. "I'll get permission to call you more. We'll call and talk like this. Just..."

"How often?" I ask, grasping for any solid foundation I can find with him.

"I'll see, but daily if I can pull it off." He says. "Okay?"

"Okay." I nod.

"Elsie... You know I..."

"Stop." I cut him off. "Don't make this harder by saying something you'll regret later."

"I would never regret telling you that I..."

"Just don't." I interrupt him again, talking faster this time. "I'll talk to you later. Let me know if you get permission to call and when."

Then I snap the computer closed and fall back in my chair.

Tears rim my eyes, and I take in deep breaths, trying to calm my racing heart.

"It's gonna be okay, Elsie," I tell myself. "You're gonna be just fine."

23

MARSHALL

June 23 — 25 Weeks 1 Day, Acorn Squash

Coming home after another hitch away on the rig is a weight off my shoulders.

For the past 20ish days, Elsie and I have kept in touch as much as we can, and each time she says goodbye, I can see the shimmer of tears in her eyes.

It's becoming harder and harder to be away from her and the baby, but I can't just abandon my career and not provide for my family.

As much as I know I'm in love with Elsie, I still can't bring myself to admit that to her. The fear of not hearing those three words back is too intense to take the risk.

But a part of me also fears the risk I'm taking by not admitting how I truly feel about her.

However, being back home takes those fears away, even temporarily.

"Honey! I'm home!" I yell as I come through the front door of the apartment.

"Living room." I hear Elsie call back.

Dropping my bags in the entryway, I stride into the open living room to find a very clearly pregnant Elsie lounging on the couch.

Elsie is lounging in sweatpants and a loose t-shirt that drapes over her belly, which has finally popped with her pregnancy. Her fiery hair hangs in soft curls around her face and highlights the pink glow she has on her skin.

"Fuck, you're beautiful," I say under my breath.

"Oh, shut up." She snaps. "Pregnancy sucks, and I feel awful."

"You're showing now," I say, admiring her rounded stomach as I walk around the edge of the couch to kneel before her.

Immediately, I'm on my knees before her with my hands outstretched.

"May I?" I ask, gesturing to her stomach.

"Sure." She says softly.

Reaching out, I place my hands on her and find her body has changed.

What were once soft curves in her tummy have now hardened into a proper baby bump. The stretch marks I adore on her skin have multiplied, with new reddish-purple lines appearing among those that have already settled into their light white stripes on her already pale skin.

I give myself a moment to just let my hands roam her body, and when I finally look up at her, there's a softness on her face that I've yet to see there before.

"You're incredible," I say softly, leaning in to give her a kiss on the lips. "Fucking incredible."

"I'm really not." She tries to say.

"No. Don't do that." I reach over to cup her face and lean in close. "You're doing one of the hardest things nature asks of your body. You're creating life. Don't discredit yourself. I know it's hard, but you're fucking amazing for doing it."

She frowns. "Has my body really changed that much? I barely notice anymore."

"I guess time away makes me notice the changes more. But, yeah, you're at 25 weeks, and you've definitely popped."

"You still keep track?" She asks, her eyes lighting up with emotion. "When you're away, I mean."

"Of course. I keep track with the app on my phone and listen to our baby's heartbeat every night before I go to bed." I admit with a shrug.

A silence fills the space between us, and I let her study me without looking away.

I need her to see how much this means to me. How much *she* means to me.

"Ugh." She groans alongside her grumbling stomach. "I fucking hate being pregnant. I'm always hungry or tired or gassy or some other gross bodily function. I want to be done with this."

Standing, I take her by the hands and help her up from the couch until I'm looking down at her where she stands.

"You're almost halfway there. You've got this." I say, leaning down to give her a kiss on the forehead. "Now. What do you want for dinner?"

"Whatever is fine." She says warmly.

"You sure?" I ask.

"Yeah."

I head over to the kitchen and start looking through the fridge and pantry for ingredients to make dinner.

Locating everything I need, I start making street tacos for dinner.

Elsie sits on her usual island stool and watches as I get into the rhythm of cooking.

When dinner is ready, I bring everything over to the dining room table and lay out our feast. Elsie follows with plates and napkins as we both settle in at the table to eat in comfortable silence.

After both of us demolish several tacos, Elsie breaks the silence.

"I have a doctor's appointment tomorrow if you want to come," she says. "We can find out the gender if you want."

"Wasn't that appointment supposed to happen at your 20-week check-up?" I ask.

"Yeah, but it was right before you were about to leave again, and I just couldn't mentally handle it."

"Why didn't you tell me? I would have gone with you." I say.

"I know. I know..." She pauses in a way I don't like. "I keep thinking that you're going to change your mind."

"Elsie..."

"No. Hear me out." She sighs. "You're 29. You have so much life ahead of you, and I just keep feeling like I've trapped you in this."

I sit quietly as she composes herself, my heart thundering in my chest, and I desperately want to interrupt to reassure her.

"I keep worrying that you're just being a good sport about this and doing the right thing, kind of thing. I worry you don't actually want this. That you don't..." She trails off, heavy words left unsaid. "If you don't want this, I'd let you go, you know."

My jaw clenches at her words. "Stop that. Stop giving me an out and expecting me to leave. I'm not going anywhere." I reach for her hand and lace our fingers together. "Never."

June 24 — 25 Weeks 2 Days, Acorn Squash

The soft eggshell on the walls of Elsie's doctor's office, combined with the oversized canvas prints of parents smiling with their kids, has nerves balling in my chest. The moment we entered the building, all of the ease and comfort of our morning routine together fled, and now I'm just *anxious*.

Every time I accompany her to an appointment, this dread takes over. Thoughts that something could be wrong with my precious ciruela azucarada swirl through my head like a hurricane gaining speed. *My Sugar Plum is everything, including their mother.* None of them are founded in reality, but the anxiety is still there.

I blame the creepy smiling faces on the walls.

When the nurse calls Elsie back, we both go through the regular routines of her appointments before being left alone in the patient room.

Thankfully, this one just has framed pictures of babies on the walls.

"Stop with the foot tapping, Marshall. It's going to be fine," Elsie says calmly.

"How do you know?" I ask, rising from the chair where I sat to pace the room.

"I just do. Now, sit." She commands, and I quickly lower myself back into the seat.

Thankfully, it doesn't take long for the doctor to come by and begin going through the things they need from Elsie, but I stay in my corner, silently panicking all the while.

I think back to my conversation last night with Elsie, how she's convinced that I'm going to abandon her and our child.

I grew up in a large family with my mamá, papá, and sisters. I know what it is to be surrounded by love. To have the stability that comes with having strong familial relationships. Even after losing my dad, it made our family stronger. We grew closer together. We leaned on each other, just like I want her to do now.

While there is a part of me that's terrified about the changes that come with having a kid, building a family with Elsie sounds like a dream, not a nightmare.

So much could go wrong between now and when Elsie gives birth. There's so much more that could happen afterward.

"Marshall?" Elsie's voice draws me out of my spiral.

"Um. Yeah." I say, shaking my head.

"Do you want to see the baby?" She asks, with an annoyance in her voice, which tells me this isn't the first time.

"Of course," I say, rising to my feet and taking a few steps to her side.

At some point in my panic, the doctor and nurse brought out the ultrasound machine and prepped Elsie for the scan.

Taking Elsie's hand, more for my comfort than hers, I glance up at the screen where the ultrasound is shown, and my breath stops.

I've seen photos before and heard their heartbeat, but nothing compares to the awe of watching your child move around on a screen like this.

My gaze hones in on the minute movements of the baby growing in Elsie's womb as the sound of the heartbeat, one I'm extremely familiar with echoes around the room.

"That's our baby girl," I whisper.

"Marshall. You don't know that." Elsie teases back at me before turning to the doctor. "But I think they could tell us if you're right."

"Would you like to know for sure?" The doctor asks.

"No. I don't need to know for sure unless Elsie wants to." I say, tearing my eyes away from the screen to look back at my daughter's mother. "I already know what I need to know. She's ours."

Elsie gives me a smile that warms my heart, and I look back at the screen where our baby is displayed.

"We're gonna be parents," Elsie says, the same awe in her voice that I feel in my marrow.

"We're gonna be a family," I whisper.

The rest of the appointment goes by in a blur, and before I

know it, Elsie and I are headed to the car to take her back to the office for work, after which I'll head home.

To *our home.*

My family's home.

It's as though everything in the world around me ceases to exist at that exact moment, and everything goes still and quiet.

Nothing is more important to me than this family I'm building with Elsie.

With that thought, everything becomes clear.

"Marshall. You need to start the car if you expect us to go anywhere." Elsie says from the passenger seat beside me.

I glance over at her, taking in her soft features and the small smile she has on her lips as she looks at me teasingly.

"I'm quitting my job," I say, turning on the engine.

Her eyes grow wide. "What?"

"My job. I'm going to quit." I say, finality in my voice as I back out of our parking spot and head in the direction of Elsie's office. "You asked me to quit. That's what I'm doing. I'll email my boss tonight."

"Okay." She responds tentatively.

"I want to stay home and care for you and the baby," I explain, glancing over at her as I drive. "I have worked my ass off, and I have more than enough saved up to help support us."

"That's really not what I'm worried about here, Marshall," Elsie says, blank-faced when I glance over.

"Then what worries do you have?"

"Look, I know I asked you to quit your job. You know I don't like you going out to the middle of the Gulf for weeks at a time like you do or being gone so much. But it is your job, and it's part of who you are. I am trying to come to terms with it. This feels sudden. Surely, you don't intend just to become a stay-at-home dad."

I continue to drive without response.

"Oh, my goddess. You do. You really do." She says, mouth agape. "Marshall!"

"We can talk through the details later, but my mind is made up, Elsie," I say sternly.

I know she won't ultimately fight me on it, but she still pouts in the passenger seat for the rest of the trip back to her office, where lunch is waiting for us.

Silence continues through our lunch, and then Oliver knocks at the door.

"Reminder that your meeting about the site tour is in fifteen minutes." He interrupts, relieving some of the pressure in the room.

"Oh!" Elsie says, finally looking up from her papers and food at her desk. "Pregnancy brain's a bitch sometimes. Thank you, Oliver."

"Welcome." He says, backing out of the room and closing the door behind him.

"What's this for?" I ask, curious about her work.

"A client we're courting wants me to go out and do a visit with them on one of their rigs that we're surveying." She explains.

"What?" I ask, bewildered.

"Yeah. That's what we do. Or at least the first step." She continues going into the science, oblivious to my mounting frustration. "The Gulf of Mexico is known for its rich deposits of crude oil and natural gas. It's created the perfect environment for coral reefs to thrive."

With every word, my pulse increases, and my hands grip tightly at the seat beneath me.

"Salt deposits in the Gulf rise up on the ocean floor, which creates pockets of crude oil and natural gas where companies build their offshore rigs." She explains. "You should know this, Marshall."

She chuckles, and not even the music of her voice calms me down.

"So, these deposits rise high enough in many cases to create the perfect environment for coral to receive just the right amount of sunlight. Plus, due to the distance from the coastline, they can maintain the perfect temperature that saves the coral in heat waves which bleach many other ecosystems." Her words start to muddle together in my ears. "We go out and evaluate different rigs to see if we can basically manually start reefs up around these rigs."

I stay silent, unable to say anything for fear of hurting Elsie with my words.

"Marshall? Are you okay?" She asks, finally looking at me and away from her papers.

"I want you to give up doing site visits," I say firmly.

"What?" She squeaks.

"You heard me." I take a deep breath. "You don't like when I'm out on rigs? Well, I don't like you being out there anymore. I want you to stop doing site visits for work. Hire someone else to do them. Hell, I'll do them for you."

"Marshall." She starts.

"No. Hear me out, Elsie, please." I glance over at her, where she sits across from me in her high-backed desk chair. "You and la pequeña ciruela azucarada mean more to me than anything." *The little sugar plum.*

"That doesn't mean I can stop doing my job, Marshall," Elsie says, her defenses rising.

"I'm not asking you to stop doing your job, Elsie. I'm asking you to hand off doing this one thing. No more travel. That's all I'm asking." He pleads. "When you asked me to quit my job, you said it was because you didn't want our kid sitting on the porch steps waiting for their father to come home. I'm asking the same thing. I don't want our family to have to worry about you every time you leave on a trip. I don't want our child to grow up with that fear. And I don't want to live with it myself."

Her expression flashes through so many emotions that I can't keep up with them. I can see her wanting to fight me, and my shoulders don't relax even when I see the moment when she makes her decision.

"Okay. I'll see what I can do." She sighs. "There may be times when I'm unable to get around it, but I'll do my best."

I let out a breath of relief. "Thank you."

24

MARSHALL

July 12 — 28 Weeks, Eggplant

One thing I am looking forward to is being home for more than a month at a time, the fact that I'm able to spend time with Elsie and be a part of her life in a way I might not be able to if I was still working on the rig.

I love being a part of every aspect of her life and her pregnancy right now.

Today, we're driving from our apartment in River Oaks to the Medical District to get her blood pressure checked and do her Glucose Challenge Test (GCT), that's typical at this point in her pregnancy.

"We're going to be late," Elsie grumbles from the passenger seat of my truck.

"We'll be fine. This is how traffic works, Elsie." I tease. "Just because we're not thirty minutes early doesn't mean we're late."

"Thirty minutes early is on time." Elsie retorts.

"For you." I chuckle.

She's grumpier this morning than usual, and her fuse is a little shorter than normal, but her surliness is only cute to me because of the way her face scrunches and how she pouts.

We're crawling slowly through the side streets, avoiding the freeway this morning because of a major accident.

I take a turn down a side street to see if we can sneak through the neighborhood and gain some time.

Instead, about halfway down the street, we're caught behind another row of cars trying to turn onto a larger street.

Waiting patiently for the car in front of me I start looking around at the houses around us.

"This is a nice neighborhood," I say, taking in the million-dollar mansions with more traditional ranch-style houses peppered between. "I love the older homes, though. Like that one down there."

I point down the street a bit, where an older home sits with a "For Sale" sign in the front lawn.

"It's quaint," Elsie says, looking up from scrolling through her phone to distract her from the time.

We inch our way down the street, my gaze continually going back to the home.

"I love that it has a big front yard. That would be great for playing around with the kids." I murmur to myself.

But Elsie overhears me and chokes out, "Kids?"

I cringe internally, knowing I've fucked up already.

It's what I imagine for us, though. A home, a *life* with Elsie, filled with family and love and laughter.

Because there's no doubt in my mind that this woman is my forever.

"Hypothetically, I mean." I chuckle and shrug. "It's just... That's the kind of house I think I'd always imagined living in with my family."

"You have your whole life planned out, don't you?" Elsie says, looking between me and the house.

She would never say it out loud, but her tone makes me think she doesn't mean *my* life as much as *our* lives.

She'd be right.

I am envisioning our life together.

"By the way, you'll need to get a suit for Coral's annual fundraising gala," Elsie informs me, changing the subject.

"A suit? Really?" I chuckle before looking over at her to see her flat expression. "Oh. You're serious. Okay... Yeah, I don't own one, but I can go pick up a suit."

"You don't own a suit?" She asks, aghast. "We'll go by my tailor after this appointment."

"Your tailor?" I ask. "I don't need a bespoke suit, Elsie."

"Over my dead body, will you be showing up to my gala wearing a suit off the rack!" She says with conviction. "Or, at the very least, we're getting something fitted to you."

Her tone is much like how she takes control and commands me in the bedroom, making my cock thicken at her words.

"As you wish, my Queen."

25

ELSIE

August 3 — 31 Weeks, Coconut

"Remind me why I had to stuff myself into this suit again?" Marshall teasingly complains from beside me. "There are plenty of people here in regular dress clothes."

I look over at Marshall, looking ever so handsome in a dark gray suit that I had my tailor prepare for him. His hair is combed back and, for the first time in my memory, looks neat and styled to perfection.

Marshall's standard uniform of blue jeans, tight-fitting t-shirts, button-ups at the club, and boots makes me drool on a regular basis. But there will always be something about seeing a man in a suit that takes my breath away.

Tonight, Marshall is no exception.

"Because I'm the host, and my date should follow the dress code I set forth on the invitation," I say, rolling my eyes.

"Fine, but you owe me." He pouts with a smirk on his face that tells me I'm likely to enjoy the favor I owe him.

Tonight's gala is for the philanthropy arm of Crude Coral,

which helps fund grants for scientists who are doing research and making conservation efforts into ocean life, specifically coral reef restoration.

Every year, we invite executives from our client list and other notorious philanthropists in the city to join us for an evening at the aquarium for a night of frivolous fun. They spend the night seeing and being seen, and the 501c3 arm of Crude Coral benefits from their generosity.

So far, the evening has gone well, and we've raised nearly our entire goal for the event, but there's still a fair amount of glad-handing to be done before I can call it a night.

"Is that Derek Bonner?" Marshall whispers into my ear in awe.

"Who?" I ask, glancing around the room.

"The biggest guy in the room," Marshall says, nodding over to the left side of the room where a man has amassed a crowd.

"Oh! Yes. Derek." I say, waiving at the man in question just as he glances over in our direction. "He's a friend."

"You're friends with one of the best left tackles in the league?" Marshall asks, his jaw agape when I glance up at him.

"Well... kind of. His husband, Emir, is on our board. You never met him when you lived with Gunnar?" I ask with a shrug. "I've gotten to know Emir and his husband quite well over the past few years. His and Gunnar's security firm consults with us on all our projects."

Marshall is, for once, speechless.

"I'm guessing you're a fan?" I ask with a chuckle.

"Fan? Fan! Elsie... he's a queer *icon*. He was one of the first openly bisexual professional players in the league." Marshall scoffs. "That man could step on me, and I would say thank you."

"Ah. A boot-blacking kink. I see how it is." I giggle.

"Elsie." He says, pinching me in the side. "He's genuinely inspiring to so many people, especially young athletes. I have a few guys on my old crew whose kids *idolize* him."

"Would you like to meet him?" I ask, glancing over in the direction of the couple, who are now making their way toward where we are standing.

"Oh no," Marshall says, a slight panic in his voice. "Are they coming over here? And, of course, I look like a penguin."

I laugh, and several heads whip in our direction, shock on their faces.

"Elsie." A thick Turkish accent permeates the space between me and Emir. "Lovely to see you, dear."

"Emir." I smile. "Thank you for coming. Derek, it's good to see you again."

"You as well." The massive man says. "And congratulations! We didn't know you were expecting."

"Thank you. I haven't really been advertising it anywhere, but I'm very excited." I reply sweetly.

"And who is this," Derek asks.

"This is my..." I trail off, and Marshall gives me a wide-eyed look before gathering himself and saving me from my blunder.

"Marshall. Marshall Law." He says before I can make a total fool of myself. "I'm the arm candy tonight."

Both the other men let out deep chuckles.

"I like your humor, man," Derek says with a smile and an extended hand to Marshall. "Derek."

"Nice to meet you," Marshall says, a bit of awe still in his voice.

Emir chuckles again at the exchange before introducing himself to Marshall.

"Well, any friend of Elsie's is a friend of ours," Derek says with a genuine smile. "She's been a wonderful friend to both of us. I'm very grateful to know her."

"He's only saying that because I told him where to get delicious cheap margaritas." I giggle, smiling widely at my friends.

"And strong ones at that," Emir replies, offering a smile back to me in return. "Elsie, may I borrow you for a minute? Business."

"I think Marshall and I are capable of entertaining ourselves for a while," Derek says, causing Marshall to light up at the opportunity to talk to one of his idols.

"Yeah. Y'all go talk numbers or whatever." Marshall says, beaming.

Emir leads me to the side in one of the alcoves so we can speak more privately.

"I've heard concerns about one of your current projects, Elsie." He starts, his face stern and serious now. "Whispers have gotten to me about one of the clients you've been courting, and it doesn't sound like they're happy."

"What?" I ask, trying to control my expression.

"There's been a few board members who have raised concerns about your performance as of late." He glances between Marshall and down at my belly. "I'm guessing Marshall is the father?"

"Yes."

"As your friend, I can honestly say I'm thrilled for you. But as your advisor, I think there are those who are conspiring against you right now. Those who are questioning your capability to lead and would like to see you replaced." He says cautiously.

"What would you suggest then," I ask, turning all business once again.

"I think you need to arrange a meeting with the client the board is concerned with to set up a trip to their site." He says, very straightforward, before glancing down at my baby bump. "I understand that circumstances may not be ideal, but I think this is the best solution."

"Okay," I say, my mind already frantically searching for a solution to everything. Then terror indeed strikes in my chest. "Emir, I made a promise to Marshall, though, that I wouldn't travel."

He can't hide his grimace quite quickly enough to keep me from panicking.

"I can't..." I say, my breath starting to shorten. "It would devastate him if I went back on my word."

"I'm sorry," Emir says softly. "I don't see a way around it. *You* are the face of this business. It has to be you."

"Okay. Okay." I say, my hand flying to my belly when I feel a kick, likely spurred on by my heightened blood pressure. "I'll figure it out. It will be fine."

"You're sure?" He asks with genuine concern.

"Yeah. It has to be." I say, my resolve solidifying.

"We should get back before people start asking questions," Emir says, glancing around the room.

"Yes. Right." I nod. "Just give me a minute, please."

"Of course." He replies, giving my shoulder a quick squeeze. "You look lovely, by the way. Absolutely luminescent. And I like your new man."

"He's quite a character." I chuckle.

Emir gives me a small smile before going to retrieve his spouse, which leaves Marshall free to wander over to me with a concerned look on his face.

"Everything alright?" He asks when he's only a step away.

He reaches for my hand, and I let him take it with a squeeze. The small gesture calms my racing heartbeat just a bit, but the panic of knowing my company is in jeopardy doesn't dissipate.

With Marshall's hand already in mine, I give him a slight tug and start walking out of the room we're in.

I just need a minute alone. A minute to gather myself and think. A minute to find a solution to this new problem.

Marshall, thankfully, follows me along without protest.

We walk down a hallway, and I try doors as I go, searching for one that's unlocked.

Finally, one of the handles gives, and I pull Marshall into the room. It opens into an empty coat room.

"Everything okay, Elsie?" Marshall asks, genuine concern in his voice.

"Yes." I pause, catching myself. "No. I need…"

My mind is moving a million miles a minute. I need something, but I can't tell what. Nothing makes sense.

"Elsie," Marshall says, cupping my face in his hands to get me to look at him. "Tell me what you need."

"I need… I don't know what I need." I say, exasperated. "I need…."

I look at the man before me, a man I want desperately, a man I know I can quickly lose myself in a moment of pleasure with.

"I need you."

26

MARSHALL

Her words echo through my skull and have my heart bursting out in song.

I need you.

I know from the bright flame in her eye that she means physically, but there's a part of my heart that can't help but dream she's telling me more. That I matter to her more than just for how well I can fuck her.

Something has her distressed, and if I can help take some of that stress away, then I will.

"Tell me exactly what you need, princess." I purr, dragging my thumbs across her cheeks.

"No. Not princess, queen." She says, her voice just as regal as the title she owns.

"Of course, my queen," I say, leaning down so my lips are barely a breath away from hers. "Now, command your toy as you please."

"Take off your pants." She commands before looking around the room.

I strip off my jacket and start undoing my belt as she continues to look for something as she waddles around the room.

"What are you looking for?" I ask.

"A chair." She replies. "Ah! Found one."

"What do you need a chair for?" I chuckle.

When she brings it back from around the corner, she gives me a deadpan look.

"I'm going to sit down, blow you until you're hard, and then you're going to push me up against that door and fuck me from behind until I come. That's what I need a chair for."

My jaw drops a little at her utter confidence and complete seriousness.

"Now, pants off." She says, pulling the chair up before me.

I quickly unbutton my pants and let them drop down along with my briefs as she sits down in the chair.

"Chair is actually a really smart moo..." My words are cut off by her hand and mouth wrapping around my already hardening length.

Looking down, Elsie's auburn hair is falling around her face, and I run my fingers through her locks to pull it back, giving myself the most beautiful view of her lips wrapped around my tip and her hand around my base.

The view alone is enough to make me come, but I'm here for her needs, not my own.

"Fuck." I groan. "You're way too good at that."

She comes off my cock with a pop and grins up at me. "I'm learning how to make you squirm."

"Yes... you are." I moan when she goes back to her efforts. "You're doing so well, my queen. So fucking well."

She continues her ministrations, circling the head of my cock with her tongue and bobbing up and down my length in time with the movement of her hand.

Every sensation has me wanting to grab her by the hair and thrust my cock down her throat, but this is for her, and I give her the room to play with me as she pleases.

My whole body is buzzing with energy as she works me over. Every nerve in my being is on fire with the sensation of her warm lips around my length.

But it's the look in her eye, one of pure sinful enjoyment, that has me nearly coming on the spot. Then she sucks me down her throat, and the tightness of being that deep in her truly has me on the edge.

I tap on her shoulder lightly. "Enough." I groan. "I need to fuck you. *Now.*"

Elsie pulls off me with a grin as wide as the sky, glowing with satisfaction.

The worry in her expression from earlier has been erased, and there's a gratifying feeling that can't quite be pinned down at the knowledge that I helped her like this.

Bending down and wrapping my hands around her wrists, I help pull Elsie up from the chair with a kiss on the lips.

When she pulls back from the kiss, I'm breathing heavily.

I'm desperate to be in her, to fuck her until her anxieties are completely gone. There's nothing that means more to me than this woman's happiness.

"Hands on the door," I tell her.

She rolls her eyes at me in response, and I chuckle in return.

When she turns around, I'm reminded how much tinier she is than me.

"Hold on," I say, grabbing the chair and moving it in front of her. "Kneel here."

She looks back at me with a little smile, and my heart fills with light.

Goddess. She's so beautiful when she smiles.

That's how I want her, always.

"Thank you." She says, pulling up the bottom of her dark green dress so she can kneel on the chair.

Once she's situated comfortably on the chair, I reach for the hem of her dress and pull it up slowly to reveal her body to me.

"No underwear? Naughty girl."

I run my hand up the back of her thigh until I reach the globe of her ass and give it a light squeeze.

"Fuck, I love your body." I groan. Swinging back, I give her a smack on her ass, and she jumps a little at the sensation. "That will never get old."

I run my fingers through her center to find she's already wet for me. Stopping at her clit, I circle her sensitive nub until she's squirming under my touch.

Taking my throbbing cock in hand, I run my tip through her folds until I find her entrance.

"I'm gonna fill you up and have you coming all over my cock." I ask, teasing her opening with light pulses of the tip of my cock, just enough for her to feel it but not enough to enter her yet. "Is that what you want, my queen?"

"Just fuck me already." She practically growls.

"Yes, my queen." I chuckle.

Pressing in, I groan as her warmth surrounds me. My spine straightens as I push further into her cunt, and my head goes empty.

"Fuck. I need you." I say, thrusting in harder. "Your pussy takes me so well."

When I bottom out, she moans loudly.

"Quiet, my queen. Don't want anyone to hear us, do you?"

"Toys don't talk." She snarls over her shoulder. "Good toys do as they're told. Now, *fuck me.*"

Pulling out and thrusting back in, I take up a punishing pace. I drive myself into her harder with each plunge into her heat, and each movement draws out little grunts and groans of pleasure from her.

Just as I feel her walls clench around me, so close to the edge of her bliss, I slow down and pull out agonizingly slowly.

"Fuck." She moans, drawing out the vowel. "Marshall."

"Oh, it's Marshall again?" I tease, pushing back into her slowly and pulling out again. "Does that mean I can talk now?"

"Fuck no." She snaps. "I need you to make me come, not talk."

"Alright then. One orgasm coming up." I thrust, and I can practically feel the glare radiating from her.

I keep my pace slow as I work her back up, and with each press, she grows tighter around me.

When I pick up my pace, I really feel her clench around my shaft, and it nearly drives me to the edge, but I hold off as best I can.

"Please." She cries. "Make me come. Please."

"Goddess, how I love when you beg," I murmur in response, reaching around to pull up on her belly and pull her back onto my cock. "Gonna give you my cum. You're gonna take every last drop of it like the queen you are."

"Marshall." She begs.

Thrusting in harder now, I move my hips, slamming into her ass with each push. Our skin slaps together in a rhythmic sound that matches her cries of pleasure.

"Take my cum like the queen you are. I'm going to have you walking around with my cum dripping down your thighs." I manage to grunt out. "This cunt is *mine*."

Then I feel it the moment she crashes over her edge of bliss. Her walls clench tightly around me and don't let me go. I can barely move, but I continue to press in and out of her. On the final wave of her orgasm, she clenches so hard that she nearly pushes me out of her pussy completely, and the sensation sends me over the edge.

It feels like my orgasm lasts forever as I shoot out jets of cum into her cunt. Waves of pleasure crash through my body with such electricity that it feels like my body is fried, every last bit of energy leaving me in a final moment of release.

I stand there for a minute, just my tip buried inside of her, as her cunt flutters around me. When I finally withdraw completely, the sight of her pussy, dripping with my cum, almost has me hard once again.

Gathering up as much of my cum as I can, I swipe my left hand through her folds and push it back into her where it belongs.

"I will never get tired of seeing you dripping with my cum." I pant out, pressing my fingers in deeper. "And the idea of you walking back into that room with my mark on you? It nearly has me hard already."

She lets out a breathless laugh, then moans when I press against her most sensitive spot.

"Stand up," I instruct her, keeping my fingers right where they belong as she gets up and puts her hands onto the top rail of the back of the chair.

While I stroke softly at the spot deep within her, I lean into her ear to murmur. "Next year, our daughter will be with the babysitter, and I'm going to drag you back into this coat room, and we're going to make this an annual tradition."

I nip at her ear on the last word and press into her walls hard, sending another shiver of pleasure coursing through her body.

"Marshall." She moans as I withdraw my hand from her pussy.

When I prompt her to turn around to face me, she looks up at me with eyes full of pure energy and lust.

She sways a little, and I catch her with my clean right hand.

"Open," I say, and she drops her jaw for me to slide my cum soaked fingers in her mouth. "Suck."

She pulls on my fingers, sucking hard and circling my fingers with her tongue.

"Every drop of my cum is yours, my queen. All of it." I say, satisfaction blooming in my chest at the vision forming in my mind. "Every August, I'm going to fuck you in this coat room. Then, for the next nine months, I will worship your body as you grow our next child. All so we can have another beautiful baby with your crystal blue eyes and that smile I love so much."

Her eyes widen, and I can see fear building in her expression. She starts to speak around my fingers, but I drive them deeper down her throat, and her eyes flutter closed, her mouth automatically going to suck on my fingers again until they're clean.

When I free my hand, she finally opens her eyes, pure satisfaction and contentment radiating from her every pore.

Cupping her face with my clean hand and pulling her into my body with the other around her waist, I promise her. "I know I scare you when I say stuff like that." I bring her face into my chest as my fingers snake into her hair, the baby bump the only thing keeping us apart, and I feel her tighten against my body. "But I'm not going anywhere. I've got you."

She looks up at me from where she's cradled against my chest.

"Marshall. You can't say stuff like that." She protests, shaking her head and trying to push away from me. "You can't mean it."

Her movement only makes me tighten my arms around her.

"I can, and I will." I assert.

She takes a deep breath as though ready to fight me, but I cut her off with a kiss to her hair, and she softens under me.

"Okay." She says softly.

"Okay?" I ask.

"You can keep telling me, but that doesn't mean I'll believe you."

"Then I'll keep telling you until you believe me. Got that?" I say with another kiss to her hair.

"Got it." She replies with a slight chuckle.

We stand like that for a while, me holding her while she rests and catches her breath in my arms. I snuggle down into her warmth, taking a deep breath of her rich, spicy scent.

"I should go clean up." She says quietly into my chest. "And you should get dressed before someone catches you with your pants down, literally."

"Off." I joke.

"Right, pants off." She giggles.

A real giggle from the woman everyone else knows as the ice queen.

But not me; to me, she's just my queen.

Mine.

I get dressed as Elsie straightens her dress and tries to tame her unruly curls.

"You look beautiful," I say when I'm finished buckling my belt, and she's still fussing over her hair.

She looks over at me with a small smile. "Thank you."

Once we're both presentable-ish, I open the door and follow her into the hall, only to find Oliver standing there.

"Oliver?" She asks, confusion furrowing her brow. "Why are you standing there like a guard dog?"

"Because *someone* decided to sneak into a coat room to fuck in the middle of their gala." He says, rolling his eyes. "And you weren't exactly discreet about it."

Elsie blushes a beautiful, rosy color, making me grin.

"And I'd rather you not end up in the paper for fucking at a fundraiser." He scoffs. "Or get fired for letting it happen."

"Sorry." She says meekly. "It won't happen again."

"Yeah. I doubt that." Oliver chuckles.

"Me too," I say, smirking at Elsie, which earns me a scowl.

"Right. Okay." She says, collecting herself and putting her cool mask back on. "Well, I'm going to visit the ladies' room and... tidy up a bit."

Oliver's smile is quickly shoved under his professional demeanor, but his genuine happiness for Elsie sneaks through in the glitter of his eyes.

"You're good for her." He admits as we watch her walk away.

"Really?"

"Yeah." He says, turning to me with a smile. "In the years I've worked for her, I've never seen her happier. We're rooting for you. So long as you stay out of the office."

"We?" I ask.

"Yeah. Me, Selene, and the rest of the office, basically. We've all noticed." He suddenly grows more serious. "You hurt her, though, and I'll have your balls."

I let out a loud laugh, drawing the attention of the few people who were passing us to leave and head home.

"Noted," I say with a wink.

Contentment fills me with the knowledge that others see just how good Elsie and I are together.

She may not believe it yet, but she will.

In her own time, she'll come to admit that she wants me.

Needs me.

Loves me.

Almost as much as I love her.

27

ELSIE

August 12 — 32 Weeks 2 Days, Pineapple

Guilt is not an emotion I'm intimately familiar with. It's just not something I've ever made room for in my life. I pursue what I want and accept the consequences of my actions when needed.

For the first time, the overwhelming feeling of guilt and a bit of shame in my chest is battling with my head for dominance.

I'm doing my job. It's as simple as that.

I keep trying to justify to myself that I'm doing the right thing, but there's a pervasive feeling that today is a mistake.

It feels like a betrayal of trust, even if I don't intend it to be.

"You sure you want to do this?" Oliver asks through the phone.

"I have to." I sigh. "If we want to keep this client, I need to be at this inspection."

"We could send someone else. You're eight months pregnant. You're not supposed to be traveling. They would understand." Oliver is quiet for a minute before speaking again. "It's the only thing he asked of you."

"What Marshall doesn't know won't kill him." I snap back. "Sorry. I'm just..."

"I know." He takes a fortifying breath. "I'm going to tell this to you as your friend, not your employee. If you do this, it's going to blow up in your face."

"I know," I reply.

"You know I'll support your decision, but the marshmallow has kind of grown on me. I don't want to see him hurt either." Oliver says solemnly.

"Marshmallow?"

"What? It fits. He's like a big marshmallow, sickeningly sweet and adorably squishy." He laughs.

I chuckle before I can help myself and before reality sets back in.

When Marshall quit his job, his only ask from me was that I stop traveling and begin to prioritize our chid, our family, more.

The reminder of the joy on his face when I agreed flashes through my mind and doubles the intense tightness in my chest.

I know without a shadow of a doubt that Marshall cares for me.

I can tell he's stopped himself from admitting he loves me several times now, but I know why.

He doesn't know how I'll respond.

Which is fair, considering I don't know how I'd respond either.

I care about him. I do.

Wanting what's best for him and treasuring the time we've had together is one thing, but building a life with another person is an entirely different.

Relationships aren't dependable. You can only depend on yourself.

Protest as much as he likes. There's nothing he can say that would change my mind.

It's better to be alone than to rely on another person.

The car rolls to a stop, and my driver opens the door, letting in the ear-shattering sound of helicopter blades whirring through the air and picking up speed. My driver helps me out of the SUV and steps to the side, letting me waddle off in the direction of the waiting helicopter.

When I spot the executives I'm meeting with, I give them a wave and a small smile, but a faint noise from behind me has me stopping in my tracks.

"Elsie!" Marshall's voice calls out over the whir of the helicopter blades spinning. "Elsie!"

I look back to find the gorgeous man jogging to catch up with me.

I've always loved how tall Marshall is and how he makes me feel safe when he towers over my 4'11" frame, but right now, the long strides he's capable of have anxiety clawing at my chest.

"Marshall?" I yell over the noise.

"Elsie, please don't do this." He says as he approaches.

"What are you doing here?" I ask.

"Selene spilled that you're leaving. Please don't leave." He pleads.

"I'm going on a quick trip, Marshall. I'm not leaving." I say.

"Elsie, you promised. You promised to prioritize this, us." He says, placing his palm on my belly. "Getting on that helicopter puts all of this at risk. I can't watch you do that."

"Marshall. You're not being reasonable."

"*I'm* not being reasonable?" He scoffs. "Elsie, you're eight months pregnant and about to go on a helicopter to visit an oil rig in the middle of the Gulf of Mexico. You can barely walk up a flight of stairs without being out of breath, and you think this is a *good idea*?"

"And if I don't go, then we lose this client. A client we've been courting since long before you came into my life." I snap. "You don't get to make decisions about my business for me."

"That may be true, but I do get input on the well-being of you and my child." He says.

"Your child, maybe. But it's my body that's carrying this little parasite, and you don't have ownership over that." I growl. "Plus, it's not like you're in love with me!"

"Would it make a difference?" He says, his expression wide with shock.

"I don't know. But you're not. So, it doesn't really matter. Does it?" I sigh.

"Oh, but I am. I most definitely am." He asserts, his face growing serious. "But I know myself, and I know if I told you how much I love you and you weren't able to say it back... it would break me."

He steps into my space. The only thing keeping us from being any closer is our baby between us, and he cups my face.

"Please don't do this. I'm asking you not to. I can't watch you put the two things I treasure most in this world at risk. Please, Elsie."

"You're giving me an ultimatum," I say over the hum of the helicopter. "You're telling me I have to choose."

"It's not an ultimatum, Elsie. I'm setting a boundary and asking you to make a choice about how you respond to that boundary. I'm asking you to respect me enough, to care about me enough, to agree to this."

"You're being a manipulative asshole, Marshall."

"Just a regular asshole, Elsie." He smirks.

"I knew this day would come. I knew this would happen eventually." I back away from the warmth of Marshall's touch. "If you want to play the victim, fine. Leave. I don't care. I'll do this on my own. Like I planned."

Turning away might be the hardest thing I've ever done.

I can feel him standing there, watching me as I walk toward the helicopter to take off.

The feeling of his gaze on me stays the entire time that I converse with my clients, and we all make our way into the massive machine, mine more of a struggle than the others.

It's not until I feel the jolt of us taking off that I finally look back to where Marshall stands at the edge of the helicopter pad, looking devastated.

He may be right, and maybe he loves me.

But he doesn't own me.

28

ELSIE

September 8 — 36 Weeks 1 Day, Winter Melon

Every morning for the past four weeks, I wake up and walk into an empty kitchen.

I'd never admit it out loud, but Marshall's absence is messing with my head more than I would have expected.

You'd never know that two people are occupying the same space with the way he manages to both fill every corner of the apartment and yet still avoid me at every turn.

Our home is suddenly full of very helpful ghosts.

Ghosts who leave out breakfast for me every morning with my juice and supplements and who pack my lunch and put it next to my key, so I don't forget it on my way to work. They keep the house tidy and organized, do the grocery shopping, make all of my meals, and attend to my every need.

But the whole time, the apartment remains eerily quiet and empty.

And lonely.

Every day for the past four weeks, it has been like this, and each little act of thoughtful kindness has my chest aching with a longing that feels foreign to me.

I'm not used to needing people.

It's always felt wrong to need people.

But now, there's a craving for one particular human that I can't ignore.

The smell of breakfast hangs in the air, making me drool. Spotting a plate on the kitchen table full of mollettes, which reminds me of that first day when I told Marshall I was pregnant, I waddle over to sit down and begin my day.

As always, the newspaper is laid out next to my breakfast, juice, and supplements, but before I'm able to dig into my breakfast, the chime of my phone interrupts me.

SELENE

I'm kidnapping you for brunch.

ELSIE

What? Isn't brunch later this month?

It's a tradition within our friend group to gather for brunch once a month, but typically, we get together on the last Sunday of the month. Today is the first Sunday.

SELENE

We're adding another brunch then. It's your birthday this week, and we're celebrating today. Don't fight me on this.

ELSIE

Okay?

SELENE

Just get dressed in something cute. I'll be there in an hour to pick you up.

Knowing Selene, an hour could either mean 30 minutes or three hours. So, leaning on the side of caution, I quickly get up from the table and put my things away so that I can begin getting ready.

Waddling from the kitchen to my bedroom takes more effort than it used to, but once in the bathroom, I'm able to sink down onto the soft bench at the vanity.

Pulling out my makeup, I begin prepping my skin for foundation but am stopped in my tracks when I spot something in the mirror's reflection.

I turn around to find a soft-looking plum-colored maxi dress hanging off the towel bar behind me. The dress is paired with an elegant, layered necklace and matching earrings that are hanging off the hook, and beneath the ensemble is a pair of flats with a cute floral pattern that matches the shade of the dress.

I don't have to text him to know he did this.

I don't want the confirmation that he would do something like this, nor do I want to know how it plays into whatever game he's been playing with my head recently.

Ignoring the tightness in my chest, I turn back around and go about putting on my makeup and arranging my auburn curls into a more manageable pattern. However, every few minutes, my attention strays back to the outfit that has been so carefully put together for me, and the tension in my chest returns.

When I'm finished with my hair and makeup, I swing around to face my fabric nemesis.

"Just because it's pretty doesn't mean you have to wear it, Elsie," I mutter, my hand reaching out to run the soft fabric through my fingers. "You have plenty of clothes to wear."

Stomping my way into the closet, I go through the racks of clothes, searching for something suitable to wear for brunch in September.

Everything I pull out doesn't feel quite right, though, and eventually, I cave and go back into the bathroom to continue my standoff with the perfect plum dress.

"Fucking Marshall," I grumble, taking the dress off the hanger and grabbing the accessories in my free hand.

Back in my closet, I pull out the maternity bra and underwear, which he annoyingly bought without asking my size, and somehow still got it right before pulling on the outfit.

When I turn to look at myself in the full-length mirror, my breath catches.

The empire waist of the dress highlights how my belly has grown in the past few months. Instead of wrestling with the little voice that tells me my changing figure is something to be ashamed of, I feel... beautiful. For the first time in months, I feel like the glowing, expectant mother everyone dreams of being.

"Do not cry, Elizabeth Iris Snow," I say, tilting my head back to keep the tears from falling and ruining my carefully applied makeup. "Your foundation is $50."

When I've collected myself, I trudge slowly out of the closet and back to the living room to pack up my purse.

I'm scrolling through emails on my computer when Selene comes through the door, without knocking, might I add.

"Alright, mama. Let's get you to brunch!" She says, waltzing into my living space where I'm propped on the couch with my computer on my belly. "Ready?"

I frown. "I've been ready for an hour, Selene."

Before my eyes, I see her turn into a caricature of herself as she grimaces in apology. "Sorry. Got held up with something."

"Fine. But you're buying." I grumble alongside my hungry stomach.

"Got it." She smirks, helping me haul myself off the couch. "Cute outfit, by the way."

"Thanks," I grumble. "Marshall picked it out."

"I like it. He has good taste." She smiles. "Let's go, mama."

When we get downstairs, I spot Gunnar's SUV idling in the parking lot.

"Chauffeur today?" I ask.

"Ugh." Selene groans. "You get into one little fender bender two years ago, and suddenly, I'm not allowed to drive anywhere."

"It's sweet," I say as she helps me waddle over to the car.

She sighs and opens the back door for me. "Yeah. It really is."

Thankfully the SUV has handles that I use to struggle my 4'11" fat ass into the tall vehicle.

When I get settled into the seat, I look up to find Gunnar grinning at me.

"Morning." He says with a deep chuckle.

"Oh, hush." I snap halfheartedly. "You try being the size of a house and getting into this tank."

"Point taken."

Once Selene gets herself settled into the passenger seat, we're off. But when Gunnar pulls out of the parking lot, he starts heading in the wrong direction.

"Gunnar. The restaurant is in the other direction." I say questioningly.

Selene turns around in her seat to face me. "We're doing something a little different today."

Her words are meant to be reassuring, but they only make me more suspicious.

When we roll up on the city's most exclusive private country club—my father's country club— my hackles rise.

"Selene?" I ask.

"Trust me." She replies simply.

Gunnar pulls up into the roundabout at the front entrance, and an attendant opens the door for me.

I shuffle out of the SUV with the man's assistance and look around, bracing myself to run into one of my father's friends.

The club itself is gorgeous. Unfortunately, it brings back a slew of memories that are less than brilliant.

Every step I take further into the building has me even more on edge.

This is *his* domain, not mine. I'm not comfortable here, and yet I still shuffle after Selene and Gunnar as they lead me through the building to one of the salons that backs up against the back gardens.

Gunnar holds the door open for Selene and me to enter the room.

As I enter, there's a chorus of "Surprise!" that rings out in the room from all of its occupants.

All around are people I care about. The room is covered from top to bottom with baby-related decor, streamers, and balloons. Gift-wrapped boxes and bags are piled high on a table against the back wall, while the table closest to the entrance is laden with snacks and drinks for everyone to partake in.

"A baby shower?" I ask, tears gathering in my eyes.

"Of course!" Selene replies with a laugh. "Marshall said you just hit 36 weeks! It's about time we got our shit together and threw you a shower. Excuse me... stuff together."

My eyes scan the crowd to find the man himself at the back of the room, away from the rest.

Our eyes lock, and for a second, the whole room falls away.

I want to go to him. I want him to hold me and tell me everything is okay, that this tension and distance between us that's formed doesn't need to be there anymore.

But I stay put.

"Come on, mama. Let's get you settled, and we can start on the games!" Selene says.

When I'm settled in a chair at the front of the room, my shoulders relax as I take in everyone around me.

All of the Morgan family, the owners of The Playground, are

here. Naomi, Bex, and Alvie are here, along with many others from the club.

I never expected such support from these people, but they're here, nonetheless.

The next few hours pass in a blur. Baby games throw everyone into fits of laughter as people struggle to wrap baby dolls in diapers and people guess trivia questions about me and my pregnancy. I nearly cry when we go through the pile of gifts as Naomi, ever the studious one, documents each gift and who it came from. The whole party is a delight, and as time passes, I relax into the pure joy of the moment.

When everything begins to wrap up, and people say their goodbyes, a few friends stay behind to help transport gifts and food to cars.

I've felt Marshall's presence all afternoon. His gaze has been on me the entire time, which is comforting and disturbing if I didn't know him better. He's kept his distance, though, which I've almost appreciated. However, there's a part of me that still wants him to pull me close and tell me everything is going to be okay.

As we exit the Salon and are headed out to the car, a voice stops me in my tracks.

"Elizabeth?" His deep rumble echoes down the hall and rings through my skull like a gong.

I turn around, and immediately, my face goes pale at the sight of the older man in an impeccable suit.

"Father?"

"Elizabeth." He says with a plastic smile, striding up to me confidently before stopping short.

His eyes grow wide as he takes me, in all of my pregnant glory, in.

"You're pregnant." He says shortly.

"I am." I smile politely.

"I didn't realize you had gotten married." He ponders.

"I'm not," I reply shortly, my frustration growing.

"Of course not." He sighs. "Just another rebellion, of course. You never could do anything the right way, could you."

The jab stings a little too much, and I shrink back at the barb, but suddenly, there's a strong figure at my back.

"Sir." Marshall's voice rumbles from behind me as he wraps himself around me and extends his hand out to my father. "I'm Marshall. The dad."

"Oh?" My father shakes his head. "Of course, you'd do this to me, Elizabeth. What a disappointment. Not only are you pregnant out of wedlock, but the father is this *boy*?"

Marshall's hand falls to his side, curling in a fist as he pulls it back.

"Father," I say slowly. "You have no say over my life or my choices. If I'm a disappointment, then that's your feelings to wrestle with. But I don't live my life in accordance with your rules. I haven't since I cut contact with you."

"You mean your tantrum that you've been throwing? Right." He scoffs. "Don't forget who supported your naive dreams to get you where you are. Who helped you establish the company you're throwing everything away for in favor of this pitiful life you're bringing into the world? Such a shame."

When I tense, Marshall's hands come up to hold me around my shoulders, comforting me in the only way he can right now.

"Elsie, we need to go." He says softly.

"Right..." I reply, tears in my eyes.

Marshall moves to turn me away to leave, but I only make it a few steps before my father speaks again.

"Such a shame." Father tsks. "I would have thought you better than this, Elizabeth. Seeing you like this hurts me."

"It hurts your ego, father." I snap out. "That's all."

"Don't disrespect me like that. You owe me everything." He scoffs.

"I owe you nothing."

Father sighs. "You may think that now, but you'd be surprised how quickly your world can fall apart. How quickly things can be taken from you."

He gives my body a long up and down.

"Children especially need to be protected from... well..." He glances over at Marshall, taking in his tall figure and all of his tattoos. "Threats."

"Are you insinuating I'm unfit to be a parent?" I ask in disbelief. "That you would take my child from me because I'm unmarried? What a hypocrite. You were around just about as much as Mother was."

"Don't speak about your mother like that. It is a completely different situation, and you know it." He lashes out. "Just be mindful of who you spend your time with. You never know how it may impact you. Or..." He glances down at where I have my hands protectively covering my belly. "Those you care about."

With tears in my eyes, I turn and start to flee, and Marshall close behind me, his one stride matching every four or five of my waddles.

"No," Marshall mutters, stopping in his tracks. "You know what?"

Marshall's retreating footsteps have me turning just in time for me to see him land a left hook dead in my father's face, making him stumble and fall to the floor.

"Make any more comments about Elsie being unfit to be a mother, and I'll do much worse than a punch to the face." Marshall asserts. "*Elsie* is the best woman I know, and she's going to be the most amazing parent, unlike you, you asshole."

I stand there in shock as my father tries to gather himself to rise from the ground, but Marshall pushes him back down.

"You stay the fuck away from my family." He growls.

For all the years of torment that my father put me through, I've never had anyone stand up for me like that.

"Let's go, Elsie," Marshall says quietly, shaking out his injured hand and placing it between my shoulder blades to guide me away. "I'm so sorry."

I finally tear my gaze away from my father, still sprawled out on the floor, and look up at him.

"What for?" I ask, confusion lacing my tone.

"I didn't know he'd be here." He admits. "I just wanted to do something nice for you."

"*You* planned this?" I say with a squeak. "The surprise shower? That was all you? I thought it was Selene or one of the girls."

"I mean, they were a huge help." Marshall shrugs, guiding me out of the building and to his truck. "But it was my idea to do it here. And now I've punched your dad..."

"Father." I correct.

"Right, father. Well, my fist landed in his face, and I'm probably gonna get slapped with assault charges."

I break out in a genuine laugh, knowing my father would never dare do such a thing for fear of drawing the attention of his friends to the shame of being punched to the ground.

"Marshall. There's no way you could have known he would be here." I sigh. "I never told you anything other than my fond memories here."

"Still..." He bends down to lift me into the passenger seat of the truck without my usual objections.

I missed having his hands on me, and when he leans in to buckle my seatbelt, I shudder at his nearness. The musky natural scent of his cologne invades my space, and I gasp at the need it drives through my body.

The short drive home, I can't help but shift uncomfortably in my seat. Need builds between my legs with every moment I spend in the car with Marshall until my body is screaming for his touch.

When we pull into the parking garage, and Marshall comes to help me out of the truck, his hands on my hips as he helps me lower down are like gasoline to my fire of desire.

Ignoring the feeling, I waddle to the elevator, making sure to plaster myself against the opposite wall from Marshall for fear of jumping him.

When we reach our floor, I scurry as quickly as I can away from him.

"I'm going to lay down for a nap," I say as he sets down some of the gifts he brought up.

"Alright. I'll bring the rest of the stuff up, then I think I need to go for a run." He replies simply and turns before I can reply.

In the safety of my bedroom, I throw off my clothes and collapse on the bed.

But sleep doesn't come. Instead, I toss and turn, listening to Marshall come in and out of the apartment as he unloads the truck and then finally leaving for his run.

With each passing moment, my need from earlier builds into a hot inferno at my core.

Guilt keeps me from satisfying my own needs, even though I need relief more than I need air at this point.

I keep remembering the look on Marshall's face as he backed away from my father after punching him. How his muscles rippled underneath his layered shirts and his taught ass as he swung through on the punch.

Everything happened so quickly, but it truly was a noble moment.

About an hour passes before I give up on sleep and, knowing Marshall is out, slip out of my bedroom to grab a drink from the kitchen.

I'm rummaging through the fridge, looking for the homemade horchata Marshall makes for me, when I snap up and freeze at the sound of the front door opening.

"Please. Just go to your room." I pray quietly.

"No luck, princess." Marshall's deep rumble comes from behind me.

Turning around slowly, I reveal my nakedness to the most attractive man I've ever seen.

Sweat drips down his face and glistens on his blissfully naked tattooed chest, the sight making my mouth water.

I need this man. *Desperately*.

29

MARSHALL

"Need something, princess?" I ask.

Elsie is standing in our kitchen, completely naked, and my cock is already hardening at the sight.

It's been too long since I last saw Elsie, really *saw* her.

The vision of her before me is more magical than any memory I have of her.

Her breasts are full and heavy, preparing to feed our child, that's due in a matter of weeks. Her belly has swollen and taken over her entire petite frame. The stretch marks on her stomach are a reminder of every milestone in this pregnancy, and I fucking love every one of them.

I want to reach out, to touch her and caress and kiss every inch of skin I can.

But I can't do that. Not without her permission.

"Elsie, what do you need?" I ask again.

"Nothing." She says, snapping herself out of her frozen state and wrapping her arms around her breast to hide from me. "It's fine."

Noting how her eyes track up and down my figure, I take a chance and step into her space.

"Don't lie to me, princess. What. Do. You. Need." I put a little growl into my final words, hoping that they'll have her lowering her guard for me.

Elsie's sky-blue eyes turn stormy as a battle rages inside her.

"If you need me, you just have to ask. That's the rule." I pause, hoping she'll see how genuinely I mean my words. "Use me, Elsie. Let me give you what you need."

"I need you." She whispers.

I smirk, knowing I'm testing my luck. "Sorry? I couldn't hear that."

"I need you, you asshole." She snaps louder.

"Nope. What do you call me, princess?"

"Daddy." She sighs, but there's heat in her eyes. "I need you, Daddy."

"Good girl," I say, backing her into the center island.

"This isn't make-up sex." She asserts.

"So long as it isn't break-up sex, I'm game." I quip. "Whatever you need, I'm here to give it to you."

"Shut up and kiss me already." She snaps, frustration furrowing her brow.

"Yes, ma'am." I laugh, leaning down to kiss her lightly on the lips.

Electricity zaps through every nerve in my body when our lips touch, and soon, the kiss grows hungry between us.

I've been starved for this woman for weeks, for her smiles and teases, the sound of her voice, and the softness of her touch.

The satisfaction of taking care of her other necessities doesn't come anywhere near the satisfaction I get from taking care of her physical needs.

This woman is mine, even if she's fighting me on it right now.

She's mine to take care of. Mine to use. Mine to love.

And I'm going to show every inch of her body how much I mean those words, even if I still refuse to say them out loud.

I know how well we fit together, how good the sex is, but also how connected we are, how our souls intertwine to create a perfect harmony between us.

Every action I take is a part of my plan to show her just how incredible our lives could be together.

Swiftly, I pick her up and turn to stride into her bedroom to find an already unmade bed waiting for us.

"Got started without me?" I tease, setting her down on the mattress and kicking off my running shoes and socks.

"Stop with the questions and strip." She commands.

"As you wish."

Teasing her, I thumb the waistband of my running shorts and tug them down just enough to reveal the V of my hips. When she reaches out to speed up my striptease, I push her hands away and take a step back.

"If I'm gonna fuck you, then I'm going to enjoy every moment of it, princess," I smirk at the desire I see flaming in her eyes.

Slipping my hands into my shorts, I shake my ass as I turn around and push the shorts off a little bit more.

Glancing over my shoulder, I take in Elsie's beautiful face that's transfixed on my ass.

"You like what you see, princess?" I ask knowingly.

She nods, and I swear I can see a bit of drool at the edge of her mouth.

Shimmying my hips a bit, I let the shorts fall until I'm entirely bare, with tanned skin and tattoos on display.

I turn my shoulders slowly, making sure to keep the real prize still hidden from view.

"Tell me you want me," I say in earnest.

I need to hear her say it, to admit that, despite every tension between us right now, she still wants this, *us*.

All I want is this woman and the future she represents for me. Everything I've ever needed, I've found in Elsie Snow.

One day, she will admit she feels the same. I'm sure.

I have to be sure.

"Tell me you need me, Elsie."

"Fuck. Marshall." She groans. "Get your ass over here and fuck me already."

"Not until you say it." I pout.

"Fine. I want you, you needy Neanderthal." She laughs, and the whole room lights up at her joy.

I'll take it.

Spinning around, I approach and stand before her so my hardened cock is at her eye level.

Her glittering eyes look up at me, hot as the blue flame that flickers behind her irises. "I want you in my mouth."

"Then what are you waiting for? Take what you want, my queen." I smile down at her.

When her small hand curves around my dick, I moan in appreciation. She puts the perfect amount of pressure around my shaft to have me already needing more.

Taking her time, she strokes as she admires my cock.

"I fucking love your cock." She murmurs before taking my tip between her lips.

Warmth surrounds me, and every thought in my head flees at the sensation. Words turn to a buzzing noise in the background of my mind, and I can't create a single coherent thought.

She bobs up and down my shaft, taking me deep in her throat with each descent down my length. Every nerve in my body is on fire, completely engulfed in the feeling of her mouth around my cock.

Elsie does her damndest to get me right to the edge, but I refuse to come in her mouth.

Her pussy is *mine*.

"Fuck. I can't take any more." I groan, pulling myself away from her grip.

She pouts at my retreat but seems satisfied with her work nonetheless.

"Couldn't take any more, toy?"

"Oh, now look who's out to play." I chuckle. "What would my queen like next?"

"I want your cock in my pussy." She says confidently.

"Fuck, yes," I reply, striding over to the bed and pulling her chin up with one hand. "You want me to fuck you from above or from behind. What's okay for the baby?"

"Fuck if I know. You're the one with your nose in the baby books." She laughs.

Man, did I miss that laugh.

"From behind it is, then. Grab some of your pillows to make yourself comfortable." I say, giving her a kiss on the cheek and reaching for the pillows on the far side of the bed.

It's sexy as hell to watch as Elsie does her best to get on all fours and prop herself up on pillows where she needs support, but I almost love it when she whines and asks me for my help even more.

Her ass is on full display before me, and I can't control the urge to give her a thwack on her right cheek.

"Hey there!" She shrieks. "What was that for?"

"For having the best fucking ass I've ever seen," I say, leaning down to give her a reverent kiss on her quickly reddening skin. "And I've admired a lot of ass."

"Of course you have." She grumbles.

"And yours is the one I've been searching for this whole time," I say, cupping both cheeks and giving them a squeeze. "Fuck. You don't even know how perfect you are, do you?"

"Just fuck me already, Marshall." She says, looking over her shoulder.

"As you wish, my queen," I reply, lining myself up at her entrance.

Wasting no time, I push into her, and my head falls back as her tight walls wrap around the head of my cock.

"Fuck, Elsie." I groan, and she whimpers in response, already rocking back into my hips to take more of my cock.

I work my way into her tight channel with small thrusts until my hips are flush against her round ass.

When I still, she looks at me over her shoulder with a glare.

"Fuck me like I deserve, toy." She commands.

I pick up my pace, thrusting in and out of her in a steady rhythm that has her head dropping back down to the mattress in pleasure. The moans and groans she lets out tell me I'm doing something right, and I keep a steady pace.

Her walls flutter around me and contract until I feel like she's going to squeeze my dick off and keep me from continuing my pace, trapping me in place. But when she relaxes, I continue to plunge into her deeply enough to make her cry out my name.

Over and over, I push in and out of her, eliciting beautiful sounds from her mouth as I pant with effort.

Reaching around her hip, I find her clit with my fingers and press down with just enough pressure to have her crying out.

"Fuck, Daddy. I'm gonna come!" She screams.

I keep pace and match my fingers to the pulse of my hips, making sure everything is just perfect for her to go flying over her edge.

"Come for me, princess. Come all over Daddy's cock and give him your pleasure." I say, pressing closer and deeper into her center.

"Please, daddy. I need it. I need you." She cries.

I need you.

Those three little words nearly have me coming myself, but I hold back, knowing there will be more time for that.

This is about her.

Her pleasure.
Her happiness.
Her love.

30

ELSIE

A satisfied exhaustion compels me to sink further into the bed. Thankfully, before I can collapse further, Marshall pulls out of me and rocks us both so we're lying on our sides.

With his body cradled around me, my muscles start to relax, and the tension that's sunk into my bones begins to seep away. His warm arms wrap around me, and he tugs me backward to fit more comfortably among his massive frame. His hands look so big where they rest on my swollen belly, rubbing small circles into my stretch-marked marred skin.

Looking back over my shoulder, my gaze connects with Marshall's rich brown eyes, and my heart melts at the reverence it finds in his stare.

"That's all you've got?" I tease with a smile, which he returns in full.

"Nah, princess." He leans in and gives me a soft kiss, one which feels so right and yet so out of place, considering the recent tension between us. "Just giving you a chance to catch your breath."

"I don't need to catch my breath. I want you to fuck me breathless, Daddy." I sass back at him.

"Oh? Is my princess still needy for Daddy's cock?

His hands shift from where they were wrapped around my belly to now rest one on my breast while the other helps me lift my leg to open up my center to him.

A shiver runs through my body when his cock brushes my lower lips, and I squirm in place, knowing what I want is so close.

"Tell me what you want." He whispers. "Tell me, Elsie. And I'll give it to you."

I know there's a deeper meaning to his words.

I know, if I asked, he would lay the entire world at my feet and give me everything I could ever want.

He would give me safety and security, joy and hope, maybe even love.

But the growing need buzzing in my body says now is not the time for such fanciful thoughts.

Now is the time for fucking.

"Fuck me, Marshall."

"How?" He murmurs.

"From behind. Us laying here like this. And slow." I let out a sigh as he places kisses up and down my neck while his cock slides through my folds.

"As you wish, my queen." He replies.

Spreading my lower lips open, Marshall positions himself at my entrance and teases my opening with the head of his cock.

"Tease," I mutter. "Fuck me already."

Before I can let out another complaint, he's there, entering me.

Every fiber of my being feels the fullness and stretch his body brings out of me. His hips rock slowly in and out of me, and the curve of his cock makes it so he's hitting that sensitive spot on my inner wall perfectly.

Each thrust has my walls fluttering around him, begging for more, but he keeps the slow, languid pace that I asked for.

It's brutal, wanting something so sweet and slow and yet needing to be fucked brutally.

The contrast between my needs and how he moves in and out of me has me weeping and whining about my needs.

"Daddy." I moan.

It feels like he fucks me like this forever until suddenly, I'm there. The edge of bliss is right before me, but I need... I need...

I reach down and drag my fingers lightly over my clit, the lightest touch sending jolts of electricity through my body.

"Yes." I sigh, finding a rhythm I know I like on my clit as Marshall continues to fuck me slowly.

Pleasure builds in my core as I play my body in perfect harmony with Marshall's thrusts. Using his free hand that's wrapped around my shoulders, he reaches for my nipple and rolls it between his fingers.

The combination of sensations has me ratcheting up and up, closer to my peak.

Without warning, Marshall gives a hard thrust into my core that sends me over the edge. The pleasure that had been slowly building suddenly crashed like a wave on the shore.

I clamp around him, and that's all it takes for him to reach his end.

Cum flows out of me as he groans out his pleasure before slowly pulling out of me.

We lay like that for a while, panting and trying to catch our breath in each other's arms.

"Just think. This will be us every day for the rest of our lives." He says, giving me a soft kiss on my shoulder.

"I'm sorry. What?" I ask, lifting myself onto my elbow so I can properly look back at Marshall.

"I'm just thinking about what comes next. You know. And how awesome it's going to be to be able to have this all the time."

"Marshall. What are you talking about?" I ask a little bit more desperation in my tone.

"You know. Love, marriage, baby carriage." He shrugs, rising from the bed and ambling over to the bathroom door.

"What?" I ask, panic clawing at my chest. "Marshall. We've said absolutely nothing about love or marriage. Where are you getting these ideas from."

"Well, it makes sense. Doesn't it? That we get married?" He asks, pausing from the doorway.

"No. It absolutely *does not*. We're having a baby together, sure." I start.

"No. We're starting a family together."

"You keep using that *word*," I say, rolling out of bed and shuffling over to my dresser to grab clothes to pull on.

"What? Family?"

I freeze at the word and what it seems to mean to Marshall.

"Yes! That!" I cry, throwing on an oversized t-shirt to cover myself.

"What's wrong with calling us a family? That's what we are." He shrugs.

"No. We are not. We are nothing like a family." I snap, my anger rising as I turn to face him again. "We are the furthest thing from a family."

"Elsie..." He says slowly.

"No. Absolutely not." I shake my head, trying to push down the clawing panic rising in my throat. "We are having a baby. We fuck occasionally. But we are not a *family*."

"Fine. Not yet, then." His voice is soft, like he's speaking to a spooked animal. "But we could be."

My hands start to shake, and anger starts to burn under my skin.

There's no way that he's really talking about this right now. No way that he's suggesting what I know he is.

We can't be a family.

Family means failure.

It means everything I've worked for, everything I've worked *not* to be, was for nothing. My independence means nothing if he's right.

Worse off, it will end.

This vision he has in his head of us down the line is just that, a vision. It's a mirage of his own making.

"Marshall, I need you to leave," I say lowly, trying not to blow up at this man who I know only means the best.

"Elsie. Hear me out." He takes a few steps towards me, and I back myself into the dresser. "We could get married. Have a house with a white picket fence, two and a half kids, and a dog. We could make it happen. We could have it all."

"I can't," I say breathlessly.

"You can. I promise you can." He says, his eyes glittering with a dream that I can't see for myself.

"Please. Leave." I beg. "Before I say something, I'll regret."

"I'm not leaving, Elsie. That's the point. I'm not going to leave you. Not you or this baby." He says, reaching out to take my hand, which I quickly snatch away. "Elsie. You can have everything if you take it."

His expression is so earnest and open. His voice has gone so soft and tender it makes me want to scream.

"Marry me."

This is something he's clearly thought about a lot, probably from the beginning since he moved in.

He's always been so forward about it, but I never took the small comments or little actions seriously. I've always assumed that the shiny newness would wear off, and he would move on.

But here he is, before me, saying he wants to... marry me?

"I'm not like you," I say quietly. "I can't jump in with two feet like you can. I can't say yes to you because it would be a lie."

"What would be a lie?"

"All of it. Everything. And it would all fall apart because it would be a sham. It wouldn't mean anything."

"No. It wouldn't."

"Exactly."

"No. You mishear me." He takes my face between his palms. "It wouldn't be a sham because I love you, Elsie." He says with the confidence of a man who truly is in love. "And that means everything."

I choke back the sob that wants to come out of my throat and push down the tears that want to form in my eyes.

"Marry me, Elsie."

He can't mean that.

He can't say shit like that.

This isn't love.

Marriage isn't supposed to be magical and all-consuming. It's not this fantasy children are raised to believe it is.

And love doesn't solve everything.

It only makes things worse.

Love is the beginning of the end of all relationships.

Because loving someone is giving a part of yourself to them, it's being vulnerable with them.

I can't do that.

"No." I shudder. "No. Marshall. I can't."

The hope in his eyes dies out, his face falling in that exact second, and I pull away to shield myself from the backlash of hurt I've just caused that will surely come next.

"Elsie." He says, a break coming through in my name.

"I said no, Marshall. No." I whisper. "Now, please. Leave."

Marshall, with slumped shoulders, gathers his clothing and moves to leave the bedroom.

My heart stops when he pauses in the doorway and glances back at me.

I wait with bated breath to hear what he says, but instead, he just shakes his head and leaves.

Just like I asked.

He's gone.

Gone.

31

MARSHALL

September 9 — 36 Weeks 2 Days, Winter Melon

MARSHALL

Where are you?

You're not home.

GUNNAR

Selene and I are at the jewelry store picking out wedding bands.

MARSHALL

Text me the address.

GUNNAR

Marshall. You're not joining us to pick out our wedding bands.

MARSHALL

Too late.

GUNNAR

Marshall. No.

MARSHALL

I'm on my way.

When I arrive at the upscale jewelry store, I immediately spot Gunnar's massive Viking frame in the store and stride past the sales attendants to join my friends.

"Marshall?" Selene asks, her brow furrowed in confusion. "What are you doing here?"

"Dude, I told you not to come," Gunnar says gruffly.

"Yeah, well... if you didn't want me to find you, then why do you still share your location with me?" I taunt.

"He shares his location with you!" Selene gasps and punches Gunnar in the arm, and he grunts. "Why won't you share your location with me."

"Because I'm pretty sure this creep snuck into my phone to do it," Gunnar says, pulling out his phone and flicking the screen open. "And I've told you, work."

Selene pouts at her fiancé for a moment, but when he doesn't respond, she turns her attention to me.

"Okay. So, either you're here to help pick out rings, or you need something else." She states.

"Elsie's mad at me." I gripe.

"What's new there," Selene says, turning back to the case of rings before her. "What exactly happened? Use your big boy words, Marshall."

"I kind of proposed marriage after we had sex yesterday." I blurt out a little too loudly.

Everything stills for a moment as they process my words.

Then, Gunnar looks up slowly from his phone, and Selene turns around like an owl with its head on a lazy Susan.

"You did... what?" Selene asks, her voice more menacing than I've ever heard it before in the three years I've known her.

"I asked her if she wanted to get married," I say, a little quieter this time.

"I need you to be specific, Marshall," Selene says, grasping me by my wrists and looking up at me. "Did you ask if she wanted to get married, or did you ask her to marry you?"

"I asked her to marry me," I reply earnestly.

"What specific words did you use, Marshall." Selene presses.

"Marry me." I say, my voice firm and sure.

Selene goes silent, and her face is blank, which is never a good thing with her.

"Have you even told her that you love her?" Selene asks, setting down the ring she had been playing with in her hand.

"Well, yeah. Of course." I reply hesitantly with a shrug. "That was part of the marriage proposal thing."

"Thing?" Selene practically shrieks before looking at Gunnar wide-eyed. "Did he just call a marriage proposal a 'thing?' Did that really just come out of his mouth? Dime que estoy alucinando." *Tell me I'm hallucinating.*

Gunnar chuckles at Selene's dramatics. "You are, unfortunately, very much lucid."

"What? I did the right thing, right? I told her I love her and asked her to marry me. That's what you're supposed to do!" I say, becoming increasingly more frustrated the longer this conversation goes on.

"Dude." Gunnar interrupts, looking at his fiancée in apology. "If there's one thing we're taught, it's not to make big decisions after sex. Don't tell people you love them, and definitely don't ask them to marry you."

"No one told me that," I grumble.

Selene looks completely bewildered.

"Let me get this straight," Selene says, taking a deep breath. "You asked Elsie, *our* Elsie, ice queen of the oil industry Elsie, to marry you *right after telling her you love her?*"

"Yes?" I reply questioningly.

"Did you even have a ring?" She asks, gesturing with another ring she's picked up from the box on the counter.

"No...."

"You are so royally fucked, Marshall." Selene sighs, shaking her head before looking back up at me. "Have you ever even thought to ask her why she might be so opposed to the idea of marriage? Why everything she's ever achieved she's literally done on her own?"

"No?" I say sheepishly.

"Oh, Marshall. Sweet baby Marshall." She sighs. "We need to have a big sis talk, okay?"

"Okay?"

"I'm guessing we're finishing this another day?" Gunnar asks.

"Yes," Selene replies, grabbing her bag off the counter. "This requires tequila."

"Beer," Gunnar replies.

"Vodka." Selene quips back.

"Whiskey." I chime in, and they both give me incredulous looks. "What? I thought we were naming types of alcohol."

Selene turns back to Gunnar. "Vodka. Final offer."

"Deal." He says, extending his hand. "But none of the shitty stuff."

She takes his hand and gives him a firm shake. "Deal."

"What the hell did I just witness?" I ask.

"Communication," Gunnar says.

"And negotiation," Selene adds. "Two things you could stand to learn a thing or two about. But first, you need to go shopping."

"What for?" I ask, curious about where her mind is going.

Rummaging through her bag, Selene pulls out her phone and begins to type. She glances up briefly. "Apology jewelry."

After another thirty minutes of shopping and being explicitly told I am under no circumstances allowed to purchase an apology ring, I walk out of the store with my wallet and head hurting.

"Okay. Now what?" I ask, headed for my truck.

"Oh no. Not that fast. You're gonna want to be at least a little tipsy for this." Selene says, snatching my keys out of my hands. "There's no way I'm letting you drive."

I look at Gunnar, hoping for answers, but he just chuckles at me and shakes his head.

"Gunnar. To the nearest dive bar!" She cheers. "¡Vamos!" *Let's go.*

Gunnar's mental map of dive bars in the city is quite impressive. It only took fourteen minutes to arrive at this one that, from the outside, looks like it should be condemned.

"Come here often?" I joke as we get out of his SUV and head into the old building.

Inside, the little dingy bar is exactly as you would expect it to be.

It's dim enough in the bar to see and make your way around but not enough to really notice how beat up the place is. The floor is scuffed, just like all of the tables. The chairs and bar are well-worn. Everything looks well-loved, for lack of a kind word.

Selene leads me over to a booth in the corner and motions for me to slide in before she takes her seat on the outer edge while Gunnar heads to the bar to get us our shots of vodka, per their negotiation.

"How well do you know Elsie?" Selene starts.

"I mean... I've been living with her for about six months now, and we're having a kid together." I shrug and keep my eyes roaming the bar. "Surely there's somewhere else you'd prefer to be right now, Selene?"

"Don't change the subject. I'm perfectly fine right where I am." She says as Gunnar makes his way over to the table and slides in on my other side, essentially trapping me between them with no escape.

He sets down three shot glasses and a bottle of Deep Eddy's on the table and begins dispensing shots for the three of us. When he's done, he hands each of us a glass.

"To..." He starts.

"To apology jewelry." Selene giggles before taking her shot.

Gunnar shrugs, and we both take our shot before Selene starts in.

"Okay. You've been living with Elsie for six months. But what do you *know* about her?" She asks, with all seriousness.

"I know her father's a dick," I reply. "He's never been around for her. Treated her more like a political prop than a daughter."

"And what do you know about her mom?" Selene asks carefully.

"Just that she's not in the picture." I shrug.

"She died," Selene says seriously. "Giving birth to Elsie. Her mom died like right after from birth complications."

"So..." I say, hoping Selene will continue.

"Her dad didn't just use her as a prop, Marshall." Selene sighs. "He avoided being a parent to Elsie altogether. He made her invisible unless it was in the public eye. Elsie's never been loved the way you or I have been. She's never felt love herself and trusted that instinct. Because the person who was supposed to love her most growing up, the person who was supposed to teach her that, was *him*."

"Shit," I murmur. "She's not ready."

"Yeah," Selene says, motioning to Gunnar to dispense another round of shots from the already low bottle of vodka. "You fucked up."

"I didn't know," I say defensively.

"Doesn't matter, man. You need to meet her where she's at." Gunnar supplies as he hands me another shot that I down quickly. "She's not ready for that kind of commitment. It has to be her idea."

Grabbing the bottle of vodka from him, I down the remainder in a few gulps.

"Can I move back into the pool house?" I ask.

"I think that'd be best," Selene says with a small sympathetic smile.

Dropping my head into my hands, my tipsy thoughts swirl, thinking about how badly I fucked up here.

I pushed her when I should have been patient.

She's always been her very own person, independent of what anyone else expected from her. No wonder she freaked out when I started insisting on something she hadn't planned for. It means changing her life plan. Everything she thought she wanted changes if she makes a decision like this.

Hell, I'm shocked that she so quickly let me invade her life like I did.

But that unto itself gives me hope.

She needs me.

Whether she's ready to admit it or not, she needs me and what I've become for her.

She's not ready to admit it, but we are family.

I just have to get her to realize it herself.

Maybe I'm down the street instead of down the hall, but I'm not going anywhere.

Not really.

I'm here for her.

For life.

ELSIE

September 13 — 36 Weeks 6 Days, Winter Melon

It's past time I dragged myself out of bed today, but I can't manage it.

Today, I turn 35, and despite being a day worthy of celebration, I've never felt so empty.

The past few days have been tense.

Marshall is barely around. He stayed Sunday night after I kicked him out of my bedroom, but the following day, he had his bag packed and left. I only know he went to Selene and Gunnar's again because Selene texted me.

He's keeping his distance. I get it.

I also hate it, mostly because I know it's my fault.

After I forced Marshall out of my room, an overwhelming sense of regret settled into my body, though it took my brain much longer to catch up to the feeling.

I hurt him.

I broke his heart when I said no to his marriage proposal. Not even just his proposal. I broke his heart when I denied him the vision of his own happily ever after.

Today is another check-up for the baby, and I know Marshall will still be there, ever the present father, but I'm not prepared to see him.

Seeing him will bring up all the guilt I can't seem to push down. I'm not prepared to be crushed by my failure as a parent and a partner.

So, I sit here in bed, well past when I usually get up, trying to convince myself that this is all worthwhile.

Kicks come through my belly, jostling me from my mental spiral, and my hand goes to my stomach.

"Hey, baby," I whisper, smiling down at my bump. "You having a party in there for Mama?"

If nothing else, this baby is worth it.

I've wanted and worked for this for years. No matter how things came about or what complications came along with all of it, this baby is worth it.

"I'm so excited to meet you soon, baby," I tell my bump. "I only hope that I'm good enough for you."

As though she's listening to every word I say, I get a firm kick in the gut at my admission.

"Oh. You're gonna be a sass master. I can already tell." I smile. "Gonna be quite a handful for Mama, aren't you?"

A knock at the door startles me, snapping my attention away from my baby and back to the realities of the moment.

"Elsie?" Marshall's voice comes through the door.

I sigh. "Come in."

Marshall opens the door and pops his head in. "Hey. I brought breakfast. Wanted to make sure you ate something before the appointment."

"Oh, thank you," I reply, genuinely grateful for how kind and thoughtful he's being despite my cruelty toward him.

Another kick comes at my gut, and I huff out a breath before telling Marshall, "Baby has been moving around a lot this morning."

"Oh." He says, gesturing to the empty space beside me on the bed. "May I?"

"Yeah. Sure." I say, situating myself up on my pillows a little better.

He comes over and sits next to me, his gaze fixated on my belly.

"You've scheduled everything with your doctor, right?" He asks. "Induction and everything?"

"Yeah. It's on the calendar for September 25." I say with effort after a significant kick to my bladder. "She's really active this morning."

Looking up, I spot tears in Marshall's eyes.

"Here," I say, reaching to place his big palm on the spot where he might be able to feel the most movement.

"That never gets old." He sighs. "Buenos días, mi pequeña ciruela de azúcar." *Good morning, my little sugar plum.*

Another kick comes through at his greeting, and I let out a laugh.

"She's always been a sucker for your voice." I smile down at where I can feel our daughter.

"You said she." Marshall looks at me with light in his eyes. "You believe me? That we're having a daughter?"

I shrug. "You just seem so sure."

"I am." He says, his tone laced with more meaning than I'm able to handle at this hour. "Elsie..."

"No. Marshall. I know you want to talk, but I just can't handle it right now. Not today, okay?" I shake my head and chuckle. "Right now, I just need help getting up so I can go to the bathroom. Baby is being a bitch on my bladder."

"Okay." He says softly as he stands and holds out his hands to help me get up. "Come out for breakfast when you're ready."

"Thank you," I say when I'm standing. "I'll be out in a bit."

He nods and then leaves me alone in my room once again.

But being alone with my thoughts is not what I need right now. Once in the bathroom, I go about my morning routine, including a long shower underneath scalding water.

I take my time getting ready, carefully going through my curly hair routine and all of my skincare. I let myself sink into the ritual and allow it to drive out the negative thoughts that keep swirling in my mind.

When I'm dressed and ready to face the world, I force myself into the kitchen to face Marshall.

Of course, he's looking hot as hell with a tight-fitting shirt that molds perfectly to his toned body and his tattoos on display. Of course, his jeans hug his ass in a way that makes me drool too.

Marshall truly is the perfect man.

Yet I can't bring myself to accept what he's offering.

"Morning," I say, announcing my presence.

He looks up from his phone. He's seated on the couch and smiles, but the light that is usually present is noticeably absent today.

"Everything okay?" I ask cautiously.

"Yeah. Fine." He replies, though I don't believe him.

"Okay."

"Breakfast is on the table." He says, gesturing to the table as he gets up from the couch and comes to stand next to me.

I glance over to find a mini feast spread out across the table and let out a small gasp.

"Marshall. What the hell?" I ask, shocked by the gesture.

I feel his warmth come up behind me, and it's almost too much for my already over-sensitized nerves.

"Happy birthday, Elsie." He whispers in my ear, wrapping his arms around me and presenting me with a small square box wrapped with a ribbon.

"Marshall." I start, turning around in his arms as best as possible before he drops them and gives me more room.

"It's your birthday, Elsie. You deserve nice things. Please, don't fight me on this." He sighs. "I'm so tired of fighting."

I take a moment to consider my options, but the truth is that I don't like fighting with him any more than he does.

This isn't good for either of us, and I'm sure that the stress of everything isn't good for the baby.

So, I cave and reach for the box in his hand.

"Here, sit." He says, pulling out a chair once I have the box in hand.

I waddle over to sit down, and he settles in a chair across the table from me.

Taking a deep breath, I prepare myself for what could be in the box.

It's too large to be a ring, thank goddess, but not long enough to be a necklace.

Undoing the ribbon and keeping everything tied together, I lift the top of the box to reveal a small, soft jewelry bag. As though the bag bites, I reach in carefully to pull it out and am surprised at the weight of it in my hand.

"What..." I start.

"Just open it," Marshall says with a smile.

I reach into the pouch, and my fingers connect with something metal that feels like a chain. Pulling it out, I find a silver charm bracelet with two charms. The first is a small crown with diamonds embedded to make it sparkle. The second charm is a small purple fruit.

"A purple peach?" I ask.

"A plum. Para nuestra pequeña ciruela azucarada." He says. *For our little sugar plum.*

Tears start to well in my eyes. "And the crown?"

"For my princess, my queen." He says reverently, and I break out into full-blown crocodile tears. "Oh no. What did I do wrong? This was supposed to be an apology."

"No." I sob. "You did nothing wrong. This is so sweet."

I take a few deep breaths and try to control my sniffles.

"Thank you." I finally managed. "You didn't have to, but thank you."

"You're welcome." He says softly before reaching for the bracelet. "May I?"

I nod, and he takes the bracelet, fastening it around my wrist and adjusting the charms to lay neatly against my skin.

"Now eat up, and then we'll head to your doctor's appointment." He says.

This man is far too good for me.

I don't deserve his gentle kindness.

He shows up for me in a way that feels so genuinely eager, which puts me on edge more than it helps soothe my soul.

I can't accept what he has to offer.

I'm not ready.

So, instead, I focus on eating breakfast and distract myself from my somber thoughts by going through my mental to-do list.

We can deal with feelings later.

33

ELSIE

Silence lingers between Marshall and I as we sit in the lobby of my doctor's office, waiting to be called back for my appointment.

All through the rest of our morning together and the drive here, there have been words locked in my chest that I want to say but can't bring myself to voice.

There's so much that Marshall and I need to talk through, but none of it has a simple solution.

The worst part seems to be that Marshall knows exactly what he wants.

He's just like a hopeful puppy waiting for me to give him his treat.

He's so supportive and sweet that it's almost sickening.

From the outside, everything seems perfect. I have a man who adores me and a baby on the way.

So why is it so hard for me to embrace the idea that this could be forever?

Marshall has spun this fairy tale for us that I'm unwilling to embrace.

I want to trust it, his vision, and to trust him, but I just can't. Not yet.

Instead, we sit with an awkward silence hovering between us everywhere we go.

"Ms. Snow?" The nurse calls.

"Yes," I reply, struggling to get out of the low chair on my own until Marshall helps me up. "Thank you."

"No problem." He says as we both turn to follow the nurse down the hall.

"If you stand here, we can take your weight, and then I'll get your blood pressure." The nurse says.

I do as she says, and then she guides us to one of the patient rooms, this one with an adorable photo of a mom and her twins on the wall.

The nurse goes through my medical records and the standard series of questions they ask at all my appointments before leaving. Marshall and I sit alone in the room to wait for the doctor.

Thankfully, this isn't an appointment where I need to change into one of those awful paper dressing gowns. Instead, I wore a comfortable outfit that allows me to slip off my pants and pull up my top before covering myself with the paper blanket they left for me.

Marshall opens his mouth as though to break the silence that's descended upon the room, but he's interrupted by my phone ringing from inside my purse.

"Can you hand that to me?" I ask, gesturing to my bag sitting on the floor next to him.

When I have my bag in hand, I dig through my bag until I locate my phone, only to pull it out and see an unknown local number.

Typically, I don't answer unknown callers, but something about it tells me I should pick up this time.

"Hello?" I ask into the phone.

"Elizabeth Iris Snow?" A smooth voice comes through the phone.

"This is she," I say calmly, though anxiety is mounting in my chest as my heart rate increases.

"This is your father's lawyer for his estate, Mrs. Johnson."

"Estate?"

"Yes. I'm so sorry to inform you, but your father passed away last night." The lawyer says. "I'm calling to inform you of his death and ask you to come by my office."

"My father is dead?" I whisper into the phone.

Marshall's head snaps up, and his full attention is now on me as I speak with the woman on the phone.

"I just... I just ran into him on Sunday." I say in disbelief. "What happened?"

"Did you..." She pauses. "Your father was sick for quite a while. He'd been battling cancer for several months. Did you not know?"

"No," I whisper. "I went no-contact with him a few years ago. We've only had run-ins here and there for the last few years."

"Oh. I apologize. He spoke of you so fondly when I last saw him, I assumed..."

"You assumed wrong." I snap.

My father was never a kind person. He wasn't the warm father figure he portrayed himself as to the world. Everyone else saw him as this great, successful man who had a picture-perfect life.

But I know better.

Father was nothing like a real dad should be. He never showed up for me nand ever supported me in the ways I needed him to.

And yet, there's still an overwhelming sadness that's overcome me in this moment.

He's gone.

Really gone.

I'm truly alone in the world.

There's nothing to change that now.

So, I shut down the mounting sorrow that threatens me with tears and turn back to the moment.

"If you can send me an email with details, I'll come by later today if that works," I say into the phone, my voice colder than before.

"Yes. Of course." The lawyer says before confirming my contact information with me.

When I hang up the phone, it's like everything crashes over me all at once.

The room disappears around me, and all I'm left with is an overwhelming feeling of emptiness. Where you would expect grief to form in my chest, there's nothing.

I've grieved the loss of my father for years, working through the abuse and neglect on my own.

There's nothing left to grieve anymore.

He's been gone from my life for a long time.

There's no point spilling tears over a man who couldn't have cared less to be the father I needed when he was alive.

Why cry over him in death?

"Elsie?" Marshall's voice and a slight tug on my hand bring me back from my thoughts. "Elsie, are you okay?"

"I'm fine," I say, gathering myself and straightening my posture. "The lawyer said she would send me more information. So, let's get through this appointment, and then I imagine I will need to go over to her office by then."

"Elsie," Marshall says in a soft tone.

"Do *not* make this worse, Marshall." I snap, causing his eyes to widen at my censure. "I'm fine."

The rest of the doctor's appointment passes in a blur. I'm grateful for Marshall's presence as I'm barely able to hold myself together for the duration of our time once the doctor arrives, much less ask questions.

I gather the important information, me and baby look healthy, and I'm on schedule for delivery as planned.

Good.

That's what I need.

I need something good to hold onto.

And soon, I'll have the best and purest joy in the world to hold in my arms and make everything okay.

It's going to be okay.

It has to be.

34

MARSHALL

Elsie's gone cold and quiet in a way I haven't seen since before I moved in with her.

Seeing such a dramatic shift occur so suddenly has shown just how much she's changed in the past months.

She's become a lighter, happier person.

I like to think I have something to do with the shift in her life, but it's hard to remember that in moments when she goes so cold like this.

The entire appointment, I kept glancing over to her, checking in, and asking the doctor all the questions I knew she would want answers to later.

Elsie's expression never changed from the emptiness that had settled over her features when she found out the news.

Now I'm sitting on a leather couch of a fancy office, after she insisted we go straight to the lawyer after her doctor's appointment, waiting for Elsie to finish up with the woman who called her earlier.

"Marshall!" I hear my name snapped, and I look up to find a furious and very pregnant Elsie storming towards me. "We're leaving."

"Please, Ms. Snow." The lawyer says, trotting behind her.

As Elsie nears, I stand up and navigate my way out from the cluster of couches to get to her.

"Elsie," I say, stopping her with a hand on her shoulder.

I look between Elsie, who's avoiding my glance, and the lawyer, who looks distressed.

"What's going on?" I ask, leaning down to look Elsie in the eye.

Elsie turns to avoid my gaze, but thankfully, she doesn't ice me out. "We're done here, that's all."

"Okay?" I say questioningly.

"Sir. Please." The lawyer pleads, thrusting an envelope in my direction. "Take this and just ask her to reconsider."

I take the paper from her and look back at Elsie, who's frozen under my hand.

"Let's go." She says quietly.

"Okay." I stuff the envelope into the back pocket of my jeans and grab my keys out of my front pocket. "Let's go."

Elsie is quiet the whole way out of the lawyer's office. She doesn't even question me when I turn to head home instead of taking her to the office like I'm sure she would want under other circumstances.

When we make it home and are safely ensconced in her apartment, I finally risk poking the bear.

"Elsie, what happened back there," I ask as she goes rummaging through the freezer, reminding me of the day she told me she was pregnant.

She comes out with a gallon of toffee Bluebell ice cream and grabs two spoons from the silverware drawer.

"What happened is that my dad is trying to get the last word." She huffs. "That fucking lawyer brings me into her office, has me sign all this paperwork for his estate, and then tries to get me to take that fucking envelope which she says is a letter from dear old dad."

I reach into my back pocket to pull out the envelope, which is now a little creased from being folded into my jeans.

"I can only imagine what he says in there. I don't want to read it." She says, waddling over to the couch and plopping down with the ice cream propped up on her swollen belly, putting her legs up to help with the swelling.

I look down at the envelope, one that could hold any number of things within it.

Something tells me this envelope contains something that will change everything for Elsie.

I know what she's afraid of. She's afraid of falling.

Ever since I met Elsie, I've known that she shields herself from the world with her icy armor. She's a master at looking the part, just like her father seemed to in my one interaction with him.

But just like him, no one is free from gravity.

Everyone falls at some point.

What she doesn't seem to realize yet is that I'm here to catch her.

I'll always be here to catch her.

"I think you should read it," I say patiently.

"What? No." She replies with a mouth full of ice cream. "Absolutely not."

"Whatever it is, he took the time to write it to you, and I think you should read it." I reason.

"No. I'm not letting that asshole get the last word. All we ever did was fight. All he ever did was criticize me. Why would this be any different?" She protests.

"Because he was dying," I say solemnly, walking over and setting down the envelope on the couch beside her and picking up a spoon for myself. "People change at the end of their lives. I think you'll be glad you read it if you do."

"You're lucky I don't hate you." She says when I dig my spoon into the tub of ice cream.

"Oh? I wasn't sure about that as of late." I chuckle, only a little seriousness in my words.

"Marshall, I..." She starts.

"No. Right now isn't the time to be getting into our mess." I push on, hoping I can get through to her. "You're avoiding right now, Elsie. It's okay to be scared, but it doesn't mean you're not strong enough to face your fears."

"I'm not scared." She snaps, stabbing her spoon into the tub of ice cream. "I'm just..."

She drops her head onto the back of the couch, revealing the length of her neck that I so love to bite and nibble at.

I shake my head of thoughts that don't belong in this moment, refocusing on being here for Elsie.

She needs me.

Whether she's ready to admit it or not, she needs me. I plan on being here for her just like I plan on continuing to show up for her every day for the rest of our lives.

Scooping another bite of ice cream out of the tub, I ask her. "What's the worst that could happen? He's already gone. There's nothing more that he can do."

A contemplative look passes over Elsie's face as she ponders the possible outcomes.

I know what she's thinking. I recognize her hesitations now, her motivations.

Taking both of our spoons and the ice cream, which gets me a look of protest, I set them down on the coffee table where I sit and take her hand in mine.

"He can't hurt you anymore, Elsie," I say softly, rubbing my thumb on her inner wrist.

I see her pushing down the tears that want to spill, and it physically pains me to see her in such distress.

I want to comfort her, but she needs to ask me.

I can't continue to give of myself without her asking. It might break me.

"Just..." I reach over and grab the letter, placing it in the hand that I hold. "Consider reading it. If you want me to sit with you while you do, I'll be here. If you want a moment alone, just say so, and I'll leave."

Too many thoughts and emotions flash across Elsie's eyes for me to honestly tell what she's thinking or how she's feeling, but I get the sense that she's right at the edge of her decision.

"Okay." She says softly.

"Okay?"

"I'll read it, but I think..." Her face screws up in an adorable scrunch. "I think I need to be alone for this."

"Okay. I'm going to head back to Selene and Gunnar's then." I say, giving her free hand a squeeze. "If you need me, just call."

"Okay." She whispers. "Thank you."

I lean down and give her a kiss on the forehead. She melts under my touch, and a warm satisfaction swells in my chest when she does.

When I reach the front door, I glance quickly over my shoulder and see her still staring at the envelope.

This will be good for her, for us.

The path forward for us might be unclear right now, but I'm sure there is one.

Elsie is my forever.

Forever and always.

She just needs to realize that for herself.

35

Elizabeth,

I doubt you remember your mother. You were so young when I lost her. I never really thought about how it may have impacted you. All I know is that it broke me fundamentally. She died, left us, and suddenly, the world shifted. Unexpectedly, there was a human who was totally dependent upon me for everything. I thought I was ready for that, but I wasn't.

Seeing you this week, preparing to expand your own family with a new child on the way and a man who looks at you with stars in his eyes, made me realize how inept I was as a parent.

I was never prepared to be a real father to you. Not really.

I never considered what it meant to be a good parent beyond providing for you financially and making sure there was a roof over your head and food in your belly.

There were too many times in your childhood when I could see the joy drain from your face when I told you I had to go to work or on a trip. There are too many memories of disappointing you at every turn, and I think it turned me into someone I don't recognize.

I'm dying.

I have been for a while—Leukemia—and it makes a man reflect on his life.

I wish I would have reacted differently when I saw you this week. When I first saw you, with your bright hair and the glow that every pregnant woman has, I wanted to pull you into my arms and beg for your forgiveness. But every day that I've called you, my daughter has also been one where I drank a poison of my own making to protect myself from a world that taught me that vulnerability is a weakness and not a gift. That bitterness seeped out of me at that moment, and I fear that it ruined any chance I may have at reconciling with you.

I've tried to mold you into the person I wanted, or maybe needed, you to be. I tried to steer you into making the right decisions. However, those choices were my own, and I should have known better than to try and force them onto others. My judgment was of myself, never you, Elizabeth. It wasn't right, but it was all I knew then.

Seeing you at the club and how soon the family would be growing it made things crystal clear.

You are, and have always been, the center of my world and my reason for being. I love you more than I've ever been able to express properly.

My biggest regret is not showing you that to be true.

I've failed you in so many ways in this life, but I hope, when you're reading this after my death, you give me the opportunity to be a father to you once more. And hopefully, a good one this time.

Don't let fear guide your life, Elizabeth. I've seen you pursue every goal you've had for your life relentlessly, but sometimes, the greatest joys come from embracing the journey along the way. There is a life waiting for you beyond the goals that you've set for yourself. Take the time to embrace the unknown of life.

You don't need to follow in my footsteps. They're lonely and unfulfilling.

Go and find what brings you joy, Elizabeth. Surround yourself with people who add brilliance to your life, and don't let them go.

Choose to be happy, sweet girl.

All my love,

Charles Snow

36

ELSIE

September 19 — 37 Weeks 5 Days, Pumpkin

It takes me a full day before I can bring myself to open up my father's letter.

Oliver has been strict with restricting the amount of work and, therefore, stress I'm allowed to take on at this point in my pregnancy. He's *heavily* screening my emails these days and only lets me work a few hours each day before he has tech shut me out of my computer.

I'm basically part-time at this point.

But part-time work means a lot of time to myself and a lot of time with my own thoughts.

So, I've spent a full day of existing alone in my apartment with my thoughts, which is probably never a good thing.

I finally brought myself to read through my father's final words, though.

By the end, I was a distraught mess.

My first instinct was to call Marshall for comfort. To ask him to come over and fuck me to make everything better.

Sure, my father wasn't the greatest or most supportive parent to me, but he tried in his own way, I guess.

It's my responsibility to do better this time, though. I can break the pattern of taking the isolated path that my father set forth. I can do better. I have to, for my baby.

Our baby.

Reading my father's letter helps me realize how integral Marshall is to all of this. Not just because he's the father of our daughter but because he's one of the people in this world who makes me better.

His presence in my life has equipped me to be a better human and, in turn, a better mother.

Despite having read every book and journal article I can get my hands on, there's no amount of reading that can prepare you to be a mother.

Instead, Marshall swept into my life and taught me the most important lesson of all.

Love.

I'm in love with the foolish man, and it took a dead man's words to make me realize it.

Or maybe not realize it. I know I've been in love with him for a while.

But the direction he's laid out for us? The vision he paints so vividly of our family? That's a future I want *desperately*. I was just too stubborn to admit it.

Moreover, I want it with *him*.

Marshall Law is the man I want to build a life with. He's the person I see forever with because I finally have a clear picture of what a life full of joy looks like.

Achievement isn't the end all be all. I don't want to move through life looking for fulfillment in the praise I receive from Board members and awards banquets.

Happiness, true happiness, is found in the people you

surround yourself with and the experiences you build your life around with them.

That is what I want from my life.

And Marshall has helped bring so much joy into my life that I hadn't previously allowed myself.

So, I'll do everything in my power to build a life for us that is just as picture-perfect and messy as he envisions it.

I want a home filled with laughter, children, and love.

Today is a rare day where Oliver let me come into the office for a few select meetings. So I yell out from my office so my assistant can hear me from his desk.

"Oliver!"

"Yes?" He says, popping into the doorway.

"Have you heard anything?" I ask.

"No." He replies, raising an eyebrow at me. "They told you they would reach out directly. I'm not handling this one."

"Right. Sorry. Pregnancy brain." I chuckle a little, levity coming back to my life with every moment that my vision of a future solidifies a little bit more.

Just then, my phone rings and I jump at the noise.

"Speak of the devil." Oliver laughs, backing out of my office to return to his desk.

It's been nearly a week now since Marshall left me alone that day, and ever since then, I've been working tirelessly.

Only this time, I've been blowing off company business and focusing on building a future for myself... and for us.

"Hello?" I say into my phone.

"Hi, Ms. Snow!" A chipper voice comes through the speaker. "It's done!"

"Done?" I ask, hesitant to let myself be truly happy.

Not yet. Not until, I'm sure.

"Yes! Everything is in order. I can meet you at your office and hand off everything you need if you like? Or you can come to my office?" The woman on the other end of the line asks.

"If it's alright, could I actually head straight there? Have you left it there?" I ask.

"Of course. I completely understand where you're coming from." She says. "Circumstances as they are, I can ensure everything is ready for you. Then we can finish up details at a later date."

"Thank you," I say, breathing a sigh of relief. "Can you text me when everything is ready? I'd like to move quickly if we can."

"Yes. Of course. I'll send you a message when everything is done." She tells me.

"Thank you. I really appreciate you dropping everything to help me with this." I tell her.

"It helps that you know what you want." She laughs. "You've been very determined."

"Yeah. I do, don't I?" I chuckle alongside her. "Thank you."

"Of course. I'll send you a message when it's done. Shouldn't be more than an hour." She says. "Goodbye, Ms. Snow."

"Bye," I reply just before the phone call ends.

It's really happening.

Things are finally falling into place like they're meant to be.

37

MARSHALL

An address and a time.

That's all that was in the text from Elsie.

No apology. No explanation. Just a time and a place.

If I wasn't so in love with this woman or so intrigued, I wouldn't have come.

But here I am, at 6:37 pm, driving to a random address in the city.

Only, as I pull up to the address, it isn't so random.

The one-story ranch-style house is the same one Elsie and I drove past all those months ago. Not just the same kind of home I told her I could imagine building our lives in, but the exact home I pointed out.

Outside, on the front porch, sits Elsie, looking radiant in a light summer dress and her hair in perfect curls.

Goddess, I missed this woman.

The sight of her alone has my cock standing at attention and my heart thundering in my chest.

Getting out of my truck, I slowly approach where she stands in front of the house.

"Elsie," I say, greeting her cautiously.

"Marshall." She sighs with a smile. "Thank you for coming."

"Your message was rather cryptic. I couldn't resist the mystery." I shrug. "But what are we doing here?"

She glances down at her shoes as though she doesn't quite know how to do this, but then I see when she gathers her courage and straightens to look at me head-on.

"Can we go inside?"

"Do you have a key? Because I'm pretty sure it's still a crime to break into someone's house." I joke, trying to get some of the tension in her shoulders to dissipate.

"The door is unlocked." She says simply.

"Oh. So, you've done this before?" I chuckle, following her as she waddles her way into the house.

"The first time was today, actually." She jokes back, and my shoulders soften at the banter between us.

The house is exactly as I would have hoped: old.

Everything inside the house is exactly as it would have been when it was initially built. The plush carpet is worn down in all the areas that are heavily trafficked, leaving spots on the floor where you can tell someone has positioned furniture.

The house even smells its age with a slight scent of tobacco that's woven itself into the walls.

"Is it what you hoped?" Elsie asks.

"What do you mean?"

"When you saw this house..." She pauses, seeming to gather her courage. "Is this where you saw our lives together?"

"Elsie...."

"No. Marshall. I want to talk about this now. I'm ready to talk about it. Please." She says sternly, and I can't help but smile at the furrow that's settled itself between her brows in her determination.

"Okay. Let's talk then."

"Answer my question."

When I don't respond immediately, she gestures with her hand in a forward, rolling motion to prompt me to speak. "Did you see a future for us in this house?"

"I mean…" I start. "Yeah. I've seen a future with you in a lot of places. But this house is pretty cool."

She rolls her eyes before returning to her serious look again. "But you like the house."

"Yeah, Elsie. I like the house. What about it?" I ask, my frustration mounting alongside my curiosity.

"I bought it." She says plainly.

"You what?"

"I bought it." She repeats.

I take a look around at the house again with its outdated everything.

"You bought this?"

"That's what I said, Marshall." She says frowning.

"But why?"

There's a part of me that senses where she's going with this, but I need her to say it.

I need to hear her tell me what she wants.

That she wants this.

With me.

"Why did you buy this house, Elsie," I say, taking a step toward her and looking down into her piercing blue eyes.

"I… I…" She stutters.

"Tell me, princess," I say with a smirk, which earns me a frown.

A battle occurs behind her eyes, and I see the moment that one side wins and declares itself the victor.

I can only hope it's the side that is favorable to me.

"I want this." She says slowly, glancing around at the house.

"And what is this?" I ask.

"I want…" She struggles. "Ugh. Just follow me."

She turns on her heel, and it takes me a moment to register that she actually walked away from me before I'm able to process and get myself to move after her.

I follow her through the house and into the tiny breakfast nook that's just off the kitchen, where there are two stacks of paperwork.

"It's four bedrooms, three and a half baths. The front two rooms share a jack and jill. And there's a hall bath that the other two share. The primary bedroom has an on-suite and walk-in closets." She starts rambling as she rustles through sheets of paper. "The house was built...."

"Elsie, I don't care when the house was built," I say, taking her chin between my fingers and turning her to face me. "Tell me why you bought the house."

Her face scrunches in an adorable pout.

"You're gonna make me say all of it out loud, aren't you?" She huffs.

"Yes. I am."

"Fine." She takes a breath, gathering herself. "I want this. I want the house and the kids and the whole stupid future you have envisioned for us."

"Us?"

"Yes, *us*. I want a future with you. *Us*."

Warmth builds in my chest, and I smile widely at her admission.

Reaching for her waist, I pull her into my body as close as she can with her baby bump.

"You want a future with me?" I ask.

"Yes." She huffs, looking down and away from me. "That's what I want."

There's a moment of silence where I can tell she's chewing on an admission, but I wait patiently for her to speak.

"I'm sorry it took me so long to get here." She says softly, finally glancing up to meet my gaze and putting her hands on my chest. "But I want this. I want you."

I reach up to push back one of her curls behind her ear.

"That's not enough, Elsie," I say with a teasing smirk. "You know what I need to hear."

"Marshall." She whines.

"Elsie," I say in a jokingly stern tone.

"Fine." She pushes away from me and turns around. "But I'm not saying it to your face."

I take a few steps forward and wrap Elsie up in my arms so my hands can cup her belly.

"Tell me how you feel, Elsie." She sighs, her body tense, but I bring my lips to her ear and whisper, "What do you want, princess?"

A shiver rolls through her body, and she relaxes into my arms.

"I... I made a new agreement." She says quickly before breaking out of my hold and returning to the dining table. "It's for both of us to review and sign."

"Elsie..." I say, losing hold of my patience a little.

"Look." She turns to me and looks at me straight on. "This isn't easy for me. I'm good with negotiations and business deals, not feelings. I'm trying to do this the best way I know how. I love you so damn much and..."

Her eyes grow wide, and I can't help the chuckle that escapes.

"You love me, Elsie Snow?" I ask, my voice bright with the knowledge.

"Yes." She says sternly with a furrowed brow. "I love you, and it feels like such a stupid thing to have to admit."

"But you did." I point out.

"Yes. Fine. I did."

"You love me," I say softly.

"Yes, you silly man. I love you, and if you'll let me, I'd like to tell you that on occasion."

"For how long?" I ask with a smirk.

She returns my expression. "How does forever sound?"

"Show me the agreement, and I'll consider it." I laugh.

"And the house?" She asks nervously.

"It's perfect," I say, pulling her in for a kiss.

38

ELSIE

Marshall's lips against mine feel like coming home, truly home.

There's comfort, passion, and *love* in every touch of our lips.

The way his hands wander my body lights my soul on fire, and it's like I'm realizing what it truly means to need this man for the first time, with no limitations.

His hand is buried in the curls at the base of my neck, and when he tightens his grip, I moan.

Everything about how our bodies connect feels like freedom. There's a lightness in my chest that's replacing every worry I've had for the past week.

That he wouldn't want me.

That he changed his mind.

That I wouldn't be enough.

Only that's not what's happened at all.

"Marshall." I moan, need building in my core as he kisses me. "I need you."

"Oh? You need daddy or toy?"

"I need you, daddy." I manage through passionate kisses between us.

He pulls back, and I whine a pitiful noise.

"You do realize that forever means more kids, right?" He asks with all seriousness in his tone.

"Sounds like we should practice for the next one then," I say, pulling him back down to me. "What do you think?"

"Fuck yes." He breathes out before crashing his lips into mine.

Between passionate kisses, Marshall backs me into the sturdy kitchen table. When I bump into the edge, he reaches behind me and wipes all the papers off the table before picking me up to rest on the table.

When I reach for the button of his jeans, I can feel that he's already hard beneath them. My hand runs up and down his length through the denim, and the sound I draw from his lips with my touch makes my whole body pulse with need.

"Elsie." He groans.

"Not Elsie." I pant. "Not right now."

He leans down to give me another kiss, and our teeth crash together in the moment. Everything about it is all-encompassing and thrilling.

"Goddess. I missed you." He says, his hands running up and down my arms, sending goose bumps across my skin. "Can I undress you, princess? I need to see you."

"Yes, please." I breathe out. "I need you to touch me."

His fingers come up to the straps of my dress and slide under, delicately teasing the skin underneath. When he slides the straps down, the bodice of my dress falls as well, revealing my full breasts.

With awe in his face, he reaches to cup my breasts and kneed them with his big hands.

"These are magnificent. I can't wait to see our daughter feed off them."

He leans down and presses a kiss to each of my breast before getting on his knees and taking one of them into his mouth.

The warmth of his lips around my nipple sends a shiver through my whole body. The need that's raging in my core heightens at the sensation, and my head drops back.

He continues to run his tongue around and suck on my nipple before switching sides and repeating on my other breast.

Each tug on my nipple has new energy flowing through my body, but soon it's not just energy that's flowing through my breast. Liquid pre-milk begins to trickle from my nipple.

"Fuck. You taste so sweet." He moans at the taste of my milk flowing from my body.

What could have been a moment turned sour instead has my teeth aching. His reaction to how my body naturally reacts to his touch is so heartwarming that it only makes me love the man more.

My hand comes to his head, and I run my fingers through the strands of his hair to keep him close.

"Fuck, daddy. I need you to touch me, to fuck me." I groan.

He lifts his head and gives me a mischievous look.

"You want me to fuck you, princess?" He smirks, leaning back down to suckle on my nipple again and draw more milk from my breast. "Then beg for it."

"Please, daddy. I need you." I pant out. "Please."

"Good girl." He purrs, dragging his hands over my breast and down my belly.

He shifts my dress up to bunch it around my waist above my belly. When he reaches to pull down my underwear, I shift my hips to help him get them off.

Exposed to him now, I shiver when his calloused fingers skim along my inner thigh and up to my center.

"I love seeing you pregnant. Knowing I did this to you." He says, taking a moment to give the stretch marks on my belly kisses.

"I'm keeping you pregnant as often as I can. You know that, right? We're gonna fill this house with kids that look just like you."

He looks up at me with such genuine joy that I can't help but fall in line with his imagined future.

"So long as I get at least one little boy who's a carbon copy of his father." I sigh as he runs a finger through my folds and up to my clit.

"Anything for my queen." He says, his focus now completely on my center, completely mesmerized.

With that, he dives in, putting his lips against my cunt. He buries himself in my center, sucking on my clit and swirling his tongue around it in a gentle pattern of circles. The rhythm he sets with his tongue drives my desire into a roaring storm, the wave of pleasure threatening just at the edge of complete release.

Pausing his relentless efforts on my clit, he leans down to lick me from ass to clit, the sensation sending shivers through my whole body. He returns to his earlier task of sucking my soul out of my clit until I'm panting and whining with need.

"Please, daddy. I need your cock." I beg. "Please, daddy. Please."

Looking up at me, his beard glistening with my wetness, he gives me a truly devious smile.

"Does princess want my cock?" He murmurs, rising from his knees and unbuttoning his jeans as he stands.

When he gets his pants undone, his cock springs free from the confinement of the tight jeans, but his briefs still cover him.

"Yes. Please." I pant, reaching for the waistband of his underwear, desperate to free his cock so he can fuck me.

He helps me push the garment down, and his beautiful length is revealed to me. I quickly take it in hand, relishing the hardness as I move my hand up and down his shaft.

"Fuck, princess." He groans at my touch.

I tighten my grip to drag him by his cock to my core, lining him up so I can feel his tip at my entrance.

He laughs. "Eager girl."

"Fuck me. Fuck me, please." I beg.

Taking control of his dick with his own hand, he runs his tip through my folds until I'm shivering with need.

"Please." I moan just as he presses the first inch in with the head of his cock.

He's slow and deliberate with how he enters me, each push in and out dragging on in agonizing pleasure.

The way he fills me feels amazing. I feel full and *complete*.

"Marshall." I squeak when he picks up his pace. "Fuuuck."

Soon, his thrusts are relentless, plunging in and out of me at a rapid pace.

My core tightens around him every time he pushes into me, filling me up. The torrential wave that's been building in my body is almost at its crest.

"I need to come. Please, let me come." I beg, breathless.

Knowing exactly what I need to push me over the edge, he reaches down to circle my clit with his thumb, and the slightest of touches sends me over the cliff of my pleasure.

The sensation is overwhelming, warm, and gentle yet completely overpowering. Every nerve in my body is alive with energy, but I still need more.

"More." I pant. "I need more."

Both of his hands come down on either side of me to plant themselves on the table, and he picks up his pace. His hips thrust relentlessly, and he takes each drive into me as an opportunity to grind his pelvis into me, so it hits my clit at the perfect angle.

"Yes. That. More of that." I say breathlessly.

He continues to press into me, and I see when his face tightens.

"Come for me, daddy." I encourage. "Give me your cum. Give me everything."

"Fuck, princess." He groans. "Take it. Take my cock and my cum. It's yours. I'm yours."

The words light up something inside me that has my whole body reacting. A sudden flood of pleasure washes through me, and I clench down on his cock harder than before to lock him inside me. His thrusts grow shallow, barely able to move his hips anymore when he groans out his pleasure, and I feel the flood of his cum trickling out of me.

Both of us are breathless and satiated.

His head drops to mine, our foreheads touching and our lips only a breath away.

"Fuck, Elsie." He says between gulps of air. "I love you so fucking much."

Tears are forming at the edges of his eyes, and I reach up with one hand to brush them away.

Still nestled inside me, he pulls me up from where I am, leaning back on my elbows and cradles me against his chest.

"I love you too, Marshall," I whisper into his ear as I stroke my hands up and down his back. "I'll love you forever."

A small hiccup comes from him, and he buries himself into the crook of my neck so I can feel his warm breath against my skin.

We sit there for a while like this, just breathing each other in.

Then, slowly, agonizingly slowly, he pulls out of me and takes a single step back before leaning down to give me another passionate kiss.

His hands are on my belly, and when he looks up at me, I can see the unconditional love in his eyes.

"I'm gonna give you such a good life, Elsie." He says reverently, glancing between my face and my belly bump.

"I know. It's going to be the most amazing adventure." I smile, reaching out to cup his face in my hand. "You're going to be an amazing father."

"And you're going to be the best mother." He promises me, making my heart seize.

I pull him in for another kiss, and it's soft and gentle, a connection between two souls who chose each other.

Suddenly, he pulls back.

"The house." He says seriously. "Can we renovate?"

I laugh at the sudden change in subject. "If you want, of course. It's *our* home."

"Yeah, it is." He leans down to give me another peck. "I can't wait to play with our little girl in the backyard. I'm gonna build her a swing. Or maybe a treehouse."

I let out a full-bodied laugh, and suddenly, there's a kick into my gut, making me grunt.

"I think she likes the idea of that." I chuckle.

Marshall goes back to his knees and speaks directly to my belly, to our little sugar plum and our future.

"Te vamos a querer mucho, pequeña ciruela azucarada." He whispers. "So much." *We're gonna love you so much, little sugar plum.*

I run my fingers through his hair, and his gaze shoots up to look at me.

"I love you," I say softly.

He takes a deep breath. "I know. I know now. I believe you."

"Forever, Marshall. This is forever." I tell him. "No taking it back."

"Never."

"Forever."

"Always."

IF YOU WANT to keep reading, the series continues in Book 2 with *Bound*, a spicy FFM romance with *two* plus size ladies who have the hots for each other and a cowboy who's *very* good with rope!

Get your copy!

Can't get enough? Don't miss the passion, healing, and heat of Book 3 in the series, *Cherished*, and fall even deeper in love with our bride and groom, Selene and Gunnar!

Get your copy!

To stay up to date on news, sales, and releases from Shannon Elliot, join her newsletter here:

Join the newsletter!

ELSIE

September 28 — 3 Days Old

Giving birth is by far the worst pain I've ever experienced.

I thought periods were terrible, but nothing compares to what I went through in order to have my daughter.

Yes, daughter.

Marshall was, annoyingly, correct about us having a girl.

Bridgit Gabriela Law born on September 25 at 10:47 a.m., weighing in at seven pounds and nine ounces and measuring 19 inches tall.

She looked like a raisin, but I've never felt such an overwhelming and immediate love for someone like I did when I first held her.

Marshall was by my side the entire time, and much to my annoyance, and he was as positive as my pregnancy test the whole time.

By the end of the whole ordeal, I just wanted to sleep, but there was so much business during the four days I spent in the hospital.

According to the nurses, Bridgit passed her car seat test with flying colors, and they finally approved us for release.

Which is why I'm now sitting outside the main entrance of the hospital in a wheelchair, Bridgit in her car seat next to me and a nurse at my back, waiting for Marshall to bring his truck around to drive us home.

Only, the vehicle that pulls up before me is not Marshall's truck, though it's definitely Marshall driving.

Instead, I'm looking at a dark blue BMW SUV.

Marshall gets out of the driver's seat and comes around to face me with a smile on his face.

"What the hell, Marshall?" I ask, startling the nurse who's standing behind me.

"Do you not like it?" He says with a frown before picking up our daughter's carrier while the nurse helps me get up from the wheelchair and walk over to the car's open back door.

Marshall rounds the car and opens up the back seat door to click the car seat in place while the nurse kindly helps me into the car.

When he finishes securing our daughter and slides into the driver's seat, I immediately start asking questions and demanding answers.

"When did you get a new car? What happened to your truck?"

"Yesterday." He says with a shrug, pushing the button to start the car. "The truck wasn't safe enough. So, I got a new car. Mamá is taking the truck out to the ranch house so they can use it out there. It will be more useful to her than it will be for me now."

"Fine," I grumble, my eyes already wanting to fall closed from exhaustion.

Slowly, he pulls the car out of from beneath the carport awning and begins our drive home.

I'm genuinely too tired to argue with him, so I lean back in my seat, glancing over my shoulder every couple of seconds to check on Bridgit.

The car ride is quiet, and I'm grateful for the silence. My eyes drift closed for a few minutes, and when I open them again, I don't recognize our surroundings.

"Marshall? Where are we going? This isn't the way home." I say.

"We are going home." He says, his smirk smug enough for me to want to smack it off of him.

On any other day, I would fight him, but right now, I'm just too tired.

Finally, our surroundings begin to seem familiar, and I realize where we are headed.

"Marshall. We can't go to the new house. There's nothing there." I protest.

He glances over his shoulder at me, and panic seizes my chest.

"Eyes on the road." I snap.

"Yes, ma'am." He chuckles. "Just trust me, Elsie."

When we pull up to the house and park in the driveway, I finally spot Marshall's truck, or instead his old truck, in front of the house.

"Marshall, is your mother here?" I ask.

He puts the car in park and turns around in his seat.

"And if she is?" He asks with a raised eyebrow.

"I... I..."

I'm at a loss for words, for once.

"Come on." He says, unbuckling his seatbelt and hopping out of the car.

Before I can get myself unbuckled, Marshall is already unclipping the carrier from its base and taking our daughter into the house.

"A little help?" I holler after him, but instead of Marshall turning back to help me out of the car, suddenly, his mamá is before me, helping me out and lending me her support.

"Oh, mi hija! I'm so glad you're here." She says with such genuine delight in her voice that it brings a smile to my face. "I hope you love what we did with the place."

"Did?" I mutter softly.

As we walk through the front door of the old ranch-style home, I see what she means, though.

At some point in the past week and a half, since Marshall and I got the keys, someone had come into our new home and completely decorated and furnished the entire house.

As I wander further into the house, I take in everything around me and notice how even all of my books and other personal possessions have been thoughtfully displayed throughout the home.

"Did you do this?" I manage to get out.

When I turn to look at Marshall's mother, she has a beaming smile on her face.

"Marshall's sisters and a bunch of your friends have been coming over to help unpack and decorate for the past few days." She says, still smiling. "Do you like it?"

Tears well in my eyes, and my vision goes blurry as I look around.

"It's wonderful," I say through watery tears. "Thank you."

"Of course." She says, giving me a squeeze on my shoulder. "It was all his idea."

Just then, Marshall comes back into the room with a very awake Bridgit in his arms.

"Did you wake her up?" I scold.

"No!" He retorts with a smirk. "She wanted to see the place, though."

I narrow my gaze at him, but he keeps smiling his charming playboy smile.

"I'll leave you two to it," Mamá says, backing into the front entryway and grabbing her keys and purse before making her exit.

When Marshall and I are alone, well as alone as you can be with a newborn, I let myself relax fully. I hobble over to the couch, which must have been brought over from my apartment, and set myself down.

Marshall comes over and sits down next to me and settles our daughter in his arms so she can take in everything around us.

"You did all this?" I ask softly.

"Yeah." He says with a shrug. "I wanted her first night out of the hospital to be at our home."

"That's so... sweet," I mutter, my eyes welling with tears again.

I reach over and take Bridgit from Marshall's arms, tucking her in close to my chest and breathing in her baby scent.

"It's perfect," I whisper.

"This is our first night of the rest of our lives." He says dreamily, and I can't help but chuckle at his dopey expression.

We sit in a comfortable silence for a while, Marshall's arm draped around my shoulder and holding me and our daughter close while we lounge there.

"Elsie? If I ask you something..., will you promise not to kick me out this time?" He asks tentatively.

"Depends on what the question is," I say with a small smile, nuzzling into his shoulder further.

"Will you marry me?"

My eyes pop open wide, and I lift myself upright, which is a struggle when your body aches and you have a baby in your arms.

"Marry you?" I repeat.

"Will you marry me?" He asks with so much earnestness in his voice.

I'm stunned silent for a moment, and I can see the panic beginning to form in his eyes while I try to gather my thoughts and calm my now racing heartbeat.

"Elsie." He says, unwrapping himself from around me and lowering himself to one knee on the ground. "I know things have been a roller coaster between us. But this is it for me. You're it."

He reaches into his back pocket and pulls out a small box.

"I know you don't always believe me when I say it, but I love you, and I plan on reminding you of that every day for the rest of our lives if you'll let me."

Opening the box, he reveals a gorgeous emerald-cut diamond ring.

"Marshall." I breathe out, clutching Bridgit tighter to my chest but quickly loosening my grip when she begins to squirm.

"Marry me, Elsie."

The only sound I can hear is blood rushing through my ears. Nothing else permeates the blur of thoughts and questions that run through my mind in that second.

When Marshall's face starts to fall, I know I've fucked up.

"Yes!" I blurt out. "Yes. I'll marry you."

Just as fast as it faded, Marshall's smile is back, even brighter than before.

"Yes?" He asks, pulling out the ring from the box and reaching for my left hand, which is thankfully free.

"Yes." I sigh as he places the ring on my finger.

It feels so right to have it resting on my hand, and I can't help but marvel at how perfect the ring is.

More though, I look up and can't help but marvel at how perfect Marshall is.

"I'm sorry if I made you panic." I cringe. "I just..."

"I know." He says with a shrug. "It's part of your charm."

"No, Marshall." I sigh.

"Oh no. You're not taking it back already?"

I chuckle. "No. No, this time, you're stuck with me."

"Forever?"

"Yeah, sure." I smile.

"Elsie…" He warns.

"Yes. Fine. Forever." I laugh.

He rises up on his knees and gives me a passionate kiss before Bridgit starts squirming again.

"How soon before she can walk down the aisle?" I ask, looking down at our baby girl.

"If I have my way, never." His face goes serious.

I laugh fully. "I meant at our wedding, silly."

"Oh." His face relaxes. "Oh. Okay. Yeah. I think it's like after nine months?"

"Damn…" I say with a smirk. "I'm not sure I can wait that long. I guess someone will just have to carry our flower girl down the aisle."

The way Marshall's face lights up makes my whole damn week.

"Really?" He asks earnestly.

"Really," I say with a smile.

"Okay. Okay. Cool." He says, pulling himself up. "I'll text Mamá, and I'm sure between her and my sisters, we can get something thrown together soon."

"How does March sound?"

"March?"

"Yeah. Why not? It seems like a good time to renew your lease." I joke.

"Oh. She's got jokes now." He mumbles. "Fucking roommate rules."

"Hey. Those rules got you laid." I say with a wink. "A lot."

"No. Those rules got me you."

WELCOME BABY BRIDGIT!

MOVING HOUSE

HAPPY 30TH BIRTHDAY MARSHALL!

CAN YOU HEAR THE BELLS?

HAPPY 1ST BIRTHDAY, BRIDGIT!

WANT MORE OF THE PLAYGROUND CLUB?

I f you want to keep reading, the series continues in Book 2 with *Bound*, a spicy FFM romance with *two* plus size ladies who have the hots for each other and a cowboy who's *very* good with rope!

Get your copy!

Can't get enough? Don't miss the passion, healing, and heat of Book 3 in the series, *Cherished*, and fall even deeper in love with our bride and groom, Selene and Gunnar!

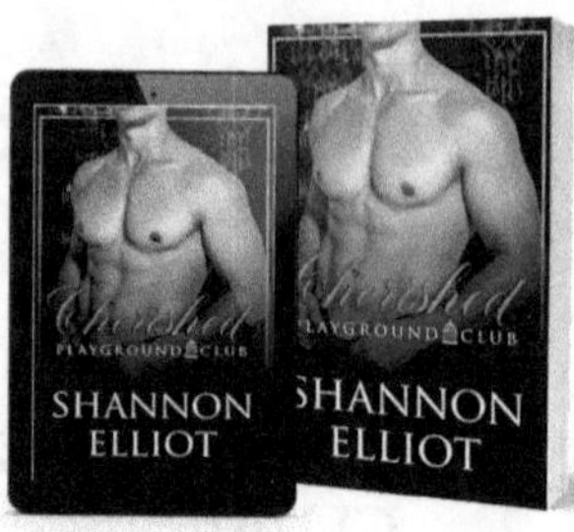

Get your copy!

To stay up to date on news, sales, and releases from Shannon Elliot, join her newsletter here:

Join the newsletter!

ACKNOWLEDGMENTS

Thank you everyone!

Becky, I cannot thank you enough. You are an instrumental part of my journey as an author. I am eternally grateful for your support and friendship. Two books down and so many more to come!

Becca. Wifey. My love. You know how much I love you. Thank you for being my partner in crime on this roller coaster. I appreciate every encouraging message and time when you make me smile. I couldn't do this without you. Love you.

Ashley, I cannot express how much you mean to me. I appreciate every moment of time and encouragement you give me. Thank you for listening to my zillion voice notes. You've made me a better writer and human. Love you.

Grace, Halla, and Hanna, y'all have been such a blessing to me. Thank you for all the work you do. I so appreciate everything you do to encourage me.

Jillian West, I consider you the Queen of pregnancy romance. To have you not only help me get unstuck with this book but also have your kind words about it as well means the world.

Gabby, you're to blame for this entire series and I'm so grateful for your support. Also, thanks for checking my abysmal Spanish.

The group chat, y'all are the best. Thank you for coming along for this adventure and supporting me at every turn.

There are other special people in my life who deserve thanks too, but I'll keep those names to myself. You know who you are.

Thank you for showing up for me like you do. (And all the inspiration too! haha)

To my family, I couldn't do this without you. Literally. Thank you. Some day, I'll pay you back for everything tenfold. For now, I hope family dinners, hugs, and Elliot snuggles are enough.

To my readers, y'all are literally the best. I am so honored you've taken a chance on me and, even more, that you stick around. I hope my stories fill your soul and make you feel seen. You are so loved by this author.

ABOUT THE AUTHOR

Shannon Elliot resides in Texas, with her fur baby and writes romance that reflects her readers whenever she's not at the dog park or curled up with a good book. Evidenced by her background in theatre, she is drawn to story-telling and the creative process. Shannon believes that diverse and inclusive stories shouldn't be the exception, they should be the rule. Happily ever after is for everyone and she aims to write romances that reflect her readers.

www.authorshannonelliot.com/pages/links

ALSO BY SHANNON ELLIOT

The Playground Club Series

Used, Book 1

Bound, Book 2

Cherished, Book 3

Descent into Darkness Duet

Angels in the Dark, Book 1

Devil in the Dark, Book 2

Standalone Novellas

Heel